On the Edge

Celebrating 35 Years of
Penguin Random House India

On the Edge

100 Years of Hindi Fiction on Same-Sex Desire

Edited and Translated from the Hindi by

RUTH VANITA

PENGUIN

An imprint of Penguin Random House

HAMISH HAMILTON

USA | Canada | UK | Ireland | Australia
New Zealand | India | South Africa | China | Singapore

Hamish Hamilton is part of the Penguin Random House group of companies
whose addresses can be found at global.penguinrandomhouse.com

Published by Penguin Random House India Pvt. Ltd
4th Floor, Capital Tower 1, MG Road,
Gurugram 122 002, Haryana, India

First published in Hamish Hamilton by Penguin Random House India 2023

Translation copyright © Ruth Vanita 2023

ISBN 9780670097319

Typeset in Adobe Caslon Pro by MAP Systems, Bengaluru, India
Printed at Thomson Press India Ltd, New Delhi

www.penguin.co.in

*This translation is for my friends Patricia Ruppelt, Rictor Norton,
David Allen, and K.D. Dickinson*

Contents

A Note on This Translation

The stories appear in chronological order, by date of composition. All words in languages other than English, including Hindi words retained in the translation, are italicized. Words that are in English in the original Hindi stories are also italicized, to indicate to the reader the way Hindi writers use English words, especially (but not only) in relation to sexuality.

Ellipses that are original to the story appear as such. Ellipses introduced by me to indicate omitted parts of the work appear in parentheses, thus [...]

As far as possible, I have tried to use English equivalents for Hindi words and idioms, and have explained significant untranslatables, such as *tumhein meri qasam*, and double meanings of terms such as *baat karna* or *joon*, in footnotes.

Some Hindi words cannot be translated into one English word. *Chaah*, for example, means both 'love' and 'desire' in the way that eros and its various forms do but no English word does. In stories like 'On the Edge', by Sara Rai, I have translated *chaah* sometimes as 'love' and sometimes as 'desire'.

Introduction

My big find for this book is undoubtedly Asha Sahay's 1947 novel, *Ekakini*. My translation of excerpts from it is the first English translation. I had almost given up hope of laying my hands on it but finally managed to do so with a little help from my friends, supplemented by the kindness of strangers.* Kuldeep Kumar called *Ekakini* 'the first Hindi novel on lesbianism' and described it as frankly portraying 'two young women in an intense lesbian relationship'. This sent me looking for the book.† On first reading, I was inclined to disagree with Kumar, because the relationship between the two women, Arati and Kala, seems non-sexual, and Arati, we are told, is in love with Vijay, the man she marries. On rereading the novel, though, I had second thoughts.

---

* As it turned out, I need not have spent months tracking down the Hindi original, because in 2022 Sudha Singh brought out a new edition from Academic Publications, New Delhi.

† Kuldeep Kumar, 'Hindi Belt: A Different Life in Letters', *The Hindu*, 17 October 2014. In his book *Strivadi Sahitya Vimarsh* (Delhi: Anamika Publishers, 2018), Jagdishwar Chaturvedi examines this novel and *Lihaf* in a chapter titled 'Lesbian Stri Sahitya Saidhantiki', along with many Western lesbian feminist works. He argues that Kala and Arati are in a lesbian relationship but Kala is the real lesbian, and concludes that a lesbian perspective is ages old in India, but it remains suppressed in normal times and comes to the surface in times of economic and political crisis (pp. 349–50).

The women's relationship is described in the florid language of romance, replete with images of passion; flames, attraction, magic, anguish, madness and intoxication (*maadak, mohak, mast, anurakt*) abound. This is the lyrical language of the little story 'Vida' (Farewell), about the parting of two close friends, which was published in an Arya Samaj women's college magazine in 1938, and which I translated in *Same-Sex Love in India* (2000).

The relationship in *Ekakini*, however, is more than a premarital romantic friendship. Kala urges Arati not to choose a male life partner (*jivan-sangi*) but to be her life partner (*sangini*) instead, telling her that she loves Arati more than a man can. This is perhaps the first marriage proposal from a woman to another woman in Indian literature (with the possible exception of some Urdu *rekhti* poems). Even if the marriage the Gandhian Kala proposes were a celibate one, as several Gandhian marriages were, it would still be a marriage. Kala's arguments are political; they are similar to the theories, in the 1980s, of those women who were termed political lesbians. She declares that womanhood and motherhood are curses, that women are treated as toys and goddesses rather than humans, that a woman is complete without a man, and that 'a new world of intoxicating revolution' is needed to erase men's ways. Yet this political statement is enlivened by emotion. 'Be my Arati, I will be your Kala,' she says.

This combination of political abstraction with fervid emotion continues throughout the novel. Although the eminent literary critic Acharya Shivpujan Sahay, in his foreword to *Ekakini*, praised the author's 'modern style', I must confess that it palled on me. Asha Sahay constantly plays on the symbolism of the characters' names and deluges us with repetitive flowery language. Though she tells a story about Gandhian activists, she gives short shrift to realism of either plot or character.

She does cleverly contrive, however, to make all the heterosexual relationships celibate. If the female–female relationships are not clearly sexual, the male–female relationships are clearly not sexual. Arati's husband refuses to sleep with her, and, even more interestingly, Kala, who refuses to marry her suitor Atul, decides, as soon as he dies, that she is his spiritual widow devoted to continuing his work for national independence. In the end, Arati refuses to return to her husband, Kala is respectably single as an unmarried widow, and neither of them has children. At the outset, Kala was termed *ekakini*, and in the end Arati calls herself ekakini. The book begins and ends with the two women's relationship, and it is dedicated to '*vishwa ki nari-murti*' (the figure of woman in the world).

Its feminism, though, is of an indigenous kind. It invokes *shakti* and *sadhana*, and rewrites several Indian motifs and narratives, from that of Buddha's wife to those of the *suhagin* and *viyogin*. This is the feminism of Mahadevi Varma, whose poem 'Panth Hone Do Aparichit' (Let the Path Be Unfamiliar), published in her 1942 collection *Deepshikha*, concludes with lines that that use the word *ekaki* and are similar in their paradoxical and Upanishadic feeling to the ending of *Ekakini*:

Jaan lo voh milan ekaki
virah mein hai dukela.

(Know that that solitary union
is dual in separation.)

Another pattern in *Ekakini* is a network of fervent attachments between women—Arati and her sister-in-law, Suman; Arati and her mother-in-law, Shanta; Suman and her ex-classmate Bijli, with whom Vijay is in love; even Arati and Bijli. The male characters form close friendships too, but they are not explored in the same way the female friendships are. There is no explicit sex between women, but there are many intimate moments. Suman adorns Arati in blue silk to meet Bijli but then flings herself on Bijli, whom she calls her 'sangini'. Arati, who misses Kala, says that she sees Kala's shadow in Bijli. Bijli, Suman and Kala later picket a liquor shop together.

This pattern of women's solidarity appears again in 'A Double Life'. In this explicitly sexual story, the two women lovers' home becomes a refuge for their abused female friend. In 'Vision', too, a blind female couple live in happy communion with other female couples. In 'Lip to Lip', love affairs are constantly formed and broken among the hostel residents, and in 'I Want the Moon', the heroine draws support from several female friends.

Romantic and erotic friendship between women goes back a long way in Indian literature. It appears in the first Hindi short story, 'Rani Ketaki Ki Kahani', by Insha Allah Khan Insha (1756–1817) and is prominent in the eleventh-century Sanskrit *Kathasaritsagara*, where women fall in love with women at first sight, and men with men, and such life-long same-sex friends are termed *swayamvara* (self-chosen) *sakha* (man's male friend) and *swayamvara sakhi* (woman's female friend).*

Hindi draws many words and concepts from Sanskrit but also many from Persian through what has come to be called Urdu but was originally called Hindi (the language of Hind, India, as distinct from Persian, the court language in Muslim-ruled kingdoms). In the eighteenth century, a set of terms developed, such as *chapti* (sex between women) from *chipatna* (to stick), *dogana* (double or other self, from the image of a twinned or doubled fruit), *zanakhi, ilaichi* (from food items exchanged in ritual unions and marriages of female couples). Some of these terms used in Urdu poetry entered Hindi dictionaries and Hindi prose. There are also local Hindi words, such as *guiyan* (woman's intimate female friend).†

---

* For this and other examples, see Ruth Vanita, 'A Second Self: Rituals and Traditions of Romantic Friendship', Chapter 5 in Vanita, *Love's Rite: Same-Sex Marriages in Modern India* (New Delhi: Penguin, 2005, reissued 2021, 2023).

† For translations of the poetry, see Ruth Vanita, *Gender, Sex and the City: Urdu Rekhti Poetry 1780–1870* (Delhi: Orient Blackswan, 2012).

Persistent Prejudices

Many Hindi literary critics are surprisingly ignorant of this long history and even of the history of Hindi literature, and several seem immune to scientific information. The Marxist critic Namvar Singh, who has been termed 'the face of Hindi' and an 'intellectual warrior',* comments as late as 2010:

> It has to be admitted that homosexuality is an exception, not a widespread practice. Whether it is between men or between women, it is unnatural. That is how it should be portrayed in literature. Some English-language writers, under Western influence, are trying to gain cheap popularity by *glorifying* this exception.†

He concludes his essay with the claim: 'We should be careful to depict perversions related to sex as an *aberration* and not establish them as a *norm* in order to obtain cheap popularity. Perversions should be viewed with suspicion.'‡

As late as 2020, another critic remarks that homosexuality is a topic untouched by Hindi literature until *Winged Boat* (2007).§ Several others, who simplistically identify the narrator, Vikram, in this novel with the author, Pankaj Bisht, attribute to the author Vikram's ideas about homosexuality as a perversion, an illness or a

---

* Ashish Tripathi, in his editor's introduction to Namvar Singh, *Zamane Se Do-Do Haath* (New Delhi: Rajkamal Prakashan, 2010), p. 1.

† 'Mukt Stri Ki Chhadma Chhavi', in *Zamane Se Do-Do Haath*, p. 123. First published in *Outlook*, 22 September 2003. The author was alive when it appeared in 2010.

‡ 'Mukt Stri Ki Chhadma Chhavi', pp. 124–25. The italicized words in the quotation are in English in the original essay.

§ Gaurinath, 'Pankaj Bisht Ke Yogdan Ka Mulyankan', *Janchowk*, 19 February 2020.

problem.* A 2020 article on lesbianism in Hindi novels by women defines homosexuality as an abnormal, unnatural perversion imported from the West, and condemns the gay movement for trying to establish a way of life that is bad for humanity, and that gives rise to diseases like AIDS and produces depression.†

Fiction writers are not immune to this kind of simplistic analysis. Several stories about women married to homosexual men are narrated entirely from her point of view and depict the husband as effeminate, oblivious of the fact that many gay men are not feminine-appearing. Other writers depict women engaging in lesbian affairs because of spousal neglect. In both types of narrative, the woman is a victim. The homosexual woman is depicted as a victim, and the homosexual man as mentally ill.

An early version of the neglectful-husband narrative is Shivani's 1972 novel *Shmashan Champa*, in which a Hindu woman falls in love with and marries a Muslim man, who turns out to be homosexual. The man analyses himself as having gradually become a girl as a result of dressing in a feminine way in the company of his homosexual friends.

Rashmi Sharma's 'Band Kothri Ka Darvaza' (2018), set in a Muslim family, repeats this pattern. The husband, who has an effeminate lover, tells his wife that he became homosexual because he was raised in a girly fashion by his mother and eight sisters. His wife's therapist, without setting eyes on him, diagnoses him as incurably impotent.‡

Reeta Das Ram's 2021 story 'Shaadi Ki Aathvin Raat' (The Eighth Night of Marriage) reads like a journalistic report told entirely from the woman narrator's point of view. A gay man

---

* Rohini Agrawal, 'Main Aisa Prem Hun Nahin Hai Saahas Jis Mein Apna Naam Lene Ka', *Pustak-Varta*, 28 May–June 2010, pp. 14–16.

† Rajkumari Sharma, 'Hindi Upanyason Mein Samlaingikta: Stri Ki Nazar Se', *Sahitya Kunj*, 162:2, 15 August 2020.

‡ *Samalochan*, 26 October 2018.

marries his woman co-worker and refuses to sleep with her. All the characters are cardboard cut-outs, but the man is particularly so.*

A 2022 novel that dwells upon the deceived wife's perspective is Amit Gupta's *Dehri Par Thithki Dhoop*. Both male lovers wallow in self-hatred and self-reproach, caused largely by disasters that have never happened in India, such as mobs stoning the unmarried partner's house and the married man losing his job at Miranda House (where he headed the Hindi department in 1990, a historical impossibility). In this novel, the male couple does reunite at the end, but the married man is permanently crippled in what reads like an unnecessarily punitive road accident.

Stories about lesbianism caused by husbands' neglect descend from *Lihaf* (1942). A horrific version of this plot appears in Rajkamal Chaudhari's 1965 novel, *Macchli Mari Hui* (Dead Fish), where a neglectful husband's returning to his wife cures her of lesbianism. He also violently rapes and impregnates her lover. The rape victim's father thanks him for curing her.

Several other less horrifying novels employ the framework of lesbianism resulting from the unavailability of heterosexual sex. In Usha Priyamvada's 2000 novel, *Antarvanshi*, an Indian woman in America takes an American woman lover when her sexual relations with her husband cool off. In Krishna Agnihotri's 2010 novel, *Kumarikaen*, a girl who is prevented from meeting boys gets involved with her best friend. In Kusum Ansal's 2017 novel, *Parchhaiyon Ka Samaysaar*, a nurse called Dorothy unsuccessfully tries to seduce the heroine, Natasha, whose husband has been rendered impotent in an accident. Natasha stumbles upon Dorothy having sex with Eliza and is horrified: 'A strange moaning, a strange smell.' Why female orgasmic moaning or smells should be 'strange' to Natasha is unclear. Has she never had an orgasm, or is a woman's orgasm with a woman supposed to be inherently different from a woman's orgasm with a man?

---

* In her 2021 collection, *Samay Jo Rukta Nahin*.

Visible, Invisible, Semi-Visible

From these strangely stunted late-twentieth- and twenty-first-century narratives, one turns with positive relief both to Asha Sahay and to Ugra, as well as to the other stories in this collection (which date from the 1960s to the present), because they try to view reality without ideological filters.

Ugra's depiction of male homosexuality shines in comparison with the medicalizing narratives discussed above because Ugra has no doubt that homosexual men are men; several of his characters are married, but whether married or single, they clearly state that they prefer men. While Ugra's narrators, and he himself in his prefatory materials, call homosexuality an unnatural vice and a disease, the author does not, in the stories, provide psychological analyses of why some men are inclined to other men. He does not imagine that all homosexual men are feminine, probably because he knew actual homosexual men and did not have to fall back on theories.

His stories are also exhilarating because they focus on the visibility of homosexuality. They depict a community of men unabashedly pursuing one another, whether in city parks, cinemas, at parties or in prison, and having a lot of fun while doing so. Ugra was not a highly imaginative writer, and his fiction is of the slice-of-life kind. It gives us a glimpse of the language and behaviour of homosexually inclined men in the early twentieth century. He portrays them as still enjoying the residual pleasures of pre-colonial Indian urbanity, wherein same-sex relations were par for the course.

Nor do the male characters in Ugra's stories diagnose themselves as diseased. By the mid-twentieth century, male homosexual characters and their families and friends frequently perform this self-hating diagnosis. In 'On the Edge', Manoranjan is depicted not as a transgender person but as a gay man. He never shows any desire to become a woman; he simply loves a man. But merely on the basis of his desire for men, the narrator diagnoses him (and he diagnoses himself) as having a woman's heart in a man's body. Homosexuality thus becomes a form of heterosexuality.

If men in Ugra's stories are fairly open about their sexual desires, women in Asha Sahay's novel are equally open about their romantic desires. This visibility is replaced by a debilitating invisibility in the post-colonial metropolitan world of the late twentieth century.

One common theme in the widely disparate stories in this collection is that of hiding and concealment, an ongoing concern with what is seen, unseen, partially seen or misunderstood and mistaken for something else. A number of Indian lesbian, gay and bisexual people born in the 1950s, '60s and '70s have told me that 'coming out' is a Western idea irrelevant in India, because Indian families often accept and integrate you, your friends and even partners without any need for labels. Having experienced and witnessed at close quarters the disastrous results of a same-sex partner being viewed or passed off as a friend or roommate, I do not accept this theory. In one case, when a woman fell seriously ill, her father took her away from her female partner, whom he saw as merely a roommate, and when she died her family took all her possessions away. The stories in this book provide evidence of how the refusal to acknowledge reality inflicts emotional damage on gay people and their families.

In *Lihaf* (1942), famously, the child narrator refuses to say what she saw the two women doing when the quilt was raised at night. Ismat Chughtai depicts lesbianism as disgusting, even abusive (the older woman tries to seduce the child narrator). In 'A Primary Knowledge of Geography', the boy narrator, Phoolbabu, reverses this revulsion when he says that the ugly acts he saw his male cousin engaging in with his wife are better not revealed. As the story unfolds, we see that although Phoolbabu is in denial, he is in fact coupled with his friend Ramaa, and everyone accurately perceives them as a couple.

Anupam, in *Winged Boat*, is an exception to this pattern of secrecy, but his refusal to hide becomes his downfall. Saleem Kidwai told me that the character of Anupam was based on a brilliant but disturbed gay man whom Kidwai and other gay men knew in the 1980s. This man worked as a journalist and also in an advertising firm, and died an untimely death. The novel's insider knowledge of the 1980s gay world in Delhi could only have come from a gay informant.

While Anupam is a convincing character, his friendship with the narrator, Vikram, is less convincing. Someone as intelligent as Anupam would be more likely to find supportive gay friends than to endure Vikram's homophobic ideas shaped by an undigested mix of Freudianism and Marxism. A passing attraction to the athletic but mediocre Vikram is understandable, but Anupam's staying in love with him is strange, unless it indicates how homophobia has damaged Anupam. Vikram briefly becomes interesting when he breaks into tears on parting with Anupam and acknowledges having walked a tightrope in relation to him. But this ambivalence in Vikram's feelings is merely glimpsed, not explored.

Another common theme in these stories is that of waiting—on the edge of acceptance, of choosing a different life, of seeing things in a new way. This theme applies to both major and minor characters, to narrators as well as protagonists.

Several of these works recount stories familiar from life—the working-class man who marries a woman, planning to continue a clandestine affair with his wealthier lover ('On the Edge'); the premarital lesbian relationship in a women's college hostel ('Lip to Lip') or a working women's hostel ('Girlfriend-Beloved'); the man who discovers that his boyfriend is married to a woman ('Shadow'). Characters in all these stories adopt disguises. Little seems to change in this regard, from the 1960s to the 2020s.

The most recent story in this collection, 'Shadow' (2022), depicts a narrator whose access to the Internet, ability to rent hotel rooms and knowledge of the 2018 abolition of the anti-sodomy law do nothing to reduce his terror of being discovered with another man. Nor do advances in media representation help him—seeing a film with a happy ending for a gay boy does not make him happy. Instead, it reduces him to tears, because he is sure he can never come out to his family; he therefore resolves never to see another film with a happy ending for a queer character.

Intensity

Fiction is not a mirror of life; it does not reveal exactly what happens in life but rather the ideas in circulation about what happens and, more important, a writer's vision about what could happen. John Keats pointed out that 'the excellence of every art is its intensity, capable of making all disagreeables evaporate'. In a similar vein, Ugra, discussing Wilde, whom he greatly admired, remarks, 'Passion that survives is power, so only one whose writings have lasting passion is a powerful writer.' Elsewhere he states that the art of Wilde 'and of any artist worth the name becomes like fire when it attains maturity'.

While some stories in this collection partake of stereotypes and formulaic patterns, I chose them either due to their close observation of same-sex desire, or because their fiery, no-holds-barred intensity counterbalances the depressing pattern of pretending not to be and not to see.

Geeta and Nanda lying together on the beach at night or making love, Geeta buying flowers for Nanda's hair ('Waiting'), the happy doodles in Sonali's diary ('Girlfriend-Beloved'), the orgasmic ecstasy in 'Shadow' and 'Lip to Lip' give the reader a glimpse of what makes the suffering worthwhile.

In 'Waiting', the lesbian relationship is the fallout of failed heterosexuality. But through acute observation of Geeta, 'Waiting' raises her anguish to a pitch that moves the reader beyond depression, into near-tragic insight: is the woman Geeta sees in the mirror her real self rather than the helpless victim who is forever waiting? So also, the febrile intensity of I–you narration in 'Lip to Lip' brings to unforgettable life not only the almost-unnamed polyamorous lesbian (she is only once called by the nickname Nanu), whom anyone who has lived in a women's hostel will recognize as a familiar type, but also the unnamed narrator who continues her lesbian life while living as a wife. This story recalls the explicit lesbian eroticism of Urdu *rekhti* poetry written a century earlier.*

Gender-segregated spaces, like hostels, dorms, prisons, girls' homes, or confined domesticity may give rise to situational homosexuality but may also allow innate feelings to flourish. The best fiction leaves the origins of sexual orientations ambiguous, as they are in life, and does not seek to pin down and diagnose people.

Two works in this collection tantalize with the delights of ambiguity. We can never know to what extent Premchand may have been aware of the ambiguity in his story 'Stigma'. He depicts two highly educated, independent women, a school headmistress and a doctor, who live alone and visit each other late at night. Miss Khurshed has acted on the stage in London. She and the cross-dressed Leela pretend to be heterosexual lovers, which deludes prying women into thinking that she is having a clandestine affair with a man. The unanswered question is, does the women's play-acting as lovers conceal an even more deeply buried secret? Leela successfully dresses as a man. When she and Miss Khurshed appear in women's clothing, is that a performance too?

The question is similar to that which arises with regard to Shakespeare's cross-dressed female characters. On Shakespeare's stage, male actors played the roles of women, and in the course of Shakespeare's plays, his female characters disguise themselves as boys to whom other female characters (also played by boys) get attracted. Are these women characters attracted to girls or to girlish boys or to boyish girls? We watch a boy actor attracted to another boy actor who plays the role of a girl disguised as a boy. For example, when Olivia in *Twelfth Night* (performed by a boy) is attracted to Viola, a girl disguised as a boy (also performed by

---

* For translations of this poetry, see Ruth Vanita, *Gender, Sex and the City: Urdu Rekhti Poetry 1780–1870* (Orient Blackswan and Palgrave Macmillan, 2012).

a boy actor), we simultaneously see a boy and a girl as well as two boys and two girls.

Surendra Verma's much-discussed, award-winning novel *I Want the Moon* reverses the misunderstanding. Gossipmongers imagine that the two women portrayed in the novel are lesbian or bisexual (both these English words appear in the novel), whereas, in fact, they are friends. Unlike Asha Sahay's *Ekakini*, where no romantic relationship becomes explicitly sexual, here male–female sex is described in explicit detail, making it clear that the woman–woman romantic friendship is not sexual. It is, however, the primary relationship in the book. Varma also clearly enjoys lesbian suggestiveness; for example, Shivani, who wanted to marry Varsha's lover, Harsh, becomes Varsha's friend and appears unannounced at her bedside while she is asleep:

> Somebody was rubbing perfumed cream into her skin. Slender fingers under her bra strap. A delicate, tender touch . . . Traversing her waist, the hands reached her buttocks under her panty, then her thighs and calves. A slight smile appeared on Varsha's lips . . . The hands progressed from her neck to her breasts, stroked her flat stomach, then began to flirtatiously play on her muscular thighs . . . 'Darling, how dry your skin is.' Shivani gently stroked her forehead, then softly kissed her lips.

A particularly Indian slant in these stories has to do with the narration from the point of view of parents and siblings, even those who are prejudiced or unkind. 'Mrs Raizada's Corona Diary' explores the psyche of a gay man's mother who departs from the maternal ideal. She is selfish, self-pitying and harsh to her son and his partner until she literally needs her son's blood. Despite the ironic contrast between her unkindness to her son (which distances her from him as well as from her husband) and her own adulterous desire for a younger man, the character is not depicted as entirely unsympathetic. Likewise, narrators in 'Girlfriend-Beloved' and 'Lado' are mothers and sisters who have mixed and changing feelings towards their lesbian and bisexual relatives. *Winged Boat* begins and concludes with the ambiguous figure of a gay man's mother; it remains unclear whether her account of him is true or an elaborate smokescreen, and whether her son is in fact dead or alive.

Geetanjali Shree's novel *Tirohit* (Under Wraps) adopts the unusual perspective of the son of two mothers. *Under Wraps* and *Ekakini* share with each other, and with 'A Double Life', a utopian yearning for a creative world not fully containable in domesticity. Kala and Arati are restlessly mobile and end up in a village far from home; Ambika and Lalna lead a semi-hidden life on a rooftop, which protects them from hostile forces. This rooftop is reminiscent of the palace that the ghosts give to the two women in 'A Double Life'. An unusual version of the utopia hidden in plain sight appears in 'Vision'.

Past and Future: Looking for Ancestors

Gay people all over the world have looked to history and literature to find others like themselves. Ugra's homosexual characters do this, referring to Shakespeare and Wilde as well as Mir. Anupam, in *Winged Boat*, finds mostly Western ancestors, the exceptions being Bhupen Khakhar and a reference to Mahmud and Ayaz in a Ghalib ghazal. A millennium earlier, a girl in the *Kathasaritsagara* also looks for ancestors in literature. When she falls in love with a woman at first sight, she tells herself that this is not surprising because they must have been connected in a previous birth and also because women in earlier literature were inseparable friends, such as Arundhati and the daughter of King Prithu.*

Vijaydan Detha's 'A Double Life' literalizes the idea of ancestors in the form of ghosts. I first translated it from Hindi in 1983, and have now updated that translation by closely comparing it with

---

* Vanita and Kidwai (eds), *Same-Sex Love in India: A Literary History* (New Delhi: Penguin, 2008), pp. 99–103.

the Rajasthani and making several significant changes. This story was written in Rajasthani but was translated into Hindi almost immediately and enacted as a play in Hindi in the 1980s. It has exerted tremendous influence in its Hindi incarnation. Despite its not being originally a Hindi story, I have included it here for these reasons, and because I consider it one of the world's most powerful and beautiful stories about same-sex love. It effortlessly integrates Indian tradition with modern debates about same-sex unions and individual preferences, although these debates had barely begun in India when the story was written.

Before her unwitting marriage to a woman, Beeja says, 'After all, marriage is a union of two hearts. If the hearts of two women unite, why should they not get married?' This is exactly what Sushila Bhawasar, a village schoolteacher in Madhya Pradesh, said about the marriage of her neighbour Urmila Srivastava to Leela Namdeo in 1987: 'After all, what is marriage? It is a wedding of two souls.'* In 2002, the Shaiva Hindu priest who performed the wedding ceremony of two Indian women in Seattle said to me in a brief interview, 'Marriage is a union of two spirits, and the spirit is not male or female.'

Bhut, the Hindi word for ghost, is also the word for the past; the past tense in grammar is called *bhut-kala* (past time). There are two types of ghosts or pasts in 'A Double Life'. One is the ghost of ingrained ways of living, of dead conventions continuing from the past. Teeja remarks that this kind of ghost prevents their friend from leaving her abusive husband and in-laws. The ghosts who help and protect the two women represent the past that inspires the future. Teeja says that these ghosts are 'the invisible, living flame of that which is to be'.

The ancient symbol of the fish as woman appears in this story as well as in other Indian lesbian narratives. This is perhaps because the *vesica pisces* or *ichthys* in many ancient cultures was

---

* Chinu Panchal, '"Wedded" Women Cops to Challenge Sack', *Times of India*, 23 February 1988.

a symbol of Goddesses, women, fertility and sexuality. Fish are associated with Aphrodite. Vishnu's first incarnation was a fish (with a female counterpart), and fish appear in sculptures of river Goddesses, such as Ganga. Some scholars think that the fish sign in the Indus Valley Civilization's script stands for woman.

Beeja's sex change from female to male recalls Shikhandini from the Mahabharata, but more importantly, the sex change back from male to female recalls Bhangaswana, also from the Mahabharata. Bhangaswana was a sage who was transformed into a woman. At first he was upset, but then he realized that women are more affectionate than men and are capable of feeling greater sexual pleasure than men. For these reasons, when she is offered the chance to become a man, Bhangaswana refuses. Similarly, Beeja, who, like Shikhandini, was eager to become a man and thought that male–female sex is the best kind, recalls her love-making with Teeja and becomes a woman again. In the Mahabharata, the woman Shikhandini becomes an aggressive and revengeful man, Shikhandin, and never misses being a woman.

'A Double Life' evokes a series of old Indian images of love—lotuses, rain, Kamadeva—but also a new one: red velvet mites. These beautiful mites, indigenous to Rajasthan, are known as *teej*, and they do not mate. They perform a dance, then the male deposits sperm on the ground, which the female picks up.

A character in Ugra's story says that everyone is naked under their clothes. Detha's story repeats this idiom, which indicates that one kind of sex is less different from another than we think. The same is true of love. When the two wives spend several nights gazing at each other, women looking through the keyhole are surprised but say, 'Well, each to their own thirst and to their own taste.' Later, the two women feel as if 'the thirst of the whole universe was encompassed in that one thirst of theirs.' Art springs from that identification of the universal with the particular.

Ruth Vanita

Discussing Chocolate*

Pandey Bechan Sharma 'Ugra'

Having supervised the porter who put my bedding and trunk in the train, I began to stroll casually on the platform. So what if I was traveling third class? I was still a '*gentleman.*'† And '*gentlemen*' board the train only when it starts moving. At least that's the way '*gentlemen*' of my age in my country behave!

When the guard and the engine both whistled to assure us that the train was about to leave, someone called out to me from the compartment, 'Come aboard, sir. The train is about to leave.'

I: 'I'll come—there's no hurry.'

---

* First published in the magazine *Matvala,* 13 December 1924. My translation first appeared in *Same-Sex Love in India* (2000). The translated title retains the pun from the original title 'Chocolate Charcha'. 'Chocolate' is the slang term Ugra says was used for both male homosexuality and a male beloved. The primary meaning of *charcha* is to talk about or discuss, with the implied meaning of practising an activity. A secondary meaning of the word is to smear or spread something on the body, just as a secondary meaning of 'discuss' is to consume something. I translate the word *charcha* in the story in various ways, depending on the context.

† In English in the original. All English words in the original are italicized. To indicate satirical intent, I use single quote marks here.

He: 'What's the use of wandering about like that? It's a crime to board a moving train.'

I: 'It may be a crime, but all the guards in the world are seen boarding trains only once they get moving. Isn't that a crime?'

He: 'Come on, brother. Why talk of guards? They are railway officials.'

Just then, the train whistled for the last time and started moving. I leapt on to the train, entered the compartment and occupied my seat.

Having glanced around at my fellow passengers, I began reading my newspaper. Remember, 'gentlemen' do not read *Leader, Forward* or *Servant.** They enjoy only the *Statesman* or the *Pioneer.* I was reading the *Statesman.* It is a characteristic of train passengers to do whatever others are doing. If one sings, all the rest hum along. If some people go to sleep, everyone prepares to sleep. Seeing me reading a newspaper, the rest decided to do so too. A man who appeared to be from the United Provinces took *Matvala* out of his pocket and began to read it. Before he had read a couple of pages, another man, who seemed to be highly orthodox, said to him, 'Why do you read *Matvala?*'

'What do you mean? Do you consider *Matvala* an impure paper?'

'No doubt about it. It's probably the most impure paper not just in the Hindi world but in the whole world. Have you ever noticed the discussion of chocolate in it?'

'Ever noticed it—of course, I regularly notice it. So you consider *Matvala* the worst of all the world's papers just because it discusses chocolate? Ha ha ha ha! Looks like you've only heard about the world but never seen any of its papers. You would faint if you read some of the papers in Western countries. Why are you so unhappy about the discussion of chocolate in *Matvala?*'

'You ask why I'm unhappy? Can it ever be a good thing to preach about such disgusting matters as chocolate?'

---

* Names of nationalist newspapers.

'*Matvala* is preaching?' Its admirer grew somewhat excited. 'It's our society that is degraded. It knows well that many wicked beings are piling boulders of chocolate-love on its chest every day. Every child in this society knows what the practice of chocolate is. In every part of society there are wicked people who are predatory tigers by nature but appear to be mild cows. What is poor *Matvala* doing but exposing such people? It should be thanked for doing so.'

'It should be thanked?' responded the protector of orthodoxy. 'If it were up to me, I would hang all the writers and publishers who discuss chocolate. What's the use of shedding light on the wrong acts that society does in secret? Everyone is naked under the *dhoti*.'*

'Society doesn't hide this weakness. Chocolate is openly practised in schools, colleges, theatre companies, and Ramlila groups. Many good poets, writers, and great leaders are said to be prey to this illness.'

'That is a lie, a deception. Society can never be so disgusting.'

* * *

A handsome young man sitting at the window replied to the orthodox pandit, 'Sir, you appear to inhabit an ancient Golden Age. What you are calling a lie is absolutely true. Listen to my story.'

Everyone in the compartment looked at the youth. He was about twenty-one or twenty-two years old, extremely attractive, with a shapely face, fair complexion, large eyes and a high forehead. He went on, 'I am a third-year student in *** College. Thanks to God's wrath, there are not many nice-looking young boys in this college, so if any student is even slightly good-looking, most of the love-intoxicated fellows start chasing him. That's what happened to me.

---

* Idiomatic, meaning that we all have something to hide.

'Wherever older and in-the-know, mischievous students saw me—in class, in the common room, in the field, they would show their colours by exclaiming, "O Prince!" "He's killing me!" "*Money order*," "*Pocketbook*" and so on.* I was fed up of constantly running away from my classmates. There are many hostels in that college. The boarding superintendent lived in my hostel. I complained to him several times, but he always claimed helplessness. He said, "These boys are adults who know very well what they are doing. So what's the use of reasoning with them?" One day, in the superintendent's presence, a Punjabi student said to me, "Sir, can you solve a maths problem for me?"

'"What is it?" I asked.

'"Twenty-one plus two," he replied.

'I bit my lip in anger and kept quiet. The meaning of his twenty-one plus two was nothing but "*Give me a kiss.*"

'One day I was sitting in my room reading a book when a friend of mine came in and said, "Dinkar! Run away! A big group of boys from the third hostel is coming here to harass you. Look there!"

'I was astonished at the sight I saw.

'About sixty or seventy boys carrying a corpse on a bier were yelling something as they approached my room. Seized with fear, I ran up to the superintendent's room. They all stopped at the door of my room and began to shout, "Dinkar! Oh, beautiful Dinkar! Waiting and longing for you, your lover pined away and died.† If you come and touch him, he will revive."

'When they could not find me, they went off in search of some other beautiful boy. They found an unfortunate one somewhere

---

* The author in his preface identifies the last two as slang terms for a man's younger lover.

† The word used for 'waiting' is *firaq*; this was the pen name of Raghupati Sahay 'Firaq' Gorakhpuri (1896–1982), a major Urdu poet from Uttar Pradesh, whose homosexuality was well known.

and dragged him to the bier. That boy was forced to touch the pretend corpse of the dead lover.

'The lover was just rising from the bier, beating his breast, when the college principal, hearing of the boys' mischief, turned up! Having witnessed that scene of the nation's students' degradation, he exclaimed, trembling with rage, "You wretches! Aren't you ashamed to play such a degraded joke? All of you are a stain on this college."

'The day after this episode, I removed my name from the college rolls. The day I left, I felt like crying over my beauty. In this degraded nation, it is a sin not only to be truthful, patriotic and outspoken but even to be good-looking.'

* * *

The orthodox pandit was stunned by the youth's narrative, and I said, 'If you all do not think it improper, I would like to write a report of this incident and send it to the editor of *Matvala*.'

The youth happily gave his consent.

Stigma*

Munshi Premchand

1.

If there were a being in the world whose eyes could look into people's hearts, very few men or women would be able to face up to it. People had begun to think of Jugnubai of the Women's Home as such a being. She was uneducated, poor, old, and always cheerful. But just as a skilful proofreader's eyes go straight to errors, her eyes zeroed in on flaws. She knew at least a couple of secrets about every woman in town.

Her short, sturdy body, salt-and-pepper hair, round face, plump cheeks, and small eyes cast, as it were, a veil over the sharpness and acerbity of her temperament, but when she began talking against someone, her expression would harden, her eyes would widen, and her voice would grow harsh. She walked with the perfect balance of a cat, treading softly, and when she got wind of her prey, she would prepare to pounce. Her work was to serve the women in the

---

* 'Laanchhan' appeared in February 1931 in *Madhuri* and then in Premchand's 1932 collection, *Samar-yatra Aur Gyarah Anya Rajnaitik Kahaniyaan* (Saraswati Press, Banaras). This translation appeared in *The Co-Wife and Other Stories by Premchand*, translated by Ruth Vanita (New Delhi: Penguin, 2008). I have made minor changes.

Women's Home, but they were petrified of her. Such was the terror she inspired that when she entered a room, their laughter would turn to a whimper, and their chirping voices would be quenched, as if they felt that the secrets of their pasts were written on their faces for all to read.

Secrets of the past! Who does not wish to keep the past locked up in a cage like a ferocious beast? The rich lie sleepless for fear of thieves. The respectable have to guard their reputations in the same way. A creature which starts out tiny as an ant grows tall and strong with time, until we tremble at the thought of it. If it were just a matter of one's own doings, most ladies would have disregarded Jugnu. But the homes of one's parents, in-laws, maternal grandmothers, paternal grandmothers, maternal aunts, and paternal aunts, all have to be guarded. Who can guard a fortress that has so many gates? It is wiser to bow one's head before the attacker.

Thousands of corpses lay buried in Jugnu's heart, and she unearthed them when needed. Whenever a woman started to brag or put on airs, Jugnu's face would change. A stern look from her could make the strongest quake, yet it wasn't as if the women hated her. No, all of them met her with great pleasure and respectfully welcomed her. Criticism of one's neighbours has always been a source of entertainment for human beings, and Jugnu provided plenty of this.

2.

There was a high school in town known as Indumati Women's School. It had just acquired a new headmistress, Miss Khurshed. There was no other women's club in town, so one day Miss Khurshed came to the Women's Home. She was better educated than any woman working in the Home. She was respectfully received. From the first day it became apparent that Miss Khurshed's arrival had infused new vitality into the Home. She met everyone warmly, and her conversation was so interesting that all the women were charmed by her. She was a good singer too. She lectured well, and she had earned a name in London for her acting. The Home was very fortunate to receive such a highly talented lady as a guest. She was fair and rosy, with intoxicating eyes; her hair was cut in the latest style, and all her limbs were well shaped; it would be hard to imagine a more enchanting vision.

As she was leaving, Miss Khurshed called aside Mrs Tandon, who was the head of the Home, and asked her, 'Who's that old woman?'

Jugnu had come into the room several times and surveyed Miss Khurshed, much as a good rider observes a new mare.

Mrs Tandon smiled and said, 'She's employed here to do the top work. Do you need her to do anything for you?'

Miss Khurshed thanked her and said, 'No, I have no need of her. She seems to me the type who carries on intrigues. And I notice that she behaves not like a servant but like a mistress.'

Mrs Tandon had suffered much at Jugnu's hands. Jugnu used to call her *Sada Suhagin* (Forever Married) to stigmatize her widowhood. Mrs Tandon freely criticized Jugnu to Miss Khurshed, and warned her to be on guard with Jugnu.

Miss Khurshed grew serious and said, 'She sounds like a terrible woman. That's why all the ladies are afraid of her. Why don't you get rid of her? Why employ such a witch even for a day?'

Mrs Tandon expressed her helplessness. 'How can I turn her out? She'll make life impossible for us. Our fates are in her hands. You'll witness her skills in a few days' time. I'm worried about you; I hope you don't fall into her clutches. Don't make the mistake of ever speaking to a man in her presence. She has spies all over the place. She finds out secrets from the servants, she gets postmen to show her people's letters, she coaxes children into telling her about family matters. The wretch should have been in the secret police! God knows why she came here to harass us.'

Miss Khurshed seemed lost in thought, as if considering how she could solve this problem. After a moment she said, 'Fine, I'll set her right. Wait and see, I'll get rid of her.'

Mrs Tandon: 'Just getting rid of her will be no use. Her tongue will keep wagging. In fact, she'll defame us all even more fearlessly.'

Miss Khurshed said calmly, 'I'll shut her up as well, sister! You just wait and see. A worthless woman ruling over everyone! I can't put up with this.'

After Miss Khurshed left, Mrs Tandon called Jugnu and said, 'Did you see the new Miss Sahib? She's the principal.'

Jugnu said in an envious tone, 'You see her. I've seen hundreds of such girls. They are utterly shameless.'

Mrs Tandon said mildly, 'She'll eat you alive. Watch out for her. She told me she would set you right. I thought I'd better warn you. Be careful what you say in front of her.'

Jugnu said, as if drawing a sword, 'No need to warn me. You had better warn her. If I don't stop her coming here, I'm not my father's daughter. She may have gone round the world, but I have seen more of the world sitting at home.'

Mrs Tandon egged her on. 'Well, I've warned you. Now do as you please.'

'You watch, I'll make her dance to my tune,' said Jugnu. 'Why isn't she married? She must be around thirty?'

Mrs Tandon added another layer. 'She says she doesn't want to get married. Why should she give up her freedom to some man?'

Jugnu pulled a face. 'No one will have her. I've seen plenty of single women of this type. The cat eats seventy mice and then goes on a pilgrimage.'

Several other ladies came in, and the conversation ended there.

3.

The next morning, Jugnu turned up at Miss Khurshed's bungalow.

'Where have you come from?' the cook asked her.

Jugnu: 'I live here, son. Where has Memsahib come from? You must have been with her a long time?'

Cook: 'She's from Nagpur. I'm also from there. I've been with her for ten years.'

Jugnu: 'She must be from a high-up family? One can tell from her manner.'

Cook: 'No, the family is not particularly well placed. She's had good luck, though. Her mother works at the mission on a salary of thirty rupees. She was a good student, so she got a scholarship and went abroad. That set her up for life. She wants her mother to come live with her, but the old woman may not agree. Memsahib doesn't go to church, so the two don't get along.'

Jugnu: 'She seems to be hot-tempered.'

Cook: 'No, she's very nice, but she doesn't go to church. Are you looking for work? You could work here, perhaps. She's looking for a maid.'

Jugnu: 'No, son, I'm not fit for work now. The Memsahib who lived in this bungalow earlier was very kind to me. So I thought I'd come along and bless the new Memsahib.'

Cook: 'She's not the kind to accept such blessings. She scolds any beggar who appears. She says no one has the right to live without working. So it's best for you to quietly go away.'

Jugnu: 'You mean that she has neither dharma nor karma. So why would she pity the poor?'

Jugnu had obtained sufficient materials to start constructing her wall—the lady was from a low-class family, she didn't get along with her mother, she was indifferent to religion. Not bad for a first assault. As she was leaving, she asked the cook, 'What does the Sahib do?'

The cook smiled and said, 'She's not married yet. Where would a Sahib come from?'

Faking surprise, Jugnu said, 'Not yet married! In our community, people would laugh!'

Cook: 'Everyone has their own customs. Among them, many women stay unmarried all their lives.'

Jugnu said, in a knowing way, 'I've seen many so-called virgins of this kind. If anyone lived like this in our community, she would be spat upon. Among them, people can do as they like, nobody cares.'

Just then, Miss Khurshed arrived. It was a mild winter. She was wearing an overcoat over her sari. She had an umbrella in one hand and the leash of a small dog in the other. Exercise in the cold morning air had turned her cheeks fresh and red. Jugnu bowed low and saluted, but Miss Khurshed barely glanced at her. When Miss Khurshed went in, she called the cook and asked, 'What does this woman want?'

Untying his shoelaces before coming in, the cook said, 'She's a beggar, madam! But she's quite clever. When I asked if she wanted to work here, she refused. She asked what your husband does. When I explained, she was very surprised—that's natural. Among Hindus, babies are married off while they are still at the breast.'

Khurshed enquired further, 'What else did she say?'

'Nothing else, madam!'

'All right, send her to me'.

4.

As soon as Jugnu set foot in the room, Miss Khurshed rose from her chair to greet her. 'Come in, Ma-ji! I had gone for a walk. Is all well at the Home?'

Standing with her hand on the cushion of a chair, Jugnu said, 'All's well, Miss Sahib! I just thought I'd come and give you my blessing. I am your follower. Call me any time you need some work done. You must feel quite lonely, living on your own here.'

Miss Khurshed: 'I'm very happy with the girls at my school. They are my own daughters.'

Jugnu shook her head with maternal wisdom and said, 'That's all very well, Miss Sahib, but one's own are one's own. If others become one's own, why would anyone care about their own?'

Suddenly, a handsome and elegant youth wearing a silk suit walked in, his shoes announcing his arrival. Miss Khurshed ran and greeted him with great love, as if she could barely contain herself. Jugnu shrank into a corner when she saw him.

Khurshed embraced the youth and cried, 'Dearest! I've been waiting so long for you. [To Jugnu] Ma-ji, you can go now, come some other time. This is my great friend, William King. He and I studied together for many years.'

Jugnu quietly went outside. The cook was standing there. She asked him, 'Who is this boy?'

The cook shook his head. 'I've never seen him before. Perhaps she is tired of the single life! He's a stylish fellow.'

Jugnu: 'The two fell on each other's necks in front of me, and I didn't know which way to look! Not even husband and wife kiss in public like that. They were inseparable. The boy was a bit embarrassed when he saw me, but your Miss Sahib seemed to have gone mad.'

As if foreseeing unpleasantness, the cook said, 'It seems to me something very odd is going on.'

Jugnu went straight to Mrs Tandon's house.

Meanwhile, Miss Khurshed and the young man were talking. Miss Khurshed burst out laughing and said, 'You played your part very well, Leela! The old woman was really startled.'

Leela: 'I was afraid the old woman might catch on.'

Miss Khurshed: 'I was sure she would come today. When I saw her in the veranda from a distance, I informed you. Today, there'll be great fun at the Home. I wish I could hear the scandalmongering among the women there! You wait and see, all of them will believe what she says.'

Leela: 'You are walking into a swamp with open eyes.'

Miss Khurshed: 'I love acting, sister! It'll be a big joke. The old woman has oppressed everyone for quite long enough. I want to teach her a lesson. Come tomorrow at the same time, dressed the same way. She's sure to come tomorrow too. She won't be able to digest even water until she comes here again! Or wait, let's do it this way. I'll inform you as soon as she arrives, and you come right away, as a fine young fellow!'

5.

That day, at the home, Jugnu had not a moment's rest. First, she told the entire story to Mrs Tandon. Mrs Tandon rushed to the Home and gave the news to the other women. Jugnu was called to confirm the details. Each lady who came in wanted to hear Jugnu tell the story again. The story became more colourful with each retelling. By afternoon, tongues were wagging in every corner of the town.

One lady asked, 'Who is this young man?'

Mrs Tandon: 'It's said that they studied together. They must have had a relationship for a while. That's what I said—how could she be single at this age? Now the cat's out of the bag.'

Jugnu: 'Whatever else he may be, he's very handsome.'

Mrs Tandon: 'This is how our educated sisters behave!'

Jugnu: 'I sensed it as soon as I saw her face. She's no innocent!'

Tandon: 'Go again tomorrow.'

Jugnu: 'Not tomorrow—I'll go tonight!'

But she needed a pretext to go that night. Mrs Tandon sent for a book for the Home. Jugnu reached Miss Khurshed's bungalow at nine at night. Leelavati happened to be there at the time. She said, 'The old woman won't leave us alone!'

Miss Khurshed: 'I told you she wouldn't be able to digest even water. Go and get dressed. I'll keep her occupied. Start babbling like a drunk. Say that you want to elope with me. Behave as if you're not in your senses.'

Leela was a doctor in the mission. She had a bungalow close by. When she left, Miss Khurshed called Jugnu in.

Jugnu gave her a note and said, 'Mrs Tandon has asked for this book. It got late. I wouldn't have troubled you at this hour, but she'll ask for it early in the morning. Miss Sahib, she has an income of thousands, but she's a penny-pincher. Beggars are turned away from her door.'

Miss Khurshed looked at the note and said, 'I can't get this book out now. Come and take it in the morning. But I want to talk to you. Sit down, I'll be back.'

She went into the next room, drew the curtain and returned after about fifteen minutes, wearing a beautiful silk sari, perfume and powder. Jugnu looked at her, wide-eyed. Oh my! Such ornamentation! That young man must be on his way. That's why she's making these preparations. Otherwise, why would a single woman need to dress and decorate herself to go to bed? In Jugnu's view, there was only one reason for women to dress up—to please a husband. Therefore, dressing up was forbidden to all but married women. Khurshed was about to sit down when the squeaking of shoes was heard, and William King entered the room. His eyes seemed turned back in his head, and his clothes reeked of liquor. He unhesitatingly caught Miss Khurshed to his breast and repeatedly kissed her cheeks.

Trying to free herself from his arms, Miss Khurshed said, 'Go along with you. You're drunk.'

King held her even closer and said, 'Today I will make you drink too, beloved! You'll have to drink. Then we both will sleep, wrapped up in each other. Love becomes very lively in intoxication—try it and see.'

Miss Khurshed gestured towards Jugnu, to indicate to him that she was there, but he was too drunk to care. He didn't even look at Jugnu.

Miss Khurshed angrily freed herself and said, 'You're not in your senses right now. Why are you so over-eager? I'm not running away anywhere.'

King: 'I've been coming here secretly, like a thief, all these days; now I'll come openly.'

Khurshed: 'You are crazy. Don't you see who's sitting here?'

King looked perturbed when he saw Jugnu, and said irritably, 'When did this old woman come? Why did you come, old woman? You daughter of Satan, do you come here to uncover our secrets?

You want to defame us? I'll wring your neck. Wait, where are you going? I won't let you escape alive.'

Jugnu slipped out of the room, softly as a cat, and ran off as fast as she could. Behind her, the room rocked with laughter.

Jugnu went straight to Mrs Tandon's house again. She could not contain herself, but Mrs Tandon had gone to sleep. Disappointed, she knocked at several other doors but none of them opened, and the unfortunate woman had to spend the night as if in the company of a crying baby. Early in the morning, she rushed to the Home.

In about half an hour, Mrs Tandon too arrived. Jugnu turned her face away.

Mrs Tandon asked, 'Did you come to my house last night? The cook just told me.'

Jugnu said coldly, 'The thirsty go to the well. The well doesn't go to the thirsty. You pushed me into the fire and stayed at a safe distance. God protected me, otherwise I would have died last night.'

Mrs Tandon asked eagerly, 'What happened? Tell me. Why didn't you wake me up? You know it's my habit to go to sleep early.'

'The cook wouldn't let me into the house. How could I wake you? You should have realized that I would be on my way. How would it have harmed you to go to bed a little later? But you don't care about anyone else.'

'So what happened? Did Miss Khurshed try to beat you up?'

'Not she but that lover of hers did. His eyes were red, and he told me to get out. Before I could leave, he ran at me with his whip. If I hadn't fled like the wind, he would have flayed me alive. And that whore sat there, watching the show. It was a plan the two of them had made. It's a sin to even look at such fallen women. Even prostitutes are not so shameless.'

In a little while, the other ladies arrived. All of them were very eager to hear the new episode. Jugnu's tongue moved ceaselessly, like a pair of scissors. The ladies thoroughly enjoyed the narrative. They kept asking searching questions about each detail. They forgot about their housework, and even forgot to be hungry or thirsty. They were not satisfied with hearing the story once; they listened to it again and again, with renewed enthusiasm each time.

Finally, Mrs Tandon said, 'It's not proper for us to bring such women into the Home. All of you consider this question.'

Mrs Pandya endorsed her opinion. 'We don't want the Home to fall from its ideals. I say that such a woman is not fit to be the principal of any institution.'

Mrs Bangda piped up, 'Jugnubai was right in saying that it is a sin to look at such a woman's face. We should plainly tell her that she should not trouble herself to come here.'

The pot was just beginning to boil when a car arrived and stopped in front of the Home. The ladies craned their necks and saw that Miss Khurshed and William King were sitting in the car.

Jugnu indicated with her face and hands that this was the same young man! The whole group of women crowded behind the cane curtain to get a glimpse of him.

Miss Khurshed got out of the car, closed the *hood* and came towards the gate of the Home. The ladies all ran back to their seats.

Miss Khurshed entered the room. No one welcomed her. Miss Khurshed gave Jugnu an unabashed look and said, smiling, 'Well, Bai-ji, I hope you didn't get injured last night?'

Jugnu had seen many bold-faced women, but even she was surprised by this brazenness. The thief, stolen goods in hand, was challenging the honest person!

Jugnu drew herself up and said, 'If you're not satisfied, get me beaten up now. He's right here, isn't he?'

Khurshed: 'He's come to apologize to you. He was drunk last night.'

Jugnu said, glancing at Mrs Tandon, 'And you were no less drunk.'

Understanding the sarcasm, Khurshed replied, 'I have never touched liquor in my life. Don't accuse me falsely.'

Jugnu brought out the big guns. 'There is something more intoxicating than liquor; perhaps you were affected by that.

Why have you kept the gentleman behind the veil? Let these ladies see his face.'

Miss Khurshed said mischievously, 'His face is one in a million.'

Mrs Tandon said anxiously, 'No, there's no need to bring him here. We don't want to give the Home a bad name.'

Miss Khurshed insisted, 'He must come before you, to clear up this matter. Why are you making a one-sided judgement?'

To deflect her, Mrs Tandon said, 'This is not a lawsuit in court!'

Miss Khurshed: 'My honour is being stained, and you say it's not a lawsuit? Mr King will appear, and you will have to listen to his testimony.'

Apart from Mrs Tandon, all the ladies were eager to see King. No one opposed the proposition!

Khurshed went to the door and called out, 'Come in, please.'

The hood opened and Leelavati emerged, smiling, clad in a silk sari.

There was stunned silence. The ladies looked at Leelavati with dismay.

Jugnu said, her eyes sparkling, 'Where have you concealed him?'

Khurshed: 'He's vanished into thin air. Go and look in the car.'

Jugnu leapt forward and went to the car, examined it thoroughly and returned with a hangdog expression on her face.

Miss Khurshed asked, 'What happened? Did you find anyone?'

Jugnu: 'What do I know of these womanly tricks? [Looking closely at Leelavati] You are deceiving us by putting a man in a sari. This is that drunken fellow!'

Khurshed: 'Are you sure you recognize him?'

Jugnu: 'Yes, of course. Am I blind?'

Mrs Tandon: What nonsense are you talking, Jugnu? This is Dr Leelavati.'

Jugnu (gesturing with her fingers): 'Go on with you, saying you are Leelavati. Don't you feel ashamed to wear a sari and pretend to be a woman? Weren't you at her house last night?'

Leelavati said, amused, 'When did I deny it? I am Leelavati now. At night, I become William King. What's surprising about that?'

Now, the ladies began to see the light. Laughter erupted on all sides. Some clapped their hands, some embraced Dr Leelavati, others clapped Miss Khurshed on the back. There was a commotion for several minutes. Jugnu's face fell, and she was completely silenced. Never had she been made such a fool of and felt so humiliated.

Mrs Mehra reproved her, 'Well, Dai, has your face been blackened?'

Mrs Bangda: 'This is the way she goes around slandering everyone.'

Leelavati: 'All of you believe what she says.'

No one saw Jugnu leave. Seeing storm clouds arise over her head, she thought it best to quietly slink away. She left by the back door and ran through the alleys.

Miss Khurshed said, 'Ask her why she was so set on destroying me.'

Mrs Tandon called out to her, but Jugnu was nowhere to be found! A search began. Jugnu had disappeared!

After that day, no one in town ever set eyes on Jugnu. This incident is still narrated, and causes much amusement, when the history of the Home is recounted.

Ekakini*

Asha Sahay

[. . .] Arati sat on the sandy seashore, gazing at *ekakini* Kala, that mysterious form which she could not understand.

When Arati had seen Kala for the first time, she was repelled. Everything about Kala was disorderly. Her full, fair face in the midst of long, thick, black hair was attractive. But Kala's carelessness appeared sordid to Arati. Beauty and sordidness together! Arati was irritated, and withdrew.

[. . .] Arati brought to Kala enchanting beauty, well-ordered emotions and moments; intoxicated, Kala, leaping like a stream, embraced her. No bondage, no obstacles, no end. All was boundless and endless. [. . .] Restless and innocent Arati found a merciless line of painful experience on Kala's lips, and trembled!

Gradually, knowingly and unknowingly, she began to love Kala. [. . .] Surprised, she wanted to turn away, not look at the disorderly Kala, but she could not.

Arati was defeated, Kala victorious. In this defeat, Arati's heart experienced the sharpness of love. But Kala found in her victory the maddening agitation of intoxicated life, an unfamiliar jolt, a

---

* These are excerpts from the novel *Ekakini*, published by International Book Agency, Patna, in 1947. The title is an untranslatable word, which means a woman who is alone, on her own. It is more evocative than 'single woman'.

19

sweet anguish! So far, Kala had loved only the paintbrush and painting, but now Arati came between the paintbrush and Kala.

Kala was an embodiment of devotion.[*] Kala loved Arati, worshipped her. Arati burned, inflamed. Attraction took form in Kala's heart. The artist Kala inscribed Arati's love on the curtain of her heart. The snapshot of love supported by immortality!

A strange magic—an unimaginable experience! Kala and Arati traded lives, they became one. A boundless curiosity— neither dawn nor sunrise, neither blossom nor bee, neither flute nor honeyed forest, neither youth nor unrest—wild Kala and cultured Arati!

Arati and Kala's childhood passed like that of two flowers on one bough. Breaking the tender nest of childhood, two images with one form unknowingly moved towards the intoxicating palace of youth. [. . .]

Young Arati had a mother's love, a father's affection, the desires of the world, learnt the sharpness of circumstances, but although she wished to, she could not overcome her heart, master her heart.

Kala mastered her heart—mastered the world. Not for her the unknown aspirations of youth, the lone land of curiosity, the restless jolt of incompletion! She was complete, holding herself in her own hands. The dream of childhood retreated before the insistent moment of youth. Youth brought to Arati a lack—a tumult. Youth brought to Kala completion—dedication. Arati found a world of curiosity and enquiry, Kala found criticism and analysis. The monarch youth gave to queen Arati the red dawn of attractiveness but gave Kala the radiance of pride and dignity. Arati wanted her life to be the *arati*, the worship, of a God, and Kala wanted to create the artistic image of a world-artist.[†] Arati

---

[*] The word is the untranslatable *sadhana*, generally used to mean spiritual dedication, devotion and commitment.

[†] The word can mean an artist of international stature; it can also mean an artist who creates worlds.

finally became an *arati*,* burning every moment in the desire for a
God. Kala lived each moment by imbibing the nectar of the Gods.

[*Arati is a rich man's daughter and has been in love since childhood with
Vijay, who is now a nationalist and is in prison. His mother arranges
their marriage, and he agrees, although he is in love with Bijli, also a
radical and also in prison. After marriage, Arati will move from Delhi
to Banaras.*]

Binding Arati in her fair arms, Kala said, 'Arati!'
   Arati looked at her, unblinking. Blending into her, Kala
said, 'Arati!'
   Lifting Kala's chin, Arati said, 'Kala Rani!'†
   'You'll leave me, won't you?' Kala said, agitated.
   Arati looked at her affectionately. 'I'll have to.'
   'But why?'
   Arati laughed, her soul lost in the tinkling of hopeful laughter.
   'You want a male life partner, Arati, not a female one. But will
he love you more than I do?' [. . .] Won't you listen to me? Don't
marry [. . .] I know you are eager for closeness with a man. [. . .] I
know that a man cannot give his heart to a woman as fully as she
can to him! [. . .] To change from a human woman (*manavi*) to a
Goddess is to change from an image to stone. A woman is crying
out for a woman. Don't ignore this longing cry, Arati! Be my Arati,
I will be your Kala! [. . .] Light up my life like worship (*arati*)
offered to a God, untouched like the tuberose; I will become the
radiant art (*kala*) of your life, like a new era. I will paint your beauty
with my immortal brush. [. . .]'

---

* *Arati* means a worship ceremony, wherein a flame is waved before the
images of a God or Goddess.
† *Rani* means, literally, queen. Women often attach it to the names of
women they like, as a form of endearment.

'A woman wants to rule the house [. . .] Kala, a woman wants
motherhood!' [. . .]

'Womanhood, motherhood, these are a curse, Arati! [. . .] I
agree that love is a mother's tenderness, a wife's bliss, the heart of
the universe. Yet I say, Arati, don't marry! [. . .] To erase men's old
ways, we need a new world of intoxicating revolution [. . .]'

So saying, Kala swept out of Arati's room like a whirlwind . . .
a tempest of revolt . . . the maddening music of revolution . . .
a startling newness . . .

[*Vijay's sister Suman is entranced by Arati's beauty in a white khadi
sari. She gives her a string of pearls and a picture of Vijay. Kala tells
Arati not to take it as she does not yet have a right to it.*]

Arati stood like a statue. She cannot oppose Kala. Kala has greater
authority over her than does the man in the picture [. . .]

Sudha said, 'Kala Rani, you are being unfair. When you get a
picture of your prospective life partner, every part of you will cry
out with eager longing.'

Kala laughed in ridicule . . .

'A picture of my life partner! Sudha Rani! Forget it . . .'

'Take it, Arati,' Kala said, her pride crashing like a meteor, and
she grew sad like a statue of renunciation. She felt that Arati was
forgetting her, distancing herself. Kala's self-sufficiency smouldered
in the embers of unfulfilment. She thought, woman belongs to
man, not to woman.

[*Kala stays over at Arati's request. In the night, Kala sees Arati gazing
at Vijay's picture.*]

Kala laughed an ugly laugh. 'A man's victory, a young man's
victory . . .'

Arati was embarrassed!

'Kala, believe me, I feel as if this image has been in my heart
for ages.'

'That's just your sentimentality.'

'Won't I be complete when I get him, Kala?'

'Complete? Aren't you complete now? Your days are yours, your nights are yours, your emotions are yours, your sweetness is yours. Your own laughter, your own tears, your youth, your womanhood. If you are empty now, can you ever be full? Once you marry, you will have to empty yourself out every moment. You will give up maidenhood for married life, give up womanhood for motherhood, give up life for stumbling blocks. You will give up youth to become a toy.' [. . .]

Arati began to cry. [. . .] 'Embrace me, Kala! I am yours and always will be yours!' [. . .]

Kala was alone. [. . .] Brushes and paints called out to her, but she did not hear. She wept. She had brushes, colours, emotions. But where was that picture her heart desired? Where is my companion [*sangini*] who supported my feelings? Where is my Arati?

[*Arati gets married and moves to Delhi. Suman, Vijay's mother Shanta, and even Bijli adore Arati, but Vijay does not cohabit with her despite his mother's reproaches. Arati falls ill and is unable to sleep.*]

Arati burst out crying.

'Mother. Call Kala.'

Today, Arati knew how divine Kala's desire was. She had broken Kala's heart and neglected her. Kala! Kala!! Her heart called out. [. . .]

'Kala will put me to sleep, mother. Kala is artistic, she knows how to cast a spell, mother!'

Shanta laughed and said, 'Then my sweet daughter-in-law will be captured by an enchantress.'

[. . .]

Kala heard that Arati was unwell. Her heart seemed to stop. Her dignity reproached her. Her dignity had kept her away from her friend [*saheli*]. [. . .]

'Kala!' cried Arati in a weak voice.

'Arati!' Kala held her to her empty heart. Arati's sadness ebbed. Kala's emptiness was filled.

Kala saw that Arati's lotus eyes were tired, as if there was no dawn for them. Her pink cheeks had withered, her red, flower-like lips were white like jasmine, she seemed to have shed all her adornments. Kala moaned in agony.

Arati saw grief in Kala's eyes, wounded pride on her face, strangled laughter on her lips. The ever-forward-moving Kala seemed lost, fatigued, sad, uninterested. [...]

The married woman [*suhagin*] and the one separated from her lover [*viyogin*] became one. Tears met tears, grief met grief. Kala met Arati as if dignified distance [*maan*] met love and respect met effort.

[*Kala encourages Arati to revolt and confront Vijay; Arati insists that love involves sacrifice. Finally, Arati talks to Vijay and realizes that his heart belongs to Bijli. Arati instructs Kala, who is now ruling the house, to get Vijay married to Bijli, and she runs away from home. She takes refuge in a village temple, starts living with a village woman, Rupa, and her family, and works to educate village children and women: 'Woman found support in woman's shadow.' Vijay marries Bijli but is haunted by Arati. He finds her, but she refuses to return, saying she belongs to Krishna in the village temple and is happy there; she blesses his union with Bijli. Vijay loses interest in Bijli and yearns for Arati. Meanwhile, Atul, a revolutionary, falls in love with Kala, who refuses him. He dies in the struggle, and then she decides that she worships him, and is his widow and the daughter-in-law of Mother India. Kala goes to the village to meet Arati.*]

Kala embraced Arati. How unprecedented, how blissful was this union! Arati's tears fell into Kala's lap. How tender, how vital was this union! How maddening, how replete with imagination! How alone, how silent! How tearful—like the emptiness of afternoon, the last watch of the night! [...]

Kala hid her face in Arati's bosom, as if it were her refuge.

[*Kala tries to persuade Arati to return to Vijay (this was before laws were passed instituting monogamy for Hindu men) and to work for the country. Arati says she doesn't need to return to Vijay; she can worship him wherever she is.*]

Lost in amazement, Kala said, 'What are you, Arati?'

In trembling tones, Arati said, 'Ekakini!'

[. . .] Between heaven and earth, Kala saw the compassionate figure of woman! The power [*shakti*] of life, lone woman by herself!

A Primary Knowledge of Geography[*]

Rajkamal Chaudhari

'Will you go to see P.C. Sorcar's magic show?' I asked Ramaa's mother. '. . . Sawing girls in half, a display of Sputnik . . . all kinds of illusions—will you go?'

She had spread palm leaves on the veranda and was enjoying the shy warmth of morning in the first week of December. She smiled at my usual careless demeanour, my blue half-pants and T-shirt . . . the old scarf tied around my neck.

She drew the pillow closer, turned towards me and said, 'Ramaa has gone for tuition . . . He's very weak in maths. Why don't you help him?'

Ramaa's full name is Ramaavallabh Narayan Singh.[†] He is the best-looking boy in our school and the most feminine. We, that is, he and I, sit at a double-desk every day in section B of class ten. Mathura Babu, the Hindi teacher, has nicknamed us the twins. One day, during tiffin-break, Mathura Babu called me to him and

---

[*] 'Bhugol Ka Prarambhik Gyan' was probably first published in the mid to late 1950s, when most of Chaudhari's stories appeared. This translation is from his *Pratinidhi Kahaniyan* (New Delhi: Rajkamal, 1995).

[†] Ramaavallabh is a boy's name, meaning 'the beloved of Lakshmi', that is, Vishnu. But when shortened to Ramaa, it means 'Lakshmi' and is a girl's name.

said, 'We are putting Ramaa into section C. You don't have any objection, do you?'

Everyone knows that it wouldn't matter to me even if Ramaa were put in section D. I am a carefree sort of boy. I don't covet Ramaa or any other nice and beautiful thing. I am not interested in any sport other than football and hockey.

When Ramaa heard that he would be put in C section he came to me and started crying in front of all the boys. His complaint was that if I was not with him, the boys in his class would harass him for indecent reasons.

I was staring at Ramaa's mother. In the almond-coloured light of morning, her whole body shone like a garland of rays. Her sari was pulled up quite a bit on the right side. The brownness and sturdiness of her thighs attracted me. My own mother was usually unwell and fragile, as if she would disintegrate at a touch . . . She keeps coughing late into the night and cursing the world, the family, God and my father. Perhaps she won't manage to outlast the terrible cold of this year, 1944 . . .

'Why are you always so dirty . . .? Doesn't Savitri wash your clothes? Why don't you oil your hair?' Ramaa's mother asked, seeing me standing in my habitually carefree style. I decided for the seventeenth time that I should not look at the naked ankles of this tall, broad, heavy, thirty-two to thirty-five-year-old woman. Ramaa's mother's name is Manmohini Devi. She lives in our neighbourhood. Ramaa's father was a police inspector. He was killed in combat with the dacoits of Rajauli.* Manmohini Devi lives alone with her only child. She has her own house and some ancestral property in the village. My father often said, 'Any other woman who suffered as much as Ramaa's mother would have hanged herself or joined a *kotha*.† Her husband, the inspector, used to drink two bottles of liquor every day and eat two *ser* of meat all

---

* A region of Bihar that was notorious for criminality.

† Become a sex worker.

by himself. He was always in debt . . . It was Ramaa's mother who somehow kept the household going.'

But when the topic came up, my mother, Savitri Devi, would talk of other things, things that I do not understand, even though I am in class ten. According to Savitri Devi, Manmohini Devi is a fallen woman, because were she not, she would definitely have protected her marital status. 'A pure woman's purity . . . has an effect! Our Manmohini is a woman of the new age, she eats paan and tobacco, even though she's a widow, she wears coloured clothes, and . . .' My mother is not able to finish her sentence.

When I stand in front of her, she never speaks of Ramaa's mother. She knows Ramaa is my friend. She knows many things about me because she's my mother . . .

Many boys in my class were *homosexual*. Such boys are usually teachers' favourites. Ramaa, despite being feminine in appearance and nature, was not favoured by the teachers. Perhaps this was because he was a boy from the city; his father was in the police department . . . and he understood the looks of his classmates and his teachers.

He immediately understood what a man was thinking about him. As far as I remember, he also knew how to take unfair advantage of this knowledge. He would rob rich boys of their money . . . but this could not be called robbery, because Ramaa was extremely cowardly and robbing someone requires courage. Ramaa was afraid of everyone except me. He trusted me because I protected him from other boys. Armed with this trust, he would often pick quarrels with other boys but never in my absence . . . Once, when I was absent, two boys from class eleven harassed him a lot. After that, he would not set foot outside his house after dark. But Ramaa was not weak or thin. He was well-built and healthy. We both were the best *centres* in our school's football team. I've never seen anyone run as fast with a football as Ramaa did. But having taken the ball up to the goalpost, he was not able to score a goal . . . Hundreds of times, I've seen Ramaa stand despairingly at the goalpost, protecting the ball with his feet.

His feet lacked strength for the kick, and Ramaa would give up; I would snatch the ball from him and score the goal. And people would say, 'Today the loving pair scored five goals after half-time.' People said many things.

I didn't dislike being with Ramaa neither did I like it. Yes, at the NCC camp and on other such outings, I did the bad act with Ramaa a couple of times, either out of anger or to dominate the other boys. But I was not attracted either to him or to any other boy or girl. I preferred beating people up, watching sports and playing football. Several times, I gave Ramaa eight or ten slaps and stopped visiting his home.

Then his mother would come to our house to cajole me. My mother was somewhat afraid of Manmohini Devi. She never criticized her to her face . . . That my mother is double-faced pleases me.

Suddenly, Manmohini reached out a hand and snatched away my scarf. Just as the great warrior Karna in the Mahabharata had armour and earrings, I had this scarf that one of my mother's sisters had knitted. This red-and-yellow woollen scarf protects me in many straits. In quarrels and fights, it helps me to lasso somebody's legs and haul at someone else's throat . . .

When it was snatched away, I felt naked. Like a modest girl I tried in vain to cover my neck with my hands. I had not bathed for the last four or five days. Having been wrapped in the scarf for that long, my neck had several layers of dirt on it. Suddenly the red rays of the sun shone on my bare neck. I felt as if small insects were crawling on my neck and buttocks, and thousands of boils had erupted there . . . Writhing, I began to rub my neck with both hands, scraping off the dirt, and I sat down with a bang on the straw mat, near Ramaa's mother's feet. She was laughing at me but stopped when I fell on the mat.

'*Arey*, what's happened . . .? What's wrong?' She sat up, drew me towards her, put my head and half of my body in her lap, and began to stroke me.

I closed my eyes and said, 'Nothing, nothing's happened,' and continued to have my neck and back scratched by her. But I was laughing to myself. My lips were pressed together, my face was distorted by imaginary pain, and seeing Manmohini Devi's agitation, I was laughing to myself. It was clear, however, that my writhing and sitting down on the mat with a thud was a performance. I have had to put on several such small and big performances since I was eight or ten years old.

If I break a glass, even now, at this age, and though I am the most mischievous and sharpest boy in class ten, I stand in front of my mother and cry. If I do not pretend to cry, mother will level a filthy and extremely vulgar idiom at me, while father will call me into his room and give me a two-and-a-half-hour-long boring speech about discipline, character and ideal celibate studenthood. My father has memorized all of M. Smiles's book about people of high character. After the lecture, he will repeat that story about an English boy who, obeying his father's command, stood in a corner of the ship and did not move by a hair's breadth even after the ship caught fire. 'Make this boy your ideal,' my father always said.

'. . . Good character is a person's greatest adornment . . . Every night, before going to sleep, remember how many good deeds you have done today and how many mistakes you have made.' Whenever I made a mistake, my father would come up with some such sage statement that was fit to be inscribed, framed, and hung up on a wall.

To protect myself from my mother's idioms and my father's speeches I had taken to playacting . . . My mother Savitri Devi's favourite saying was, 'The devoted wife spends her life at the stove, whores go on pilgrimage,' generally referring to herself and her friend and neighbour Manmohini Devi. My mother is remarkably skilful at creating idioms that are a tremendous help to her in defeating her women neighbours in verbal battles. She doesn't hesitate to use them against my father either.

That is why, when my scarf was snatched away and Ramaa's mother pressed it to her nose and began smelling it, I panicked. My scarf stinks of sweat and dust. I thought she would feel like vomiting after smelling my scarf, and would throw it at me and tell me to get lost . . . In the grip of this fear, I had pretended to writhe around.

Manmohini Devi did not throw the scarf at me. Instead, she placed my head in her lap and began to stroke my forehead and neck. Then she said, 'What happened, Phool-babu? Did an insect bite you?' My eyes were closed, and her large, shapeless breasts dangled above my nose. I tried to look at her from the corners of my eyes, but I couldn't see anything, nor was I able to open my eyes.

Phool-babu is my pet name. I can never remember the name, consisting of five words and containing eight ligatured letters, that is recorded in the school register as my name. All I know is Phool-babu. This Phool-babu, despite being fourteen or fourteen-and-a-half, has never seen a woman up so close . . . Ramaa's mother leant over my face and my chest like a huge rock. I was thinking about my name. Phool-babu . . . Ramaavallabh . . . Priyadas-babu, the doctor's son Kaminidas; Chandmal of Bhushan Bhavan— we are the best players on our school's football team. We were unconcerned with studies. I had not started smoking but thanks to Ramaa and Chandmal, I had acquired all the other bad habits. Chandmal would pilfer money from home and our problem would be: how should we spend so much money . . .? Once, our school watchman, who, in a way, was the manager of our football team as well, took us with him to Kamaalpur to drink toddy. That day, Chandmal had twenty or twenty-five rupees with him. In 1944, twenty-five rupees was a lot of money.

After drinking toddy, Sukhlal the watchman asked Chandmal for ten rupees and then said, 'Sirs, you keep sitting here . . . I'll be back soon.' Kaminidas began to smile when Sukhlal said this. He

was the oldest of the four of us and was a close friend of Sukhlal.
He had come with Sukhlal to Kamaalpur several times before.
Kaminidas understood where Sukhlal was going with the ten
rupees . . . that's why he was laughing, but we three were silent . . .

Kamaalpur is a settlement of Pasi and Musahar people at the
foot of a small hill, and is surrounded by a forest of toddy and
date palms.* Huts made of straw, bamboo and tile were scattered at
considerable distances in the shade of the hill . . . dark women and
naked children . . . a group of pigs roamed the open ground. Three
or four locally bred dogs sat near our hut. It was not yet dark but
soon would be.

Drunk on toddy, Chandmal returned and said, 'I have eleven
rupees left. Ramaa, keep this.' Ramaa looked at me. Chandmal
put a ten-rupee note in Ramaa's hand. Putting one rupee back
in his pocket, he said, 'We'll have to pay the rickshaw puller
one rupee.' Ramaa held the note out to me. Kaminidas began to
sing a Bengali song. 'O beautiful bride, when will night come,
sweet night!' . . . Chandmal put his head on Ramaa's thigh and
fell asleep with his arms around Ramaa's waist. His behaviour
made me angry for sure, but drinking too much toddy had made
my stomach swell up and made my limbs lethargic . . . At that
moment, I did not feel up to pulling the legs of this one-*maund*-
forty-five-*ser*-heavy boy and dragging his corpse on foot from
Kamaalpur all the way to Patna Junction . . . But reading my
expression, Ramaa pushed Chandmal away . . . The real event
started after Chandmal lost consciousness.

After a short while, Sukhlal the watchman entered the hut, a
cigarette between his lips. Behind him came a woman, who was
about eighteen or twenty years old . . . She sat directly in front
of me and tried to make herself acquainted with each one of us.
Sukhlal said, 'Phool-babu, this hut belongs to this woman, that is,
to her husband. They are Pasis.'

---

* Both Pasi and Musahar are Dalit communities. The Pasis were
traditionally toddy palm climbers and the Musahars were rat-catchers.

Sukhlal smiled a little. The woman came forward, picked up a glass and filled it with toddy. She gulped down two or three glasses of toddy, and then asked Sukhlal for a cigarette.

The sudden advent of this heroine on the stage worried me. I had some understanding of why this woman had been brought here, but I was suspicious. I put the ten-rupee note in the pocket of my half pants and stayed alert. Sukhlal said, 'I've paid for the toddy. Ten rupees was enough for everything. I've given Birichhiya Pasin,* that is, this woman, seven rupees. One and a half rupees for each of you, and one rupee for me. Do you agree, brothers? What do you say?'

'They won't agree . . . They are students in a government school, they won't agree,' said Birichhiya Pasin, laughing shyly as she drank the left-over toddy from the glass. Then she began spreading out leaves on one side of the hut.

Stroking my forehead, Manmohini Devi said, 'Come, let's go into the house. I'll massage you with oil and bathe you. Let's go.'

. . . I hesitated. The sight of Ramaa's mother swaying like a snake to this blandishment ('Come into the house') reminded me suddenly of that hut in Kamaalpur and Birichhiya Pasin spreading out fresh palm leaves to make a bed in that hut.

The memory made me feel that I might jump off the veranda, run into the open ground in front and, the next day, stand on the road shrieking, 'Help! Save me!' No, this shouting 'Help, help' is largely inaccurate . . . Yes, it's true that before Birichhiya Pasin I had no personal experience of sex with a woman. But I had seen my mother and father, and also one of my maternal cousins and his wife doing these ugly acts. The maternal cousin's name was Bhavanand, and he was twice my age. I used to sleep in his room when visiting my maternal grandparents, and his wife would come into that room after everyone had fallen asleep . . . At first, I thought they were fighting and beating each other up. But later one day I

---

* Pasin means a Pasi woman.

felt that they were doing what that Hindi teacher Mathura Babu
had tried to do with Ramaa.

Bhavanand and his wife, my maternal sister-in-law, would
growl like animals, leap and jump, and hurl the filthiest abuses
at each other as they practically wrestled. On these occasions,
my old grandmother, sleeping in the adjoining room, would
cough loudly . . . One night it was raining. Lightning flashed into
the room several times, and what I saw in its light is better not
revealed. I shut my eyes in fear. It seemed to me that my sister-
in-law was sitting on brother Bhavanand's chest and murdering
him. Later, I saw a picture of the mother of the world, Kalika,
sitting on Bholenath's chest . . . This first experience is still
inscribed on my brain.

And with it is inscribed the fear of being murdered like
Bhavanand Bhai . . . Birichhiya Pasin says, 'Sukhlal, go and stand
outside. If my man were to come along . . .' Sukhlal happily went
outside. Kaminidas was looking at Birichhiya with greedy eyes. He
had already tasted this blood. He knew its taste . . . Chandmal was
snoring away. Ramaa had now understood the whole game but was
afraid, and he wanted to stand up and come close to me.

'Who will come first?' Birichhiya stands up and stretches. She
takes off her sari, folds it, and lays it aside . . . It is not yet dark. In
the last rays of the sinking sun, this woman looks completely black,
like a silhouette, and extremely ugly.

Under the sari, she was wearing a red loincloth, like that of
Hanuman. She asked the question again . . . Ramaa came and
quietly sat down next to me. I was frightened and upset . . . What
was to be done now? Kaminidas said, 'Phoolbabu . . .? Phoolbabu,
shall I go first?'

Birichhiya had removed the bridle of her red loincloth. 'A
black mare with a red bridle*'—this idiom that I had heard my

---

* This is an incorrect version of the idiom 'an old mare with a red bridle,'
which refers to an old woman dressed in an inappropriately flashy way.

mother use suddenly came to mind . . . I had a strong desire to put
my fingers in my mouth and start throwing up . . . and vomit all the
toddy from my stomach on to this woman's naked body. And then
fall unconscious. But at that moment Birichhiya said, 'O Babu?
Your name is Phool-babu? You come first!'

Ramaa gripped my arm tightly with both hands, as if Birichhiya
Pasin was calling him, not me . . . Sukhlal the watchman looked in
and gestured to us to get done fast . . .

My mother Savitri Devi . . . my maternal sister-in-law . . .
Ramaavallabh . . . Birichhiya Pasin . . . and now Manmohini Devi,
pressing my left hand, said, 'Sit down on the bed . . . Don't be shy.
You are a son to me, just like Ramaa.' So saying, she pressed me
to her waist, smelled my forehead, and began patting my cheeks. I
tried to get my neck away from her and, moving back, said, 'If you
speak to my mother, she will allow me to go to see P.C. Sorcar's
magic show . . . Would you like to go? You, I, and Ramaa?'

Manmohini Devi began to laugh the way madwomen
laugh, the way my maternal sister-in-law used to laugh, sitting
on Bhavanand Bhai's chest . . . the way Birichhiya Pasin had
said, gathering me into her arms like a sack of potatoes, 'Oh my,
my! What a sweet name it is, Phool-babu, Phool-babu. I will
take you for a ride on an aeroplane . . .' Laughing, Manmohini
Devi sat down on the bed. Then she said, 'I'll take you wherever
you want. P.C. Sorcar's magic is nothing . . . I'll take you in
an aeroplane to foreign lands. There are great magicians there
who will, in a moment, transform you into a strong, forceful,
virile twenty-five or twenty-six-year-old young man. Will you?
W . . . i . . . ll you?'

I began to scream. '. . . I won't go . . . No, I won't go.' But
no sound issued from my throat. I wanted to pretend to faint
and collapse on the ground. But as if someone had tied me to
an iron pillar, I couldn't move. I was frozen like ice . . . shrunken
like a tortoise's neck. I was in such a state that I could not even
turn around to look at Ramaa . . . Shame . . . surprise and terror.

What else could be done but to close one's eyes and allow the monsoon river's water to flow over one's head!!

* * *

I forgot to mention that I am, in fact, even more cowardly than Ramaa. Ramaa at least had the courage to stand up and run out of the hut. He didn't stop . . . I didn't even have the strength to do that . . . I was so afraid.

This fear is in my blood. And this blood gives me the ability to attack. When I'm afraid I do not run away. I try to attack when I get the chance. Football is based on this principle. One should not run away even when one is most likely to lose . . . One must look for an opening. But even after acknowledging this principle, the truth is that I am a cowardly boy, and to conceal this fear I perform all kinds of brave acrobatics in football and mischief in school.

I keep protecting Ramaa from the other boys because inside me this boil keeps ripening: 'I am a coward . . .' I am happy when Ramaa is with me. I feel I am not a coward because here is Ramaa, who goes to school under my protection and plays football, thanks to me.

But Ramaa was not with me. I was alone, and I was furious with Kaminidas, who was emptying the last dregs of toddy into his glass from a clay goblet, and with Sukhlal the watchman. These two had cast me in this demonic play . . . What to do now? O God! What to do? I felt as if pieces of glass were embedded in my back.

In that one moment, I was filled with terror, rage, disgust, guilt, pain and fury. I said to myself, 'Now I must save my life.' Having decided this, I let my body go slack, stopped my breath, and began playacting.

How does a man lose consciousness? How does he gradually drown and sink into death? How does his weight, the blackness of his body, the poison in his eyes gradually increase? All this I knew.

When no other performance works, I put on an act of dying. The play that Shivshankar Bholenath performs lying under Queen Kalika! My eyes grew fixed, my breath stopped, my hands, feet, arms, knees . . . the grammar of my whole body grew cold, like a dead black snake. The grammar of my body . . . gender, voice, conjunctions, abbreviations, all of it.

Manmohini Devi kept trying to bring me back to consciousness and to warm me up. She said, 'Don't worry, Phool-babu, I'll massage you . . . I'll apply scented oil made by Maha Bhringraj Company.'

But the snake was dead . . . I picked up the scarf lying on the bed and wrapped it round my neck.

Waiting[*]

Rajendra Yadav

When people have lived through a situation repeatedly, they get used to it. But this is not true of Geeta, and even today, waiting is the worst torture for her. She is split in two when it comes to waiting—one part of her waits calmly, untroubled, while the other part, torn by nerve-racking tension, starts at every sound. She is not able to focus on anything; sometimes she starts cleaning the house, while at other times she sits down, spreading out books and papers, as if arranging them will make the time pass. When all her strategies fail she lies flat on the bed and, putting the pillow over her face, stays still as if unconscious, her ears alert to sounds downstairs, waiting for a rattling at the door.

How carefully she had explained to Nanda: 'Listen, I'll wait for you. Don't eat out and don't keep me waiting and hungry for too long. Listen, Harsh, don't stay out too . . .'

She was standing at the door upstairs, and they were on the landing below, where the stairway turns. Harsh, with his hand on Nanda's bare waist, looked up. 'Arey, Didi, don't worry! I won't let her delay us. Is this any way to behave—keep looking at saris in showcases while you are sitting at home, hungry?

---

[*] 'Prateeksha' was first published in October 1962. I translated excerpts from it in *Same-Sex Love in India* (2000). This is the first English translation of the whole story.

All right, ta-ta.' He waved his other hand, which was holding a cigarette, over his head.

Nanda smiled at Harsh's mischief, put two fingers on her lips, sent a flying kiss to Geeta and bounded down the stairs.

'Naughty one!' The words escaped Geeta's lips. Harsh can talk his way out of anything. She kept looking at the stairs and smiling as if enchanted. The mingled sounds of shoes and sandals reached the ground floor; the door latch opened and closed with a click. A wave of perfume remained.

This has been going on for the last three or four days—when the door clicks shut, it snaps off the sound of their voices and footsteps like a length of tape and flings it behind. The footsteps grow fainter in the narrow alley, then the noise on the street, the trams creaking and ringing, the buses honking and the conductors' bells are audible; and starting suddenly, Geeta realizes that she has stopped wiping her face and is standing at the door, towel in hand. That is when her waiting begins.

Now it feels as if this has been going on for years. How quickly Harsh has opened up to her, but Geeta remembers that when she first met him he did not dare smoke in her presence. And now? Now he grabs and kisses Nanda in Geeta's presence. He catches hold of her two plaits, turns her to face him and embraces her; and Nanda, emerging freshly bathed from the bathroom, hangs her clothes out to dry on the clothesline, smiling at Geeta the while as if indicating some secret or perhaps issuing a challenge . . . Now Nanda keeps humming all the time when she is awake. If she doesn't sing, songs from Radio Ceylon play in her room, and she often sings along with them. The wretch knows any number of songs by heart. She has seen all the Hindi and English films that are showing in Calcutta now!

Ever since Harsh has come, Nanda seems to have gone crazy. She is not on earth; she is floating in the air, above time and death. Why would she pay any attention to the fact that Geeta exists? As soon as he leaves, she will start up again with her 'Geeta-di,

Geeta-di.' How quickly this girl changes colour! It doesn't take her a moment! When will this Harsh leave? Who knows how much time he has taken off from work? It doesn't look as if he will leave any time soon. By bringing him here from the hotel, Geeta has increased her own pain. When they are with her, she pretends to be happy, laughs at their antics and jokes, and sometimes teases them, but the anguish within her thickens. She doesn't feel jealous, as she was of Miss Raymond. When the Miss Raymond interlude happened, something roared within her like a lioness. Seeing Harsh and Nanda together pleases her even as feelings of helplessness and inferiority gnaw at her . . .

What time is it? Geeta starts when she looks at the watch on the table, as if she had forgotten all about time, even though she had removed her watch and put it in front of her so that she would be aware of the time. A quarter to ten. Looking at the food on the table, she thinks it has gone cold. No sign of them yet—is the film so long? They must be roaming about at the lake, arms around each other. As soon as they had left, Geeta had started cooking, and just half an hour ago, she had laid the meal on the table. She had kept Khoka's mother waiting so that after they ate, the dishes could be washed, otherwise they would lie dirty until eight the next morning. How long could she be kept waiting? Khoka's mother had asked, 'When will this mister leave? He smokes a lot. Wherever you look ashes lie scattered. Who is he to her?' Showing disinterest, she had shut down the topic. 'He's her husband, what else? He has come to coax her into going back to him. Just wash the cooking pots and the spice-grinding stone. The dishes can be done tomorrow morning.'

Geeta had sat down at the dining table with a book, trying to keep herself busy. The china dishes and white plastic covers dazzled her in the light of the bulb dangling above. The recently mopped floor shone; through the open door, half the bed was visible in front of the dressing table and the other half in the dressing-table mirror. This mirror would be the witness of her night-long vigil. She wonders greatly at the way she has helplessly accepted the situation and not only endures the brazen behaviour of these two but swallows so much humiliation. The frightening thing is that she doesn't have any complaints. Later she may feel angry, but when they are with her she feels as if they are two small children whom she must look after, feed and provide for.

She knows how they will enter when they return, blaming each other for their tardiness, proffering excuses such as the unavailability of a taxi or the crowded buses, or, if all else fails, saying that it was raining heavily. Calcutta is so big a city that it can rain in one area while there is no sign of rain in another. She knows where Harsh will sit at the table. When they pick at their food, Geeta will jokingly say, 'You've eaten out again, haven't you?' And looking at each other like offenders, they will both break into smiles. Looking at them, Geeta, charmed, will forget to eat. Seeing or imagining them together arouses in her a strange tenderness, the kind one feels for a child. They become for her a symbol of cheerfulness and at that moment, the ever-present guilt in her heart dissolves. She does not remember that this is the Nanda for whom she has made enemies of all her relatives, damaged her reputation everywhere, and in relation to whom she always feels that she has tried to obtain some false moments of happiness at the cost of an innocent girl's life.

It was Mrs Kunti Mehra who had first spoken of her. 'Didi, there is a poor, lonely girl. She's staying here at someone's house but is in great discomfort there. She's a typist in a firm. You are alone these days, she could stay in one of your rooms. She'll be company for you . . . No, no, she won't disturb you at all. She's so simple and sad that she speaks very little.' Nanda did indeed look helpless and simple when Geeta first met her. She had a pretty face and a clear complexion. But there was an awkwardness about her that wasn't temperamental but was derived from living in a small town and being isolated. She wore her hair tightly pulled back and never let the end of her sari go below her waist. She thought this was the

way to look smart . . . With what difficulty Geeta had changed
her tastes! Geeta herself wore simple white clothes, but when she
went out with Nanda she wanted people to look twice at the girl.
That was when the first contradiction surfaced in Geeta. Without
consciously willing it, she gave up her preference for simplicity
because of Nanda, and today that same Nanda—a sleeveless black
blouse, a sari from Bangalore with a peacock-feather design, its
end floating down to her heels, a string of plump white pearls,
and hair loosely coiled in the shape of the number eight—what a
figure and what *grace*! These days, she is lost in dreams, floating on
air as she walks along, as close to Harsh as she can get. When she
had stretched her fingers towards Geeta after touching her lightly
lipsticked mouth, something had tugged at Geeta's heart and for a
moment Harsh's presence felt intolerable to her.

Khar, khar, khar. Geeta sat straight up when the door
rattled—they were back, perhaps! The book in front of her was
still open at the same page. She closed the book and stood up,
holding on to the table, waiting for the door latch to open or for
Nanda to ring the bell if she had forgotten the key upstairs. She
felt like going down to open the door. The door rattled again
when she reached the stairway. Oh, it was the cow downstairs.
She must have shaken her horns. Who knew whose cow this
was? She stays there all day and wets and dirties the ground in
front of the door. Anyone who goes in or out drives her away, but
she comes back. For some reason, Nanda is very afraid of her.
Whenever she comes home with Geeta, she always hides behind
Geeta, protecting her sari and treading carefully. 'Didi, do get
someone to drive her away. She shakes her horns whenever one
comes near her,' Nanda would complain.

She stopped. If they had returned, Bose Babu's dog would
have barked. No, it's not them. At night, one hears the taxi meter
ping on the street outside. Geeta didn't know whether she should
go down, open the door and stand there, waiting, or whether
she should again try to read her book. Hesitantly, she went into

Nanda's room. The door was half open, and the open space was covered by a heavy, checked, handloom curtain. What if they did not return at all, and she had to once again go through all those difficulties? Geeta suddenly felt so sure of her suspicion that she moved the curtain and went into the room. She pressed the switch, the room was flooded with light—no, everything was just as usual, scattered and untidy. She felt like laughing at herself—if they had taken anything away, she would have seen them do so. But what had Nanda taken with her last time? She had left without anything. But when she had bade them goodbye on the stairs, she would have noticed something. In one and a half to two years, she has not managed to teach Nanda how to live in an orderly manner. She looked around. The usual pile of saris, blouses and petticoats on the towel stand, a line of disordered slippers below, a new sari, half unwrapped, hanging on the radio, an attaché lying on the bed on its side, full of bangles, ear studs and plastic necklaces. These days, Nanda does not use the dressing table in Geeta's room. She has put two trunks under the full-length mirror on the wall, and on one of them lie scattered all her items of make-up, a lipstick with its red beak jutting out, and a comb with a bunch of hair stuck in it ... If she does get married to Harsh, how will she manage to run a house? She doesn't allow the maid into her room. Every fifth or sixth day, Geeta insists on tidying up the room.

Will Nanda actually marry Harsh? Looking helplessly at the walls, Geeta began to imagine a time when Nanda would not be in this big, three-room flat. Today, hangers with Harsh's bush shirts and shirts hang here and there from hooks meant for calendars. A hanger has even been stuck on the bolt of the lattice window, on which dangle Harsh's socks and Nanda's bra. With what diligence Nanda washes Harsh's clothes in the bathroom and spends hours ironing them perfectly. She is always either bringing him tea or snacks or washing his shaving equipment without being asked, or looking for a needle to sew on his buttons. If she could, she would even bring his bathing water into this room. She wants

to keep 'her Harsh' all to herself, away from others. Had Geeta
not promised to let her have her way in all these matters, Nanda
would hardly have agreed to leave the hotel and come here! That
is why Nanda is a lion. Geeta longs all day for a sight of her
face. These days, Nanda doesn't get up before eight o'clock, even
though the sun rises at five. Then she hurriedly bathes and rushes
to office. She always eats lunch with Harsh, somewhere outside,
and in the evening they either make plans to go out somewhere
straight from there, or if they do come here, Geeta gets to meet
them for a short time over tea. Nanda comes here mainly to
change her clothes. Then they go off together, and Geeta is left
with a cloud of powder and scent, and a brief, 'All right, Didi, ta-
ta.' Descending the stairs, the sound of people and car horns, and
a restless waiting . . .

Harsh has asked her a couple of times, but Nanda has never
said, 'Come on, Didi, come with us today to the cinema or for
an outing.' Yes, before the hotel business, she did once take her
to dinner at Sky Room, but that was only to introduce her to
Harsh. That too because Geeta had said, 'You keep singing songs
about Harsh. Won't you introduce me to your Harsh, Nandan?'
Ever since Harsh moved here from the hotel, Nanda has forgotten
about Geeta's existence. Geeta tries to figure out whether this is
her own fault. Was it a mistake to allow them so much leeway just
because she wanted them to live here, regardless of how they lived?
Then she tells herself that had she not given them this leeway,
Nanda would definitely have gone back to the hotel. Is she in her
right mind? She has gone absolutely crazy. Does she get any work
done at office? Anyway, it's just a matter of a few days now. Harsh
has to go back to work. After all, he can't stay here forever. Then
I'll teach the girl a lesson!

Despite drinking down all this unrest and irritation as if it were
blood, Geeta cannot understand why, from the first day until today,
she feels somewhere a deep satisfaction when she observes Harsh
and Nandan's uninhibited behaviour and impassioned surrender.

The morning after Geeta had brought the two of them home from the hotel, she made tea, but neither of them got out of bed, and it was now eight o'clock. She kept doing one chore after another, hoping that Khoka's mother would not arrive and find them still in bed. She hadn't slept all night. She couldn't go to sleep without Nanda. The door to Nanda's room was open, the curtain half drawn across it. Finally, she knocked at the door a couple of times and said, 'Get up Nanda, it's eight o'clock, tea is ready.' All she heard was a faint whimper and a sound of grasping and snatching. The third time, Nanda said, 'Didi, please bring it in here.' The same way she always says it, as she lies in bed. She must be lying just the same way, Geeta guessed. Geeta replied, as she did every day, 'All right, I'll bring it. I was born to serve you, it seems.'

A cup in each hand, she pushed the door with her foot and entered, the curtain wrapping itself around her. Harsh sprang up with a start and covered himself with the mosquito net. He was busy searching for his slippers when Nanda turned in bed, stretching and yawning, put her arms round his waist and pulled him down again. Pushing her arms away, Harsh muttered, 'Stop it, Nandi, Geeta-di is here.' Her eyes still closed, Nanda tightened her hold and replied in a sleepy but pettish tone, 'So-o what? As if she doesn't know—my Didi is "great", she doesn't bother about such things.' Highly embarrassed, Harsh remained seated. Pretending to be absorbed in balancing the cups, Geeta stepped forward. Trying her best to act natural, she said, 'Here, take your tea.' Without raising her eyes she saw that Harsh was wearing a shirt with Nanda's sari wrapped around his waist, and Nanda had on only a petticoat and blouse. She had now slid down and put her head on Harsh's thigh, and her long thick silken hair flowed from the pillow to the edge of the bed. It was hard for Geeta to contain herself—this was Nanda's daily habit. When the two women slept together, the milkman would knock at the door downstairs and Nanda would wrap her arms around Geeta's waist to prevent her from getting up and would put her head in her lap like a demanding child. Her soft, thick hair would flow over the bed just as it was flowing now. Geeta would stroke it lovingly and say, 'Let me get up now, Nandan, the milkman must be cursing us. If he goes away, how will I make tea for you?' But she felt a deep satisfaction in stroking the somnolent Nanda's hair, and she knew that Nanda enjoyed it too. The sight of Nanda's hair awakened the habitual stirring in her hands—perhaps Harsh doesn't know how Nanda enjoys having her hair stroked in the morning!

Highly embarrassed, she hastily put both cups in Harsh's hands. As she was turning to go, Nanda called out, 'Arey, Didi, listen!' When Geeta stopped in her tracks, Nanda, without raising her head from Harsh's lap, tried to open her sleepy eyes and said, 'Are you annoyed, Didi? Look at me, Didi!* If you don't look, I will know that you are upset!' Geeta forced herself to turn her head and look, and could not help laughing. 'How often can I get upset at your doings?' Perhaps there was an element of complaint in her tone.

'Then bring your tea here, Didi, do!' Harsh, who had now relaxed, said.

'Yes, yes, Geeta-di!' Nanda said in wheedling tones. 'Won't you do as your Nandan says?'

Pretending to be angry, Geeta said, 'Go on with you. Khoka's mother is ready to leave.'

But when she was sitting in the kitchen, drinking her tea alone, the question remained in her mind: why was she unable to oppose this indecent behaviour? Why, indeed, did she feel a type of fulfilment when she witnessed their intense happiness? Observing their uninhibited behaviour in her presence, why did she feel a generous satisfaction in not obstructing someone's climactic pleasure? Ever since Harsh came, she has been asking herself

---

* *'Tumhein meri qasam, Didi.'* An idiom indicating deep affection. It means that if the addressee does not do what the speaker wants, the speaker will suffer a misfortune.

how her ego and dignity have allowed her to become so negligible in her own house! Why has Nanda become such a weakness that she wants her before her eyes at all costs? Harsh is here only for a few more days . . . her heart beats with fear lest someone ask her—Geeta, you are so stern in matters of conduct, you don't even like girls to laugh and smile when they walk on the street. You have made so many rules to stop teachers and girls from being fashionable. And you . . . if anyone knew, what would they say? No one has questioned her about this, but one day, hooking Nanda's bra up at the back, she had said, 'Look, Nanda, how low I have had to stoop for you. That's why I've stopped inviting anyone over.'

Turning round, Nanda flung herself on her neck. 'Didi, *you are so large-hearted!*' Geeta's eyes filled with tears. 'Yes, keep cajoling me with words, it costs you nothing!' She got annoyed . . . She feels a ticklish satisfaction at the sight of Harsh and Nanda together. She identifies either with Harsh or Nanda, or else stands at a height rejoicing in the sports of these 'children.' But later, a brokenness steals over her. Nanda's humming and moving around the house as if to the beat of a dance, the fluid, pleasurable contentment spilling from her every pore, her remaining sunk in dreams and smiling to herself . . . all of this seems like burning evidence of her own humiliation and incapacity. A weight like that of a soaked blanket keeps wrapping itself around her heart, and the constant sense of being alone and unnecessary overshadows her spirit. The depression like solidified darkness, which was her daily companion before Nanda came—which used to keep provoking her to commit suicide, and feeling which she had asked herself, 'What should I do with this life? And why?'—used to just make her cry and feel suffocated, but now it has returned, making her feel that past and future are two black walls which keep approaching one another and squeezing her between them, so that she cannot look beyond them!

How terrible it is that Harsh has snatched away her Nanda, and she feels neither anger nor jealousy! Just the acceptance

of defeat. Perhaps even Nanda feels sorry for her. She had feared
that Didi would raise a storm as she had in the case of Miss
Raymond. Some demon had taken possession of Geeta that day,
and she had taken leave of her senses. Why does she not feel such
a challenge in the case of Harsh?

Nanda had become very intimate with Miss Raymond and
would often put on a sari, turn this way and that to look at herself,
and ask Geeta, 'Didi, how will I look if I start wearing skirts?' or,
'Didi, isn't this long hair a nuisance? Won't it be a relief to cut it
off? Just brush it and be ready in a moment!' Every day, Geeta
would tell her, 'Nanda, come home on time. We are going to dinner
with Mr and Mrs Vishwas' or, 'Let's go to the fine arts exhibition
this evening' or, 'There's a function at so-and-so college' or, 'Let's
go to the lake or to a movie . . .' Nanda would promise every day
like a good girl, 'Yes, Didi, today I will come home exactly on time
. . .!' But every day, Geeta would be ready in fresh white clothes
and would move around, having taken out Nanda's favourite outfit
for her, and would keep looking out of the window at every sound
and scattering things around in anger. At nine or ten o'clock the
bell would ring softly, like an offender, or the latch would rattle—
'Didi, what can I tell you, Miss Raymond forced me to . . . she just
wouldn't leave me alone and first she looked for cardigans in New
Market, then she wanted to go to Melody Room . . . then we had
coffee at Kwality,' or—'This Raymond is too much . . . today was
the last day of Disney cartoons . . . I laughed till I wept . . . had
you been there you too . . .' But seeing Geeta glaring at her, her
tongue would falter and she would fall silent. Geeta would turn
over and cry softly, and Nanda would wheedle her, 'Didi, please
forgive me this one time!'* They would not speak for a couple of
days. Nanda would come home on time for a day or two, and then
the same sequence of events all over again! Ignoring the possibility
of losing her reputation, Geeta spoke to the managing committee

* The original is, *'Tumhein meri qasam.'*

to get Nanda a job at her school. She could have approved the appointment herself had Nanda not failed the BA exam. Then she could have supervised her all day. Nanda began going with Miss Raymond to her house every day and started learning to dance. She would practise there and return home only by nine or nine thirty. It was a long way off too, as she had to first catch bus number 3 to Hajra junction. Geeta would complain to Mrs Kunti Mehra, 'I worry only because I'm afraid these low class Christians will mislead her.* So far, she has seen big hotels and the world of dance only in movies, and is very attracted to them. She's pretty, many people will try to lure her away. Today it's Raymond, tomorrow it will be someone else. These stenos and [telephone] operators are not to be trusted. I hope she hasn't started drinking. I just read in the *Statesman* that some old Englishwoman used to entice simple girls by exposing them to glamourous lifestyles and then would get them drinking. After that she would procure customers and run a business . . . this girl is alone, she's like my daughter so . . .' But she didn't dare say all this to Nanda.

One Sunday a quarrel broke out. Geeta said plainly, 'Nanda, we live in a decent neighbourhood. This coming home so late and roaming around everywhere cannot carry on. I want to live in peace. You too must be unhappy here. It's best if you shift to Miss Raymond's house.'

Nanda raised her chin and said rudely, 'Geeta Didi, I'm not indebted to anyone. I pay for my board and lodging. Don't interfere with my right to decide whom to meet. It would be best for us to understand our rights.'

Speechless! Geeta's hand stopped moving on the paper that she was checking. Her ears burnt! She gaped at Nanda. Nanda continued powdering her neck and back with a puff. Ignoring the rudeness, Geeta said, 'Nanda, you are dazzled by the world of

---

* The word used for Christian is *kirantan*, a slang term for a low-class convert to Christianity.

Lindsay Street, New Market and Park Street, so you are talking about money. You know that I let you live here not because I can't afford the rent and need your contribution. I let you live here because you came whining with Mrs Mehra, saying that you could not live with a married couple who ended up fighting because of you. I thought you were a simple girl and would stay in one room, and that you wanted a homely life. Today you have grown wings ...'

'Thank you very much, Didi! I'll be grateful to you as long as I live! I was in trouble, and I came to you.' Nanda's voice was tearful.

Geeta, too, had come close to tears when she had spoken of Nanda going away. Wiping her eyes with her sari, she said, 'What I'm saying is for your own good, Nanda.'

Nanda smiled sarcastically at the mirror—she knew what kind of good and how much of it Didi wanted for her. If she must live with such constraints, what was the point of coming here from Bilaspur? Her aunt, too, in the name of her own good ...

Geeta was upset all of the next day. They had quarrelled, got angry and stopped talking many times, but neither of them had suggested living separately. She regretted having spoken so harshly. The girl came from a small, suffocating town, so she could not resist the attractions of this new and open life. She would roam around a bit and come back here—where else could she go? But now Geeta could not imagine a life without Nanda. Why would she care to come home early, whose scattered clothes would she gather up, whose money clip would she keep carefully aside? Whom would she persuade to eat, putting morsels in her mouth as if she was a child and ... the biggest question, how would Geeta sleep without her at night? She felt afraid at the thought of sleeping alone in her bed; the possibility of being alone made her heart sink.

She feels that she has always loved people unilaterally, but no one has ever fully reciprocated her love. Somewhere she had heard that love is by definition one-way. In a long-term intimate friendship or love, two individuals never love one another equally. There is always one who loves and another who is loved.

When she feels like it, Nanda makes a great show of affection, but she has never really loved Geeta. Yet Geeta had fought with her own brother's wife because of Nanda. Her sister-in-law had hoped that Geeta would adopt their Pintu . . .

Anyway, she would go and ask Nanda's forgiveness. The fault was hers; she should not have spoken so harshly. She felt like getting up and going home right away, although she knew Nanda would return only in the evening. She raised her hand to call Nanda's office, but then she remembered that there was a managing committee meeting tomorrow. Several important decisions were to be taken, so she had Mrs De sit in front of her and help her prepare the report, and she kept giving papers to the auditor. She didn't want to speak to Nanda in the presence of Mrs De and the clerk. There were already any number of rumours about her and Nanda. And Mrs De . . . the auditor at least was an outsider . . . It got later and later. She came home on the school bus. It was ten. She alighted and ran down the alley like a madwoman. The windows were dark. Nanda puts on all the lights because she's afraid of the dark. Hands trembling with excitement, she inserted the key and lifted the latch. When she switched on the light, she saw a note on the floor—I am going as you ordered, Didi. Please *redirect* my mail to this address. I will send my share of the expenses as soon as I get my salary. Below was written Miss Raymond's address on Iqbalpur Road.

Geeta turned around at once. The driver was reversing the bus in a narrow spot. Geeta called out, 'Listen, Bihari Singh, Stop. Do you know where Iqbalpur Road is?' By the time Bihari Singh thought about it and said it was somewhere near Mominpur, Geeta had boarded the bus. 'Let's go, we'll enquire on the way.'

Nanda was taken aback to see Bihari Singh and Geeta. She did not know what to say. Without looking around, Geeta asked sternly, 'Where are your things?' Then, indicating the suitcase in a corner and the bag on the sofa, she said, 'Bihari Singh, take all this down to the bus!' By then, another woman had issued from the bathroom and was looking in astonishment at these three. Geeta said in a practised, authoritative voice, 'Nanda, go sit in the bus. Get up!' The voice was so irresistible that Nanda got up as if hypnotized and went ahead. Geeta made her get on the bus first and then sat down. Bihari Singh was on the other side and Nanda in the middle.

After Bihari Singh had brought up the luggage and left, Geeta bolted the door and went straight to Nanda's room. As Nanda raised her head from her hands, Geeta pounced on her, slipper in hand, and began showering blows and abuses on her. Geeta kept talking and hitting her. 'You will calculate how much you owe me? Have I ever taken anything from you, you bastard? I've been defamed by the whole world and fought with everyone I know because of you—why should I let you go away? I'll tear you to pieces! When I die you can go where you please . . .' At first, Nanda tried to fight back, but she was defeated by that tempestuous rage. She kept suffering the blows and crying out: 'Didi, I'll die . . .! Didi! Didi! I beg of you . . . I'll never do it again . . . Forgive me, Didi!' She kept protecting herself with her elbows and crying, like a small girl. Finally, Geeta flung the slipper aside and collapsed on the ground, like a felled tree, sobbing and gasping for breath. Nanda lay limp in her arms, and Geeta covered her throat, temples, lips and arms with kisses, crying, 'Nandan! Nandan . . . Nandan . . .! My Nandan! Forgive me, my queen . . . I can't live without you, Nandan! I'll do whatever you say. You can do as you like, go where you like, but don't leave me and go away! Who else do I have in life besides you, tell me, Nandan? I'll take poison if you leave me.' All night, Geeta lay clinging to her, crying and asking for forgiveness.

* * *

Remembering her passion and her entreaties that night, Geeta's eyes filled once more with tears, which spilled over on to her cheeks. She found herself back at the dining table, running a finger over the letters on the cover of the book. She would wait another half hour, and then bolt the door and go to sleep. To hell with both of them.

She had feared that a wall might spring up between Nanda and her after that episode. But she found, with a glad sense of surprise that was new to her, that they became even more intimate and inseparable thereafter. Geeta procured a fortnight's leave for Nanda, and they went to Puri for a week.

Every day their plan to see the sunrise was postponed to the next morning, because despite all their efforts they could not wake up early. Yes, they would wander around all day. They spent two or three days at the Jagannath temple. Looking at the images there, they would smile at each other with secret meaning. Hand in hand, they would walk along the seashore, holding their sandals in their hands and enjoying the waves tickling their feet. Nanda would laugh and call out, 'Arey, Didi, hang on to me.' They would lie for a long time on the sand. Neither of them spoke of what had passed; both of them forgot about it.

That night, at nine o'clock, they lay on their stomachs, supporting themselves on their elbows, in front of the hotel, in the lonely moonlight, at a little distance from the waves, and letting the sand run through their hands. The boiling, layered waves sent white foam into their hair and returned, while sometimes here and sometimes there in the sea, a mountain of water crashed and dispersed. Geeta's glasses were repeatedly washed and dimmed, sticky with moisture. The roar of the sea awakened a strange excitement in mind and body.

After a long silence, Geeta asked tenderly, 'Your aunt beat you a lot, didn't she, Nandan?'

'Yes. How do you know?' Nanda replied with a sigh.

'Just like that.' Geeta lay flat again. Gazing at the sky, she said in a natural-sounding voice, 'That day you cried out several times, "Chachi, I beg you, I won't do it again."'

Tears rolled down Nanda's cheeks. Her lips trembled for a while, and then she said, 'I've suffered a lot, Geeta Didi. My father sent me to my uncle's house to save me from my stepmother's ill-treatment. But there . . .' She sighed deeply.

Geeta drew the weeping Nanda to her, put her head on her breast and stroked her temples for a long time. Tears fell from her own eyes too.

'The scar on my chest, which I said was caused by a boil, was actually given to me by my aunt. One day, I told my cousin that I was thinking of going away with Harsh or by myself. She told her mother, and after that, Didi, I lay moaning in pain for a week. She burnt me with a hot spoon, saying, "Here, I'll draw out your youth."'

Geeta's stroking hand kept comforting her, and she continued to speak with pauses. 'Don't you think, Didi, that some people are born ill-fated? There is nothing but a lonely darkness in their past and future, and they get nothing in life?'

Then Geeta felt as if this was not Nanda lying on her breast but someone speaking from within herself. Nanda continued, 'Harsh was two years senior to me in college. We acted in a play together, and our friendship grew deeper. He had told me from the start that he was already married and that after he graduated with an MCom, the rest of the rituals would be completed. But I was so crazy, I said, I don't love you just to get married . . . Now he has a child too, but, Didi, I never feel that Harsh is not mine.'

Geeta thought to herself: that's why you went off with Miss Raymond! She had heard many times about the love affair with Harsh and knew that letters from one H. Khanna came for Nanda. Whenever she was inundated with love for Nanda, a doubt would lick at her like a serpent's tongue—somewhere there was a Harsh who would snatch away her Nanda. When she heard Nanda lovingly talk of Harsh, she would usually feel deeply sad, but today, in the moist atmosphere of the sea, she felt there was really something profound and ideal in Nanda's love.

Nanda was saying, 'He works in a bank in Delhi. But even if he were in London, I wouldn't feel that I am far from him . . . I tell you truly, Didi, if it were not for Harsh there and you here, maybe ... maybe I would sprinkle kerosene oil and ...' Geeta put a hand over her mouth and stopped her. At the same time, she felt that these speeches, even if they were not a pretence, were certainly imbued with a temporary sentimentality. Yet she was affected by them and said, 'Why do you say that, Nandan? You have saved me too, otherwise I don't know, I don't know ...' Swallowing, she continued, 'Everyone in my family, or among my acquaintances who has a child, used to think that I would adopt it and put my provident fund and insurance in its name ... I was so tired of their selfish calculations, Nandan ... Now I don't enjoy anything without you ... Whom do I have of my own? I had one brother, who is now in a lunatic asylum ... I was the daughter of a high-ranking officer. Papa had my tutor tied up in a sack and beaten by the servants while I was locked in my room and could only bang on the door. I can still hear his stifled voice—Geeta, I will come to fetch you ... wait for me ... my revenge was that I never obeyed my father. I kept studying and studying and waiting, and now I feel as if waiting has become a way of life ... I don't feel as if waiting for him is useless because he doesn't exist ... No, this is not the sentimentality of love. The truth is that when I got tired of waiting I found that life had passed me by, and my joy in life had waned ...! When I turned thirty-five I felt as if I was waiting again, but I didn't know for whom. Sometimes, now, I think, you were the one for whom I was waiting.' She took off her glasses, put them on the sand, covered her eyes with her arm and burst out crying. Sobbing, she said, 'I am old now, Nandan. You are my daughter, beloved, companion, husband, everything ... When I die, take everything and settle down with your Harsh.' Tears of self-pity continued to flow from her eyes. 'All I have is yours.'

'Didi, don't talk like that, Didi!' Nanda slid up on to Geeta and kept kissing her lips, eyelashes and earlobes. As she looked at the tears shining on Geeta's cheeks in the moonlight and at her closed eyes, the thought came to her that Geeta might look like this when she died. Pushing the thought away, she kept repeating, 'I won't go anywhere, Didi . . .'

The tide was high, and the waves were close to them now. When a huge wave rolled up and wet the sand just below them, they stood up and brushed down their clothes.

That night, binding Nanda's naked, surrendered body with her eager arms and excited breath, repeatedly kissing the coin-shaped scar on her right breast, Geeta kept saying like a madwoman, 'Nandan, don't leave me . . .! I'll die without you, Nandan!'

Later, feelings of guilt and self-hatred might nibble at the conscience like so many mice, but at such moments neither Geeta nor Nanda could restrain herself. Nanda would get so wildly excited that she would take to scratching and biting.

Whenever Nanda awoke that night, she found Geeta stroking her hair spread over the pillow, her shoulders or her back. Perhaps the sensation awakened her. She lay awake, gazing at the ceiling, listening to the roar of the sea, and then slowly fell asleep. Her eyes opened again before dawn. Sleepily, she embraced Geeta and asked, 'You didn't sleep all night, did you, Didi?'

'I don't know what has happened to me . . . I want you to keep lying like this while I gaze at you and stroke your hair, your cheeks . . . I feel as if someone will snatch you away from me.'

Nanda didn't say anything. She felt slightly bored. As if thinking of something, she said, 'Do you know something, Didi?'

'What, Nandan?' Each time she said 'Nandan', it was as if she wanted to pour out her love on her.

'Mrs Mehra told me once,' Nanda said, 'that a rumour is spreading like wildfire in your college that . . . that I am your daughter.'

'And so you are!' Geeta said caressingly.

'Oh, not like that! They think you loved someone, and I am his child. You had me educated in a hostel and have now brought me here. You are anxious to get me an appointment in your college . . .' Nanda said, watching Geeta to weigh her reaction.

'I know,' Geeta said with a deep sigh. 'That's why I haven't taken you to college. Otherwise would I have let you work in that firm as a typist for a single day? Is that any place for decent people?'

Nanda came back to her point. 'Is this true, Didi?'

Laughing in pain, Geeta replied, 'If it were true, wouldn't you have known? Have I hidden anything from you?' Geeta grew emotional. 'If it were true, my daughter would be your age . . . or three–four years younger . . . we both met for the last time in '39. That was the year the war started . . . The girl would have been twenty to twenty-two.' Geeta turned on her other side, and Nanda felt as if Geeta was sobbing. Throwing herself on Geeta's back, she turned her shoulder towards herself and said, 'Geeta Di . . .! Didi! Look at me, Didi.'*

'I don't like to think of those things, Nanda.' Geeta kept crying.

'I'm here, Didi, your daughter, your younger sister, your . . . Nandan!' Nanda kept coaxing her as a mother or older sister might, and she wondered whether her own future would be like Geeta's present. She kept saying, 'Didi, I'll never leave you, I'll never go away.' Holding Geeta's grey-sprinkled head in her arms, she kept patting it as if caressing a small girl who had fallen and hurt herself. But deep beneath that pure emotion was someone calculating— she has an insurance policy for ten thousand rupees, at least ten to twelve thousand in her provident fund, and probably fifteen to twenty in her bank. What are Didi's expenses? She has no servant, she doesn't spend much on food. She wears white clothes. She, too, would start saving up, and one day she would say proudly to Harsh, 'Here are fifty thousand rupees—start a factory, a farm, whatever you like. Let's start life afresh. Or let's buy some shares and a house in some small town . . .' And Nanda's eyes filled with tears at the thought of this happiness.

Geeta began to comfort her. 'Why are you crying about my sorrows, you silly girl?'

---

* 'Meri qasam hai tumhein.'

When she got up, Geeta felt as if all that had happened was a dream. They stood on the balcony, their saris wrapped around their shoulders, under which they were wearing only their brassieres. It was a foggy day, so the sun was just a small ball of light over the sea. The sea was leaping and growling as usual, the sand was wet up to the point where the waves had advanced last night, and a white line of dried foam marked the shore. The claw-prints of crows on the wet sand were like a line of sewing. A wooden boat lay upside down.

Her elbows resting on the railing, Geeta slid her sari a little off her shoulder, laughed and said, 'Look how hard you bit me! There's a mark here. Do you lose your mind at that moment?'

Nanda felt embarrassed. But she laughed, mischievously stuck out her tongue, and turned away to look at two fishermen in the distance who were carrying a net loaded on a rod. A fisherman clad only in a small loincloth and a tall cap was talking to a rickshaw puller at the door of the hotel. In the distance, two dark fishermen wearing the same kind of caps were leading a family by the hand to bathe in the waves. A gentleman was sitting on the shore washing his head with both hands. When a wave approached, he fled in fear. She thought that if she ever came here with Harsh, she would insist that he take her into the water and bathe her without the fishermen's help. Then she eagerly said, 'Come on, Didi, let's bathe too.'

When they returned home, their routine resumed, but Nanda never came home late. The two of them would visit new places or stay at home, chatting about college and office. On her way back from work, Geeta began to pick up garlands of tuberose and jasmine for Nanda's hair.

One day, Nanda said, 'Geeta Didi, Harsh is coming day after tomorrow, for some official work.'

'Here?'

'No, he'll stay in a hotel. He wrote to me not to make plans for any evening.' For the first time, Nanda felt that her meetings with Harsh would not be accompanied by the fear of her aunt like playback music. They would be able to meet freely. In a wheedling and coaxing tone, she said, 'I'll get late. Didi, don't take offence. It's just a matter of a few days, Didi.'

Geeta lifted her chin affectionately and said, 'Silly, don't I know your feelings? But you will introduce us, right?' And a cloud of sadness arose in her.

'Oh, of course, of course!' Every part of Nanda's body was blossoming, and every nerve tingled with waiting. How would she survive until day after tomorrow? She felt like going and sitting at the station right away!

'But look, Nandan, don't make it too late ... We are two women living alone here. As it is, people keep scrutinizing us. They keep a watch on every visitor of ours. And I can't bear waiting!'

'Do you think I'll stay out all night? I'll be worried about you!' Nanda was arranging her hair with a plastic brush at Geeta's dressing table . . . as she spoke, the clip she was holding between her lips fell down.

Geeta first saw Harsh at Kwality. He had invited her.

'You could have stayed at our place! Nanda, do invite Harsh to dinner at least once!' While exchanging such pleasantries, Geeta was evaluating Harsh in the light and shadows of the restaurant. Hair parted on the left and puffed out like a film actor's, half-framed glasses, a cream-coloured silk shirt, and a black bow. He was quite fair, had a small mole near his nose, and dark glasses peeked out from his buttonhole. Geeta felt that Harsh took considerable pains to look good. She wondered whether she would have liked such a man when she was Nanda's age. He must be thirty now and would have been twenty-five when he met Nanda. She felt bad because Harsh was a more formidable rival than Miss Raymond. Whenever she observed Nanda, who, like an enchanted peahen, was immersed in each word Harsh uttered, his every movement and gesture, her heart grew heavier.

Harsh was telling her, 'Every letter she writes is full of Didi, Didi. When she starts praising you, she loses count of pages. My Didi looks after me like this, my Didi loves me like this . . . I went to Puri with her . . . All this made me eager to meet her Didi.'

'Don't believe anything she says, Harsh. She is a little turncoat . . . But yes, she does keep singing songs of you all day!' She almost felt like complaining to Harsh about Miss Raymond, but she was pleased by his praise of her. She began to feel as if she was much older and Nanda was her daughter, and she was interviewing Harsh as a prospective husband for Nanda to see whether or not he could make her happy. Embracing Nanda, she said, 'She is crazy about you. Since the day before yesterday she has been displaying dozens of saris and hairstyles to me. Today, her room is in apple-pie order, but usually it's a total mess. Today, she has bunches of tuberoses in vases . . . Didi, does this blouse fit me better or that chocolatey one . . .? Harsh loves brick-red . . .' Nanda kept twisting Geeta's fingers, but Geeta kept smiling and talking. She did not like the way Harsh had kept his dark glasses attached to his buttonhole. What bad *taste*, like that of a college boy!

Nanda had turned red and kept tossing her head to show her displeasure. With trembling hands, she kept drawing lines using her fork on the white tablecloth and saying, 'Enough, Didi, enough, please!' Geeta had never seen Nanda so shy and embarrassed before. This was not the Nanda she had known for so long.

Harsh looked affectionately at Nanda's face, lovingly put his hand on the hand holding the fork and said, 'No, Didi, she's a simple girl. She worships you.' Harsh did not see what Geeta's and Nanda's eyes exchanged at that moment, and continued, 'I was worried about how she would live in such a big, new city. I was not in favour of her living in Bilaspur. She was anxious to leave, and I thought she was right. I had talked to the Delhi branch of her firm and managed to get her a job, but I didn't know how she would live there alone. If I could have kept her in Delhi, I wouldn't have let her leave for even a day. I arranged for her to stay with a friend here, but then new problems arose. What wife would want to invite danger by keeping a young, beautiful girl in her house? I was thinking of coming here, but then I met Kunti Bhabhi, who said she would make arrangements right away. She must have had you in mind. I breathed a sigh of relief.'

Harsh was talking with the authority of a husband. These two were far gone indeed. Geeta wished she were a man and could talk of Nanda with such sensitivity and possessiveness. She sighed to herself.

'Once I met Kunti Bhabhi, you didn't bother to come for a whole year!' Nanda complained. She had looked down shyly when he said 'young, beautiful girl.'

'Uff, I've been explaining to you since yesterday but . . . your brain is like a dog's tail.' Harsh looked at Geeta. 'Tell me, Didi, is it so easy to go wherever one pleases? And I have a lioness at home.'

'That is what I wanted to ask you!' Geeta took the tone of an elder in order to assess the situation. 'How long can things go on like this? You must have a plan!'

The bearer brought the soup plates, and Harsh, leaning to one side to make room for him, asked, 'May I smoke, Didi?'

'Yes, yes, go ahead!' she said, though she did not like cigarette smoke.

'There you are!' Nanda said, eyes dancing. 'He's been making signs to ask me, and I keep telling him to smoke. Why hide from Didi?'

He took a cigarette from the pocket of his coat kept behind him. 'No, I thought you might object. She has scared me, saying that Didi is the strictest of all principals. Even teachers are not allowed to wear silk saris in her college. They are strictly forbidden to have fashionable hairstyles, sleeveless blouses, scent, powder, and so on!' And with a wicked smile, he blew smoke towards Nanda.

'What are you doing?' Nanda waved the smoke away and shrank towards the back of the sofa. Geeta looked at her and thought Nanda was *over-acting*. She thought Nanda's eye movements, smiles and coyness were all highly artificial. Regretfully, she said, 'Yes, I am, but that strictness has given way because of her.'

Geeta felt something slacken within her. She was witnessing wrongdoing and assisting wrongdoing. Her Master Sahib, too, used to blow smoke in her face. The more she grew annoyed and threatened to complain to Papa, the more he would wickedly insist on blowing smoke into her eyes. Perhaps all men had this habit.

'Here, Didi, start.' Nanda shook her shoulder, and she came back to herself. She sipped the soup to test the salt . . . Would Nanda too depart from her life? She remembered. 'You didn't answer my question, Harsh?'

'I'm thinking, Didi, about how to answer.' The cigarette in one hand kept releasing smoke, and with the other he stirred cream into his soup. 'The truth is, Didi, I can't live without Nanda. You know, we met during a play at college, where I had to deliver certain dialogues. I didn't realize then that the play's dialogues would one day become life's dialogues. There was one sentence— you have become a truth, a part of my life that I cannot any longer deny . . . But the trouble is my wife. Had she come into my life four months earlier, you would have perhaps seen us in another form. My wife has no pity for any other woman. She is always sickly but extremely stubborn, and like every wife she has decided that she must bring me on to the right path. She thinks that her prayers and her quarrelling will one day give me wisdom; I will remove Nanda from my heart, get rid of my perversions, and attain peace. But how can one experience peace when one knows that someone else is dissolving each of the golden days of their life? She wants to keep all of me to herself, but I can't give her all of myself, because this one here is half my life.' Geeta saw that Harsh's face was anguished. He paused and went on. 'I keep trying to think of a way out, hoping that she will understand my pain and have pity. Truly, Didi, I recently tried sincerely to give her all of myself, I did whatever she said—but I can't live this double life any longer. She has realized that she cannot have all of me! So now she will have to give me up—*she will have to lose me whole*. I'm just waiting for some way to take myself back from her and give myself to Nanda. I just hope that her illness . . .'

The bearer appeared. Geeta waited for him to continue, but she felt a cruel satisfaction—Harsh's vocabulary and manner were those of every dishonest man . . . no one would take Nanda away from her; Nanda would stay with Geeta.

Nanda kept looking blissfully at Harsh's face and thinking that Harsh was waiting to take himself back and come to her while she would get all of Geeta's . . . she smiled unconsciously.

Geeta laughed to pass the matter off lightly. 'I hope you won't wish that for her some day!' The three of them laughed a little and went back to chatting and laughing. Harsh began to tell them about that episode in the play when the hero gets annoyed with the heroine, scolds her, and says something against her class and community, whereupon she slaps him. Laughing, Harsh said, 'Didi, she slapped me so hard that my head spun. When I asked her about it later, she said, "How else would the spectators at the back of the hall have heard?"'

When they were ready to leave, Harsh went ahead to get paan, and Nanda said hesitantly, 'Didi, Harsh says that I should come home later. He wants to discuss something with me.'

'Discussions are all very well, but invite him to our place one day!' Geeta said, breaking off a stray thread from Nanda's blouse sleeve and smiling knowingly.*

Harsh, returning with the paan, overheard and said, 'I'll come for sure now that I've met you.'

Nanda hailed a passing taxi and quickly said, 'You're not afraid to go alone, Didi, are you?'

'Yes, I am, come and drop me,' Geeta said, looking sarcastically at Nanda and taking two paans from Harsh's hand to put in her mouth. Harsh said, 'Let's drop Didi off.'

'No, no. I just said that to Nanda because she was being extra sympathetic,' Geeta said, advancing to the taxi. 'I travel alone

---

* The word for 'discussions' here is *baatein*, with its double meaning of talking or having sex.

every day.' There was no complaint in her tone. She suddenly became very generous and cheerful. Harsh held the taxi door open.

'Don't mind, Didi, if Nanda gets late,' he said softly, closing the door.

'But she won't be able to come alone. Drop her off,' Geeta said, lowering the taxi window, and her eyes shone with an undesired jest. 'It's a quarter to ten ... no more than another hour, and, listen, no foolishness!' The taxi started with a jerk. At first, she thought: what must the Sardar-ji be thinking? Then she realized that everything had been said in such an ambiguous manner that he wouldn't have understood any of it. On the way, she kept smiling, remembering the conversation at the restaurant.

That night, every car horn sounded to her like that of a taxi and every sound like that of sandals and shoes. She kept tossing and turning all night, the watchman kept making his rounds, thumping with his stick; the whistles from the station and the late and early trams and buses kept heightening her restlessness, but neither of them came. The laughter-filled atmosphere of the restaurant and her open-heartedness rapidly dissolved, while the tension of waiting turned into annoyance. Again and again, she felt like going to them the way she had that day and dragging the bitch back by her hair. Must be lying stuck to her lover . . .! False, cheating man! She'll come crying to me one day. I'll say, there's no place here for you! But this time she didn't dare drag her back. Harsh was different from Raymond. If she staked Nanda in Harsh's presence, she might be defeated . . . All night, with the pillow over her face, she burnt below and the light above, until by morning she decided that if, like Harsh's wife, she insisted on having it all, she might lose it all. Wisdom lay in swallowing her grief and giving Nanda some freedom, because Harsh wouldn't stay here forever—four days, six days . . . two weeks. He had children, he had a job. Harsh was, after all, a man, and one could not and should not gamble against him.

The next day, she could do no work at college, and, pretending she had a headache, she sat holding her forehead and thinking, until it was no longer possible to stay there, and at night she went and affectionately persuaded and coaxed Nanda and Harsh into coming to her house. She would not obstruct their freedom in any way. She felt angry enough to hit the self-seeking girl's head against the wall. How soon she had forgotten all her vows and promises! She had gone off to stay at the hotel as if she had always stayed there and would stay there for good.

And Geeta would watch Nanda wholly absorbed in washing Harsh's clothes, ironing his shirts or emptying his ashtrays with an expression of housewifely care and responsibility, as if she had been married to him for years. Nanda had never, of her own accord, ironed Geeta's clothes. If she was asked to oil Geeta's hair, she would behave as if she was being forced to work like a bonded labourer . . . It was Geeta who would wash Nanda's smaller garments when she went to bathe, or fold up her clothes with her own or keep track of the washerman's accounts . . .

Bow wow! When Bose Babu's dog barked, Geeta jerked into wakefulness. She didn't know when she had got up from the chair and come to bed, put her glasses by the pillow and covered her face with it. She put the pillow back in its place, felt around for her glasses, and half sat up, supporting herself on her elbows, eagerly listening for the downstairs latch to rattle, so that she could quickly go to the dining table and seem as if she had been reading there. She hoped she had not bolted the downstairs door. If the door did not open, they would ring the bell. Half reclining and listening, her head turned towards the door, she kept looking at the mirror. For a moment, a sort of doubt arose in her mind: was this Geeta reclining on her elbows and looking keenly at her the real one, or was the one on the bed real? This doubt ran through her like a lightning bolt so that for a moment she felt afraid, alone in this empty, brightly lit flat—perhaps . . . perhaps that Geeta looking out of the mirror, half rising at the sound of the door, is the real one . . . the reflection is this one lying outside . . .

Vision*

Ruth Vanita

I have a terrible headache again today; since morning my head has been throbbing as if someone is hammering away at it on the inside. And that old childhood fear returns: what if I go blind?

'Why do you keep reading all the time then?' Ajay can think of only one reason for my feeling unwell. 'Your eyes are weak. How many times have I told you not to read so much? It's not as if you have to pass any more exams.'

Exactly what the doctor said to my mother when I was a child. 'Madam, her eyes are very weak. She's in danger of losing her vision. You had better withdraw her from school. Fortunately, she's a girl—no point in her studying too much.'

But my mother didn't agree with him. And the truth is that these days my head aches not only when I read but a lot of the time. After sending Ajay off to work I wait for the vegetable vendor, then for the cleaning woman, and then I complete all kinds of small and big chores. By evening the ache takes full possession of me. At night, as soon as Ajay touches me, it speeds up like a train

---

* This story, 'Nazar', was written in 1983, based on my encounter with some girls at the blind girls' school in Defence Colony, New Delhi. Shaku-di is based on Pushpa Mehta, the *Manushi* volunteer who accompanied me. The narrator in this story is invented. The story appeared in *This Kind of Child: The Disability Story*, ed. K. Srilata, 2022.

leaving the station. After he goes to sleep, I listen to its steady beat. Perhaps I remain in its embrace even when I'm asleep, because I wake up with a slight pang as day dawns.

That is why, even though it's hard to get away from all the work at home, I am happy to accompany Shaku-di when she goes to volunteer at the Red Cross or at a women's association or to interview someone.

Shaku-di lives upstairs, with her son and daughter-in-law. She's about fifty, cheerful, always ready to chat. I'm the quiet type, so I like the company of talkative people. And Shaku-di is not the sort of talkative person who is unaware of anything except the sound of her own voice. Ajay and I often fall out; Shaku-di never asks questions or gives advice. She just makes me a cup of tea and talks about all sorts of things to divert me. Not touching the central question, she tries to indicate to me that since this knot cannot be untied, there is no point struggling with it.

Today, Shaku-di is going to a blind girls' home; she wants to write an article on the conditions there, because this is the Year of Disabled Persons.

'The blind boys' home is so big and has so many facilities,' she told me. 'And here, just imagine, the girls are shut up in small dark rooms like prison cells. The last time I went, the warden wouldn't let me meet the girls. This time, I won't let her stop me.'

A golden afternoon. I was ready on time, but a whole lot of visitors dropped in on Shaku-di. Finally, after entertaining all of them, she emerged, not having managed to eat any lunch.

'How far is it?'

'Just a ten-minute walk. Near the gurudwara.'

'So it's right in the centre of the colony, and I didn't even know it existed.'

'You've only been here a year.'

'If you hadn't told me, I probably wouldn't have known even in ten years.'

'Look, it's that house.'

'That one?'

A house like any other. No indication that instead of one housewife's life, many girls' lives are smouldering within.

'Look, what a jail they've made of it.' Shaku-di pointed to the shuttered windows. 'I've heard they don't let the girls go anywhere. They're not allowed to step out of the gate.'

I began to feel strangely reluctant as we approached the house. We were behaving like tourists going to observe a newly discovered species. What would they think of our arrival? I felt quite unfit to talk to them. What was I going there for, with my ignorance and my eyes?

The watchman was missing. We peeked into the office; no one there either. The ground floor was deserted. We could hear the girls' voices upstairs.

'Oh, it's 15th August today, so it's a holiday. That's why there is no one here; how amazingly incompetent they are.'

Then I remembered; of course—Ajay hadn't gone to office today. He was at a friend's house and would be back early.

Shaku-di saw her chance. 'Come on, let's go upstairs and talk to the girls. If the warden were here, she might have stopped us.'

We climbed the stairs quickly. Three open doors on the first floor. The corridor was touched by sunlight, but the rooms were dark with the comfortable darkness of late afternoon. For a moment we stood there, uncertain. Then Shaku-di stepped into the first room. I was close behind her. Right next to the door of the room was a bed, and there were two other beds as well. Four or five girls were in the room, lying and sitting on the beds. On the bed next to the door two girls lay wrapped in each other's arms, and a soft sound in a monotone emanated from them, like the rippling of a brook, like a mother's—no, just like my own voice . . .

Jayshree and I used to cycle to college together every day, racing each other. When the cycles took wing, and the sleepy morning dazzled awake to the perfume of Jayshree's long hair, her laughter, her intoxicating company, I felt as if she and I would fly like this through life, leaving the world behind, ecstatic at our own pace. Those three years spent with Jayshree now seem like the three hours of a colourful film, from which one emerges into the same whispers in the dark, the vulgar hoardings, the sharp neon light and men's sharper stares, but at that time it was no dream. It was waking reality, speaking and laughing. Reality that shook awake my half-slumbering heart, opened my eyes to many colours, unwrapped my enfolded desires and set them afloat on the winds.

At that time I didn't have these thoughts, these words, neither did Jayshree. Just feelings. How many times I wanted to tell her something, something surely very profound, rising up in my throat, and I would say, 'Listen . . .'

'Yes?'

'No, nothing.'

Weeping, that something sank back into me.

My father was transferred, and we had to part, still in that same silence. My head on her shoulder, my body blossoming. She trembled like a young tree awakened by the breeze, yet we couldn't say anything. As if our tongues had been cut out or we had forgotten our names. Yes, now sometimes words do come pouring out.

Not the couple of times when I have formally met Jayshree— on those occasions my head felt numb and my body like a chopped-off branch. But in dreams sounds rise to my lips—of the kind I'm now hearing.

'Lord knows what nonsense you keep talking in your sleep,' Ajay says. 'I can't understand a word of it.'

The girls sit up, and Shaku-di begins asking them questions. The oldest girl answers, calmly but as if on high alert. Emphasizing the terrible conditions in which they live, Shaku-di keeps asking whether she's longing to go home, and the girl keeps repeating that she is perfectly content living here and she does not want to go home.

'What work do you do here?'

'We knit mops.'

'How much do you earn?'

'Four annas a cloth.'

'That's all? Don't you want to move to the Rajinder Nagar school, where you can study further?'

'No.'

'Why not? Don't you want to study further?'

'No. What's the point of studying?'

Shaku-di is speechless. Like most of us, she considers education the only means of women's upliftment. Her father did not let her continue her education and tied a husband around her neck. I too am a bit surprised by the clarity of the answer. Shaku-di tries to expand the girl's horizons; after all, why would such a smart girl want to continue living in this prison?

'But if you study you can advance in the world, you can marry.'

'I don't want to marry.'

Shaku-di clearly thought that the girl assumed no one would marry her.

'Why? Why should you think like that? Just last month, Miss Verma, who teaches in the Rajinder Nagar school, got married. I've interviewed a lot of people there, many men as well. All the men are married.'

'No, I don't want to marry. Absolutely not.'

'But why not?'

'What's the use of marrying?'

Shaku-di did not answer this question. Instead, she began to talk to another girl. A girl from the hills, smiling, pink-cheeked. She looked like a happy child.

'What about you? You don't want to study?'

'I used to study in the Rajinder Nagar school. I was expelled.' She was shy and didn't speak with the confidence of the older girl.

'Why were you expelled?'

She was silent.

'Shall I talk to them and get you readmitted there?'

The girl shook her head in the negative.

'But why not?'

'No.'

'You don't want to study?'

'Yes, I want to.'

'Well, then?'

'I'll study here.'

'But there are no teaching arrangements here. You have to study on your own. There you will be properly taught.'

There was no answer, so Shaku-di changed the subject. 'What pretty bangles you're wearing. Who gave them to you?'

Her pink complexion turned even more rosy, and she indicated with her head the girl sitting next to her, in whose arms we had seen her lying a few minutes earlier. What love, what pride, what joy on her face . . .

Shaku-di talked a little more and then stood up to go. And I? Throughout the conversation, I had sat silent, tears in my eyes, like a guilty person.

* * *

A few days later Shaku-di turned up, rather excited.

'Manju, I talked to some women teachers there. They say that all these girls love each other and have formed couples. That day I did feel there was some such thing going on, and when I asked, the teachers said calmly, "So what? If they're happy, what is it to you?"'

Gathering all my courage, I managed to say, 'But what is wrong with that?'

'Because they are not allowed to meet boys and they need love and affection, they start embracing and kissing one another from childhood onwards, and as they grow older they want to live only with women.' She paused, and then concluded, 'I am going to write about all this in my article.'

So far, I had listened with the wariness of that girl the other day, but now the words came pouring out, not to protect those girls from our insolence, our shamelessness, but as if to protect myself.

'But, Shaku-di, if they are happy, why should anyone object? How happily and confidently they spoke that day. They didn't want anyone's pity. They shouldn't be prevented from meeting boys. But how do we know they will be happier with boys? How much happiness have you and I found with men? How many have found it?'

Shaku-di hesitated, then said, 'No, but such things interfere with children's education.'

I felt that a gulf was opening up between Shaku-di and me, which I must leap over. 'But Shaku-di, children play these sorts of games with each other in every house. They hide their play, they feel afraid and guilty. It's all a matter of how you look at it. We keep repeating what we have been told is right or wrong, but reality may be different.'

'When I talked to the teachers, they said, "We only care about the exam results and the passing rate is a hundred percent."'

'They are happy, so why wouldn't it be a hundred percent? If you write about it, who knows how the authorities may punish them?'

'All right, I won't write about this. But the misuse of government funds, the girls not getting proper food and clothing, the low wages, the unnecessary restrictions . . .'

'Yes, of course, it's important to write about all that.'

Shaku-di has left. I stand by the window. I have seen another world just a few steps away from where I live. How much I saw in a few minutes! A world I never dreamt could exist. I have lived with limited vision.

Lip to Lip[*]

Shobhana Bhutani Siddique

Madan gets up. A cigarette between his lips, he puts on his shirt and opens a window. I'm lying unclothed on this wide bed. Below me is spread a dark brown satin sheet with large pink roses all over it. A pillow embroidered with the words '*Sweet Dreams*' has fallen on the floor. A soft pillow lies under my hips. It is perfectly still outside. A breeze enters the room, bearing the perfume of your armpits, a perfume that drives me crazy even today. Madan's way of smoking is very careless—he barely touches the cigarette with his forefinger and middle finger, so that it seems as if it is about to fall. You hold a cigarette tightly in a clenched fist. I draw deeply on a Simla cigarette. When you take a drag your small slanting eyes grow even smaller. You look exactly like a Chinese merchant. Taking a last puff, you suddenly throw away the cigarette with a jerk—and the blood begins to race through my veins and continues tingling for a long time. Energy seems ready to explode from every small, big and even unnecessary action of yours. As if lava bursts from within you, emerges boiling from your fingernails

---

[*] 'Lab-ba Lab' from *Hindi Kahani Ka Madhyantar*, ed. Ramesh Bakshi, Sanmarg Prakashan, 1985, pp. 194–204. The title can mean 'lip to lip' but also has the idiomatic meaning of overflowing. I translated long excerpts from this story in *Same-Sex Love in India* (2000). This is the first complete translation.

and spreads all around you. It overshadows everything that is in
your proximity. It crushes every bone in my body. This alone is
your strength. For you are very ordinary-looking. A flat, dark face,
small eyes, a broad nose, full lips that seem ready to burst into
laughter and a long tight plait that seems to defy people. But there
is an aura around you—perhaps your eccentricity. I feel afraid
of your beauty because it depends so completely on your energy.
As soon as your energy ebbs, your beauty will begin to rot like
stale fish. Then you'll look coarse and ugly. That's why I want to
squeeze every drop from these moments. I want to suck the nectar
out of you, swallow you whole as a lizard does an insect. So that
when I leave you or when you tire of me, your attraction will have
vanished, and no one will think you worth tasting. You sit down
next to me like a fanfare of drums. Why are you looking at me as
if you've never seen me before? I consider my body through your
eyes. Small fair feet, long slim legs lightly sprinkled with golden
hair, dirty knees, full fair thighs, wide but slender hips, a slightly
darker waist with a blue mark on it from tying my salwar tightly.
Without a salwar, my waist looks less slim. Long, full, pink breasts
with two dark-brown dots, oh how delicate. A big gap between
the two breasts, more than is usual. Whichever part you glance
at comes alive. Every part begins panting like a small puppy,
begins desiring you, begins demanding you. You hide your face
between my breasts and remain perfectly still. A cry leaps from
every pore in my body and rises upwards through me. I want to
disappear, but the cry keeps echoing, like the sobbing of a hungry
cat. You take my face between your hands and look at me with
overflowing eyes. How sensitive your face becomes. The warmth
of your hands makes my skin tender, very tender. I see in your
eyes that I am beautiful. My head droops slightly to the right.
With what pride you smile. A shameless smile that begins on your
lips and spreads to your temples, keeps spreading. Your yellow
teeth shine. You find it amusing to see me in this state. Drawing
a line on my left cheek with the hand that is holding it, you

ask, 'Well, what's happening, little sexpot?' I feel terribly shy. That word vibrates through me like someone blowing on a spiderweb. The web keeps trembling. Fighting my sensations, I say 'Nothing' in a quivering voice. 'Really? Nothing?' you say, running your lips over my ear, 'And now?' A wave rises beneath my controlled voice. 'No, nothing.' And then I say loudly, 'What can happen?' You brazenly get up and bring over the mirror that is hanging on the wall. 'Look here.' When I see my face in the mirror, I feel surprise, anger, embarrassment. I hide my face in my hands and say, 'No, no, it's nothing. I have a headache, I have fever, a high fever.' You throw down my hand and hiss, 'I have happened to you.' You throw the mirror on the bed and burst out laughing. The walls and the ceiling vibrate. How distorted your sense of humour is. You don't understand that this is not a joke. You can make a joke of anything.

You are the most brazen girl in our college. The salt and spice of your attractiveness is your good health. When I walk with you I feel that I'm the most important girl in the world. You stride along, scattering energy all around you. You walk down the corridor as if the whole building belongs to you and all the girls are your subjects, and I the special slave whom you find charming. Your beloved slave-girl.

We sit on the lawn behind the college, under the mulberry tree. But not in the shade. The pink winter of October. You are talking very freely to Umesh, Sinha, Kapoor. In your presence all these boys seem like cooing pigeons. One feels like pinching their cheeks as one does a child's. Srivastava brings two dozen bananas. You lean forward and break off one. This little movement of yours seems charged with significance—more significant than life itself. Every gesture, every posture, every expression of yours seems vast, as if you have the capacity to capture, to embrace the whole world. You devour the banana and throw the skin into the air, and it gets stuck on a branch above. Ramanujam offers peanuts, first to you and then to me. You give him a come-hither look, and smile.

Oh, how I hate you for that. You run your tongue over your lips.
Your full lips start looking poisonous. The sun goes in and out, the
top of the mulberry tree shines, the lawn is chequered with light
and shade.

Sinha says, 'Yesterday Gyani said, "Look, Sinha, you criticize
me too much." I immediately said, "Sir, I also praise you highly."'
You roar with laughter, and keep chewing peanuts. Your cheeks
look slick like the trunk of the mulberry tree. I think of khasta
kachauri from Alwar. Whenever I'm angry with you, this image
comes back to taunt me. You seek the company of boys to mislead
everyone, and you send these wretched dogs off on a false scent.
I silently applaud your cunning. Umesh asks, 'Nanu, what is your
hobby?' You reply, 'Politics and *sex*.' Umesh doesn't know where
to look. To hide his *nervousness*, he says, 'Yesterday Mr Chatterjee
was really gazing at you.' You say, 'Oh, you naughty boy,' and
pretend shyness, to offset your earlier mention of *sex*. What cheap
behaviour. I wish I could tear you and Umesh to pieces; no, throw
you to the jackals. One day I'll push you down from some high
cliff. I feel ashamed of your behaviour. At such times, I don't exist
for you. You flirt with them in my presence and become the focus
of their appreciation. Even though I am prettier than you, it is you
the boys always admire, and somehow this seems natural. 'Who's
for coffee?' says Umesh, and you immediately second him. You
might refuse at least once in a way! In your place, I would have
refused at once, and then the two of us could have gone off alone
and talked to our hearts' content.

Ramanujam, Sinha and I quickly cross the road. You say in a
girlish way, 'Oh, there's a car coming.' And then Umesh puts his
arm around your waist and takes you across the road. Even after
you have crossed the road, his hand stays there for quite a while,
and you do not move away. Shameless creature. How you act the
helpless little thing to allure the boys. You always want to appear
feminine when they are around. Is it possible that you really like
boys? I look at your blooming face and feel sick. The restaurant is

so suffocating. Boys and girls, people, people, round and round and round. I want to get up and run away.

I stop talking to you. I am filled with suspicion and doubt. I hate you. Or is it that I want to hate you? So that when I come back to you after some days your strength will seem doubled to me, and I will be helpless before you, helpless with the desire to have you. You will assert your claim on me, conquer me at night and suck the pith from me, empty me out.

Whenever I stop talking to you, you spend a lot of time with Ramanujam, Umesh and Sinha. You also talk and laugh with Uma, Mehrunnisa, Kiran and Prabha, but all the time you are highly aware of me. You try to demonstrate in small ways how much you need me. Oh, how I hate the sight of you. As soon as I see you, I stand more erect and turn away my face. Your eyes are filled with pain. When I get back to my room, I feel like crying. No one tells me I am pretty these days. I wear pink, yet the boys do not look at me. I cover my face with *cream* and *powder*. 'Why are you whitewashing yourself?' the girls ask. I have to give up *powder* and acknowledge that I look yellow. Perhaps my feelings are very obvious, or else it seems to me that everyone knows what the matter is with me.

At bedtime, you come to our room to return one of Uma's books. You don't look at me. When it is your turn to serve food in the dining hall, you bring crisp chapatis for me, you throw a piece of lemon into my plate, you serve me curd and sugar twice over. These strategies of yours irritate me. But I am hungry, so I devour the crisp chapatis. I behave as if I haven't noticed anything unusual. But when my stomach is full, I feel exasperated with myself. You never dare to ask directly why I am angry with you. But you lightly brush your body against me, as we are walking along. When I don't react, your ego is hurt. I am amused by your childishness and feel quite detached from you.

But suddenly the energy vanishes from your stride. You start talking of Marx and Richard the Fourth; you begin to turn pale. The teachers and your male and female followers begin to pay more attention to me. Gradually, all the reasons why I couldn't bear you begin to fade. And then one day they disappear altogether. I have to look for reasons to continue being angry with you, but I can't find any. I feel sorry for you when you carry on your act. After all, you're doing all this to placate me. Poor thing, what techniques she uses. What right have I to be so cruel to anyone? What wrong have you done me? How pale you look! I should be ashamed of myself. I can never forgive myself. Suddenly I leave the class and run, panting, to your room. You throw aside your book (how fond you are of throwing things) and ask, 'Want some water?' These moments are unbearable for both of us. You look at me as if you've found a lost treasure, as if you had given up hope of my returning. But you should know that I always return to you in the end. You lie down on the bed. We lie for a long time with our backs to each other. It seems unnatural to start once more. But it also seems unnatural to do nothing. Sometimes your foot or your plait brushes against me. I quiver and remain still. This unintended contact excites me terribly. But you don't take me. I put up with this, although I want to pounce on you, crush you, chew your bones. The day passes. You keep reading. I hear the sound of the pages turning. Whenever the sound stops I stop breathing. Have you gone to sleep? I can never bear to look at you asleep . . .

You have really gone to sleep. You do not move at all. All my nerves are on edge, waiting. It is not yet midnight. I am turning numb, my feet tingle, I can feel the blood enter my heart and flow out in tiny blood vessels. Will my breath return? I keep counting but cannot sleep, so I get up quietly, pick up *Confessions* from the table, go into the corridor and try to read in the dim light. The words turn to ciphers, and a cold anguish settles in my stomach. Am I afraid? Or is this excitement? What will you say? How will you begin? What will I reply? Will I be able to speak, or will I choke? And you? Will you stand far off, silent, making my predicament more difficult, or will you lovingly embrace me? I will wait, head bent, like an offender. I will accept whatever punishment you mete out. I want to run away but cannot. Even if I run away, I will return at midnight to receive my punishment.

It is midnight. You take a candle and examine my face. I pretend to be asleep. Your eyes shine with victory. So you knew all along? I don't like this cool look on your face. You touch my left cheek with your hand, scratch my temples, blow softly into my left ear. Then you tap with your fingers on my eyelids. Your touch is very soft and light. My body yearns to grab hold of your touch. Helpless sounds burst from my throat. For a long time, you continue to tease me like this. When I can no longer bear your touch and begin to moan, you pounce on me like a tiger. You draw my tongue into your mouth, crush my lips and suck my teeth. Your big hands play with me for a while, and then gradually you enter me. I feel very proud. Because your lava, your energy, your blossoming health enter me. I slowly keep rising, keep rising, and then, when I climax, you are very loving. For some reason you seem very grateful when I come. Then you put your cool lips there. I am sinking into love. I feel as if my blood is slowly ebbing from a high place. I feel a slow, sweet dizziness. At that moment I realize how deprived I was all these days. You like early mornings. I wake you up, you whimper and fight me, fight yourself, for a long time, then you are defeated by my tenderness and dependence. I bite your chin gently. Overwhelmed, you hide your face in my cleavage. Yes, your mother is a whore, your father is a drunkard, lying drunk in some alley, you are my lost son—are you not?—my life. Before you come, you say, 'Who are you? Tell me who you are. Where do you live, what do you do, why have you come here, what are you to me, why do you give me such happiness, why do you leave me, why do you come back again, what are you to me, why do you leave me, why do you come back again? Tell me, answer me. Who are you, where have you come from, where—'* You talk like a mad person, first slowly, then faster and faster, merely touching some words and breathing life into others. Then your words become indistinct,

---

* All the verbs referring to the addressee are feminine in the original.

broken. You leave words incomplete and seem to sink into a swoon, then just before you come you suddenly fall silent—only your pulse throbs. I lay my head on your feet and fall asleep. The next day you have a slight headache or a hangover from smoking too much dope. How irritable you become. Your enthusiasm for life, which is so attractive, suddenly vanishes. You complain like a sick child. Was your vigour based merely on a healthy body? A little weakness and your confidence flies away like a pigeon. All the girls sit around, but you don't listen to anyone. Uma brought you two Anacins, but you refused them. You accepted a Codopyrin from me. You close your eyes and lie still when I tell you to do so. You never stay with the same girl for more than two months, or three months at the most. But we have been together seven months. It is becoming a challenge for me to keep you with me. The other girls are beginning to notice this.

A week later. You have started keeping three seats together in the class. I think you've kept a seat for Uma because she's my roommate. How blind human beings can be! One day I arrived first and forgot to keep a chair for Uma; yes, I forgot; all right, I deliberately didn't keep a chair for her. What will you do to me? You looked at me, then joined two chairs and sat between both of us.

Now Uma is always with the two of us. I am not hostile to Uma, but I don't think three people can be good friends without one of them feeling like an unwanted third. And that is what gradually happens. You two enjoy talking for hours about politics or about yourselves. You forget my presence. Uma doesn't forget. She deliberately uses her wiles to keep you entangled so I don't resent her behaviour. But you actually forget that I am sitting there. When I catch you at it, you try to hide it, but your efforts only make it more evident. New buds have appeared on the mulberry tree. How fresh they are. What pure beauty! I don't consider Uma more beautiful than I am. She is not at all beautiful. Not in the least. No, she isn't. At least, you never have liked her kind of looks. When she sits in the sun scrubbing her small feet, with what innocent wonder you watch her. Alas, what attraction there is in novelty, in new desire!

I close my eyes like the proverbial ostrich. I try desperately to explain away your behaviour. After all, why should you confine yourself to me? I am not your friend. You are interested in politics, so is Uma, but I am not. (My older sister says silliness is attractive in girls.) Sometimes, when you are sitting near me, before I have finished talking, you get up and go off. 'Oh, I have to *study* with Uma.' You and Uma *study* together till two in the morning. Sometimes you ask me something which tells me that you haven't heard what I told you a fortnight ago. You forget many important things I have told you. But I've begun to put up with these insults, because I cannot live without you, even for a moment. You have become a very personal need of mine, like the need to urinate. You always were. But in the beginning, I used to fight this need in myself. Now I cannot even fight with you. I am beginning to feel fulfilled, now that I have you. I have become very delicate, a bundle of tenderness. You are exasperated by my passivity in bed. You say irritably, 'Love me, love me.' But I enjoy lying silent. That initial mad eagerness for every free moment between classes, every night, is disappearing. Sometimes, a fortnight passes without my missing it. But you have begun to wander like a thirsty ghost. You can't sleep. Many girls have noticed your discontent and have started trying to seduce you. They never dared before. It is you who must have incited them!

One dark evening, you were stroking my soft palms. At that moment I felt all that I had imagined was false, my delusion. Your hands were solid and cold. The perfume of your armpits disturbed me. At that moment you had really come back to me. A short figure approached us. Suddenly you dropped my hand, drew away and said: 'Yes, yes, I understand your point, but I don't think you are right. In fact, I would say that—' Uma was standing next to us. 'Umey'—your lips were trembling. You stood up without another word. In the darkness, Uma's eyes shone with cruel satisfaction.

As I entered the room, my image leapt at me from the mirror. How pale I have become, how old I look, how wrinkled. How hard it is to take each step. Perhaps I have no beauty at all; it is you who give it to me. How quickly I tire these days. I don't feel like doing anything at all.

You are with Uma in my room. I'm lying on your bed in your room. Whenever you kiss her, these walls echo. You return very late at night. You look prepared for a fight. But I don't say anything. You're disappointed. You feel I am becoming indifferent to you. I know you so well. How transparent you are. Once I have sought out a reason for every action of yours, I no longer feel angry, just sad. Sometimes I feel that although you are going out of my orbit, you can never become part of Uma's being—perhaps one day you will realize this and return. You have started spending more and more time with Uma. I have withdrawn into the background. For the first time, I look closely at Uma. A very fair complexion, wide jaws that are no longer rigid these days, a small, upturned nose, small, slanting brown eyes, bright red, full—no, thick lips, brown hair. How beautiful Uma is! At night, I wait for her to return to our room. She returns, mussed-up, relaxed, happy, and lies down on her bed. I keep looking at her—enchanted. There is nothing I can do. I would like to be attracted to boys. But I feel disgusted by them, afraid of them. I remember that childhood incident. Is there not a cruelty lurking in their eyes? And then, such a complete union with them is not possible as it is between you and me. Should I get married? What will it be like? How will I feel? These days, such futile questions fill my head. But as long as you're around I can never be attracted to Umesh, Ramanujam, any of them. Because you overshadow them, all of us, these trees, this building. One laugh of yours scatters them all.

I didn't return after the final exam. What is the use of doing an MA? What great things have I achieved with a BA? I don't want to take up a job. I don't have the courage to compete in a man's world. Mother keeps insisting that I get married. If I ask for a second roti, she looks reproachfully at me; she is constantly worried about me. Every now and then she says, 'Prices are rising, how long will your father—?' Father does not say anything, but he does not oppose Mother either. He did oppose my older sister's marriage. Mother stopped sleeping with him in protest. Father was forced to give in to her. Next year, Father will retire, and Mother will have to give tuitions to make money. Madan has a beautiful body, so beautiful that it is not attractive. If his glance ever falls on my naked body, he says, 'Oh, sorry,' and turns away. I find this amusing. He never forgets to pat me before leaving for office. He takes great care of me. Gradually, I'll get used to this situation. Let's see. Everything will be fine once I have children. Perhaps after we live together for many years, I will start loving Madan. That is what everyone does. I enlarge the bindi on my forehead. Today, Madan's aunt is coming on a visit. How beautiful she is. Is my *lipstick* looking good? She will stay for two or three days. Sleeping with Madan is so inconvenient.

A Double Life*

Vijay Dan Detha

A hand claps with another hand. The clouds embrace and roar!
Touching makes for rising. Who counts and who desires? Waves
collide and produce foam. The forest fire consumes every branch.
Youth meets youth. Who sees and who knows?

May Kama, the bodiless one, be gracious and give to each one
of us two lives. Once upon a time there were two villages at a
distance of twelve and twelve, that is, twenty-four *kos*† apart from
each other. In these two villages lived two Seths who were similar
in their wealth and their miserliness. There was no limit to their
greed or to their love for each other. So united were their fortunes
that the weddings of both took place on the same night. At the
same moment, their hands were joined to those of two beautiful
brides, and at the same moment, pearls were generated in the
two oysters. In their joy, the two Seths promised each other that
regardless of which of them had a daughter and which a son, the

---

* Rajasthani title, 'Dowari Joon', first published in the 1980s and enacted
as a Hindi play at that time. This translation from *Bataan Ri Phulwaadi*
(Jodhpur: Rajasthani Granthagar, second edition 2009), volume 13,
pp. 58–90. The word *joon* can mean birth, womb (*yoni*) and life. I was
the first to translate this story into English. It appeared in *Manushi* 17,
August–September 1983, under the title 'Naya Gharvas. '

† A kos is 1.8 miles.

84

offspring would be united in marriage. Thus, while still in the womb, the two children were linked together.

Intoxicated by their love for one another and by their pride in their wealth, the Seths ignored the magical play of nature. In the ninth month, under the influence of the same planet, two girls were born. Intoxicated partly by his pledge and partly by greed, one Seth played false. He announced his daughter's birth by beating a copper plate instead of a winnowing basket. He sent the barber to his friend's village, with the news of a son's birth. Both Seths celebrated the occasion by distributing molasses.

At first, the mother thought this was a private joke between the two friends. When the time came, the facts would be revealed. Until then there was no harm in maintaining the illusion as a joke. After all, in childhood, what is the difference between a boy and a girl? It's only when the shadow of youth falls on a person that one is forced to recognize the secret of the difference.

But the father made no attempt, conscious or unconscious, to dispel the illusion. He brought the girl up like a boy. Well in advance, the child was equipped from head to toe with turban and *angarkhi*, girdle and *dhoti*. At first, the mother treated the whole affair as a game, but when the passing of time did not make the father change his tune, she grew perturbed. One day she tried warning her husband. In a tone of tender remonstrance, she said, 'How can you shut your eyes to reality like this?'

Bristling, the Seth retorted, 'Who says my eyes are shut? I am alert to every reality in all the three worlds!'

Clasping her head in her hands, his wife replied, 'If you're so alert, how come you can't see your daughter's youth blossoming in a boy's dress?'

The Seth gave a smart answer. 'Do you think I have nothing better to do than to waste time on such trivial matters?'

The Sethani's tongue responded according to habit. 'Father of our son, why are you talking such nonsense? Your daughter has reached marriageable age, and you call it a trivial matter?'

'Well, I'm not forbidding marriage, am I? In fact, no one can equal my good sense in such matters. I arranged the marriage long ago, while the child was in the womb.'

Stepping closer to him, the Sethani answered, 'What has your arranging got to do with it? Have you ever heard of a girl being married to another girl?'

'Why not? What does it take to get married? You decide to do it, and it's done. But a pledge is a pledge—it can't be broken even for fear of death.'

The Sethani's eyebrows shot up. This certainly did not seem like a joke. How should she explain to her husband a reality as clear as the sun? Was this a matter to be explained? She sat still, bewildered, but soon realized that silence could lead to disaster.

She screwed up her courage and said, 'My good man, how do you think your pledges will make up for what will be lacking in bed? Have a little sense, do. All these years I did not interfere only because I thought this was a joke.'

'I never do anything that needs to be interfered with. You'll see—we'll get a huge dowry. I'll arrange a grand marriage procession for my son. A man's word, once given, cannot be taken back. And after all, why should I have to suffer a loss because of nature's mistake?'

The Sethani sank into confusion. Either her husband was still pulling her leg or else he really was determined not to break his pledge. But her mind could not be at rest while the matter remained unresolved. Burning with suppressed anger, she said, 'To hell with your profit and loss! What about the loss your poor daughter will have to suffer in bed on account of having a father like you? Haven't you thought about that at all?'

Not a whit disconcerted, the Seth replied, 'Of course I've thought of it. When men go on business trips for eight or ten years, their wives, if they are sensible women, wait patiently. When women are married to incapable men, somehow they still the desire of their wombs. After all, a child widow also lives out her life, doesn't she? A girl brings her karma with her. She'll cut her coat according to her cloth.'

When she heard this, the Sethani was convinced that it was no joke. Her husband was not willing to untie a single knot of the web he had woven. As if in a dream, her daughter's face swam before her eyes. Through her tears, she exclaimed, 'She's our own daughter, born of us. How can we tie her to a stake and burn her like this? Once she's married to a girl, what will she cut and what will she wear? I cannot consent to such a misdeed, not even in a dream.'

Irritated, her husband broke in, 'When did I ask for your consent? I'm quite able to arrange everything on my own. I warn you, if you poke your nose into this once more, I'll kill myself. Far better to die than to break one's word. And you know very well how a shortcoming in the bed of a Seth is compensated for. Don't pretend to close your eyes to the truth that you know. The whole district knows how your dear father's name was saved from dying out. Didn't I swallow that fly, although my eyes were wide open?'

The Sethani had never dreamt that her husband would fling this taunt at her. As soon as she heard it, she felt as though her lips had been sealed. The blood congealed in her veins. It was true that everyone knew how her mother had openly indulged herself with every man in sight. Her unmanly father had stayed buried in his business and his account books, while her mother, as though intoxicated, forgot even the distinction between high and low. She had an open affair with a Bavari.* The Bavari was fair and handsome. The Sethani looked exactly like him—the same features and the same build. When the lid was suddenly blown off that seething cauldron, she was defeated and stammered, 'Do as you please.'

Her husband was very pleased at having hit the target with this arrow and settled the matter once and for all. As chance would have it, the very next day, at an auspicious hour, engagement gifts

---

* A nomadic tribe categorized by the British as a criminal tribe.

were sent to his house. He happily accepted them, but his wife felt
cut to the heart. Yet she didn't open her lips to protest. The girl's
own karma must decide the outcome.

The girl herself was naive and innocent. Neither did she think
about her karma, nor did she pay heed to her blossoming youth.
Brought up as a boy from infancy, she considered herself a boy.
Though she did not understand the meaning of marriage, she was
thrilled at the prospect of this new adventure.

She was sure that after marriage her smooth cheeks would
sprout a beard. Her fingers itched to stroke and curl a moustache.
This childish delusion was like fuel added to the fire smouldering
in her mother's breast.

One day, a girl of her own age had seen her bathing and had
realized the truth. Thinking that her friend's parents were perhaps
performing some magical ritual, she had kept quiet, but when she
saw her friend's excitement growing as wedding preparations were
set afoot, she could wait no longer. Taking her to the room on top
of the house, she said, 'Look, sister . . .'

The other interrupted, 'Hey, what's this? How come you're
calling me sister instead of brother, as you usually do?'

The girl smiled and said, 'Why not? You are my sister. So
why should you mind my calling you sister? You silly girl, you're
a woman and you dream of becoming a bridegroom? How long
do you think you can make up for your lack of manliness by this
playacting?'

'What do you mean how long? All my life. But what do you
find lacking in my manliness—in my dhoti, my angarkhi and my
sixteen-foot-long turban?'

Suppressing a smile, her friend replied, 'A sixteen-foot-long
turban can't make up for the lack of a man's equipment. You
should flatly refuse to enter into this marriage. My dear, you need
a bridegroom, not a bride. What furrow do you think you two girls
will plough together? Why can't you understand such simple facts,
even though you're all grown up?'

The Seth's naive daughter still failed to understand her. Frowning, she said, 'You're just jealous of my beautiful wife. You can't bear to see me happy.'

'What's to be done with you?' cried her friend, embracing her. 'You'll come to your senses only after you've taken a hard knock. It will be too late then. Your father is greedy for dowry, but how is it that your mother didn't explain matters to you? I can't understand how she has brought herself to agree.'

'I'll go to mother right now and ask her!' said the girl impatiently. 'She won't hide anything from me.'

'She had better not.' So saying, the friend went home, while the girl rushed to her mother and cried, 'Mother, today one of my friends said something very strange. She said that I wear men's clothes but I'm not really a man. Of course, I'm not such a fool as to believe her! I know you won't hide anything from me. Tell me, isn't she lying? I told her that it was nothing but jealousy—she couldn't bear the idea of my having a beautiful wife.'

The mother turned her face away and wiped her eyes. After a while she said tearfully, 'If that had been the case, wouldn't I have told you so long ago? These silly girls have a habit of teasing each other.'

'I'm not going to be scared by any amount of teasing,' cried the girl, filled with enthusiasm. 'Even if I were a woman and not a man, I wouldn't refuse this marriage. After all, marriage is a union of two hearts. If the hearts of two women unite, why shouldn't they get married?'

'Your father says the same,' replied her mother in a low voice.

Dancing away, the girl cried, 'Of course! My father is very wise.'

Now that she had asked her mother what she wanted to, there was no need to linger there. Off she went, tossing the fringe of her turban, leaping and dancing, while her mother remained standing like a stone statue, lost in thought, holding back her sobs.

The next day when she met her neighbour, the Seth's daughter berated her soundly. She was no fool to be misled by anyone, not

she! Proudly she declared, 'Even if I hadn't been a man, I would
have married a woman and shown you how it is done. We two
women would not have had the slightest objection to each other.'

The other girl had been married two years but had not yet
conceived. She could barely keep herself from laughing at this
nonsensically innocent declaration. She tried to explain, 'There
must surely be some intoxicant instead of water in your family well!
You silly girl, however much two grinding stones may rub against
each other, nothing will come of it. Only a man can perform a
man's function.'

'Oh come on, what great shakes do you think a man achieves,
reducing everything to sixes and sevens! It's the grinding stones
that nourish the whole world. They grind flour as well as pulses.'

At this, the other really couldn't control her laughter. She
clapped her hands and cried, through spurts of laughter, 'Oh dear,
don't you two lag behind in grinding pulses!'

Hearing her laughter, the innocent girl felt shy. Pretending to
laugh too, she said, 'Why, what's wrong with grinding pulses?'

'You'll find out when the time comes,' said the other,
smothering her laughter in her veil.

'You must have found out something then?'

'What comparison is there between your marriage and mine!'

'Well, yes, the king and the pauper are worlds apart. Even
your ancestors could never have dreamt of such a dowry as I am
going to get.'

The neighbour didn't take offence at this remark. Lightly
pinching her friend's cheek, she said, 'Why drag our poor ancestors
into this absurd babble? It's not humanly possible for anyone to
bring you to your senses.'

The innocent daughter of the Seth did not understand what
was happening, nor was she able to comprehend what others tried
to explain to her. As the appointed hour drew near, she felt swept
along by waves of impulsive delight. Finally, the long-awaited
moment arrived. After enjoying numerous feasts given by relatives

and the community, the Seth's son's marriage procession set out at last. What a fine procession it was—seven horses, eleven camels and twenty bullock carts. The groom's father was seated on a brown camel and the groom in a decorated bullock cart.

Announcing its arrival with drumbeats and music, the procession reached the bride's village. A coconut was offered at the village border. After the proper rituals, at dusk the two were seated in the pavilion. Two soft hands were joined in the hand-taking ceremony. As their hands touched, a current ran like lightning through their bodies. Two strangers were joined together for life.

In the flickering lamplight, the groom sat on the flower-bestrewn wedding bed, waiting for the bride. At midnight, the tinkle of anklets and the whispers of the bride's girlfriends were heard. Her face veiled, the bride stood on the threshold of the room. A hundred buds began to bloom in the heart of the bridegroom. So this was the joy of marriage . . .!

As the bride hesitated, her friends pushed her in and bolted the door. Slowly, very slowly, the bride came up and sat on the wedding bed, close to the groom. The groom lifted the veil and looked at her face. Here was a veritable moon hidden behind the veil! The groom's joy could hardly be contained within the four walls of the room. Stroking the bride's cheeks, the groom said, 'I had heard much in praise of your beauty, but I never dreamt of such perfection!'

The bride's pink lips opened. In a sweet voice, she said, 'You are no less beautiful. My beauty is nothing before yours.'

They gazed at each other's faces, drinking in beauty through their eyes. The women standing outside tired themselves out peering through the cracks in the door, but they could see no light except that of the lamp. They thought that other thirsts would arise once the thirst of the eyes was quenched.

But the next night showed them the same scene. The women's eyes grew glazed with staring, but they saw not a glimpse of what they wanted to see. When their feet began to ache from standing on tiptoe, they descended the stairs one by one. Shyness is all very well, but this was really taking it too far. What was the use of such shyness? The couple had wasted two precious nights. It was not as if they were babes in arms. After all, when can the thirst of the eyes ever be quenched? A moment's glance shows you the same sight that you would see if you were to gaze all night long. Well, each to their own thirst and their own taste!

The bride went to her in-laws' house, yet the groom's shyness did not abate, nor did his tastes change. The mother's anxiety continued to grow. Though it was the height of summer, this strange marriage made the mother shiver. The Seth, asleep next to her, snored peacefully, but the Sethani stayed awake, her eyes refusing to close. How were the two girls confronting the empty night, she wondered. How would the daughter-in-law feel when she finally saw the reality? Her daughter had not understood anything. She had happily set out to fall into the pit with open eyes, but the poor daughter-in-law was still unaware of reality.

In the other room, the lamp of cow-ghee was glowing softly. Stroking the edge of the turban, the bride said, 'It's hot in here, isn't it? Why don't you remove your turban and be comfortable? I'll fan you for a while.'

So saying, she picked up a multicoloured fan. The husband said, 'The turban is the chief ornament of a man. Manliness pales without it. But if you say so, I'll open my angarkhi.'

The bride continued to wave her delicate wrist, and the husband, without any hesitation, began to open the angarkhi. As it opened, the bride saw her husband's bare chest. A scream escaped her, and she collapsed on the bed. Half swooning, she cried, 'You are also a woman! Why have you taken such revenge on me—for the doings of which birth?'

For the first time, the husband's illusion was shaken, and as it shook, the vision of a whole life spent in men's clothes swam before her eyes. She now understood what the neighbour girl had been trying to tell her. The demon of illusion is able to render a person blind and deaf. One neither sees nor hears. One sees only that shadow cast on the screen of illusion which one wishes to see and hears only what one wishes to hear. Reality ceases to exist.

After so many years, her eyes now began to throb with eagerness to see the naked truth. Mad with anxiety, she tore off her turban and shirt. When she had pulled off all the bride's clothes as well, her eyes grew wide at the reality that confronted them. How was it she had not seen this reality all these years? Both bodies were built in the same way. Like a pink fish, the bride lay unconscious on the bed. And just such another fully conscious fish stood beside her. Was such a drama ever enacted since the creation of the universe?

Suddenly the conscious fish began to shake the unconscious fish and cry out, 'Open your eyes, bride. I am rid of my illusion. I have sinned against you. You can punish me any way you like.'

The bride opened her eyes. She looked around. She sat up with a start. The two fish, shaped in one mould, gazed at each other. The fish who had been a husband once again acknowledged her fault and said she would feel at rest only after undergoing the severest of punishments. She had herself invited this disaster, but the bride had unknowingly fallen into the fire. No punishment could be too severe for such deception.

The bride was a good and intelligent girl. She knew that to acknowledge one's fault and sincerely repent is the greatest possible punishment. At once she understood that all this had happened unintentionally. Then, though she repeatedly said it was not necessary, the husband-fish told her the entire story of her childhood. She realized that her father had woven this web, inspired by his false and nonsensical concept of keeping his word and by his greed for dowry. Her poor mother had tried her best to prevent it but had failed.

Lost in thought, the bride listened to the story. She said, 'I have borne the pain of this illusion only for a week, but you have borne it for years. Your pain is greater than mine. The same lightning has struck both of us. We must now face this crisis together.'

'But I was the one who became a bridegroom and took your hand. I am completely to blame. You have been deceived by me.'

Impatiently, the bride interrupted, 'You have been equally punished for the deception.'

'No, not even death can liberate me from the weight of this misdeed.'

Then the bride stroked her cheeks and said in honeyed tones, 'We two will now cross this Bhagirathi together.'*

Weeping, the other replied, 'Had I knowingly married you, there would have been no obstacle to liberation, but now I can't rid myself of remorse for this deception. Otherwise, I would have set up a matchless model of marriage between two women.'

'Nothing is lost yet,' said the bride, encouragingly. 'Give up the error of regret. We will have to find our own path to liberation. What's so wonderful about marriage between a man and a woman? Everyone knows that the sun rises in the east. Were it to rise in the west, that would be something really special!'

Then the bride opened her box and took out a set of clothes. With her own hands, she dressed the other girl. She decked her with jewels and applied collyrium to her eyes. She then put on her own clothes. Both of them began to sparkle like the flame of the lamp. Dispelling the evil eye by spitting seven times, the bride kissed the other's cheeks and said lovingly, 'Your name is Beeja and mine is Teeja.† How blessed we are that fortune has brought us together. Don't you ever say another word of regret in my presence!'

Examining her clothes with care, Beeja said, 'I hope this isn't a dream.'

Holding her in her arms, Teeja replied, 'Silly, this is a truth which has never before been revealed.'

---

* Bhagirathi is a name of the Ganga River.

† Beeja derives from *beej*, meaning seed, and Teeja from *teej*, the third day of the lunar month. Teej is also the name of a women's festival observed in the rainy season and the name of red velvet mites.

When the darkness of night was dispelled, the sun rose as usual, but the blaze that was revealed when the door of his daughter's room opened blinded the Seth's eyes with its dazzle. He seemed as astounded as if he had no idea of the truth. Like a rabid dog, he stood up and came close to both of them. Recognizing his daughter, he shouted, 'How dare you dress like this? Have you lost all respect for the family honour and for my words?'

Beeja felt like laughing at her bristling father. She replied, 'I wanted to ask you to explain the deception you have practised all these years, but now I will neither ask questions nor will I answer any.'

The father stamped his foot and, spraying spittle, said, 'You shameless creature! Of course, you can't answer my question. Under no circumstances will I permit you to dress like this. Understand that once and for all.'

Hearing the uproar, the mother came running out. She had not slept a wink all night. When she saw her daughter thus decked up, she felt as if a scorpion's poison had run through every vein of her body. It was more painful to see her daughter dressed thus than it would have been to see her lying dead. When the truth, nourished in silence for years, suddenly showed itself in this form, for a moment she was unable to bear the revelation.

As her daughter's lips opened to ask a question, she embraced her and burst into tears. Through sobs she exclaimed, 'Don't ask me anything, daughter, don't ask me. I did my best. I fell at his feet and pleaded with him, but I was just as helpless as you are. With folded hands, I beg you not to curse this father of yours.'

A smile flickered on Teeja's lips. She said, 'Are you still worried about curses? Don't worry. Neither will I curse anyone nor will she. On the contrary, we are grateful to both of you, since through you we have learnt something very valuable.'

As soon as he heard Teeja say this, the father did not hesitate. He took off his turban, put it at her feet and began to plead with her. 'Daughter-in-law, my honour is now in your hands.

Please, somehow persuade my daughter to take off these clothes and dress as she used to.'

Bubbling with laughter, Teeja said, 'You still call me daughter-in-law! Blessed indeed is this honour of yours! How will a false dress preserve your honour? So far you've done as you wished; now let us do as we wish. We only want to openly accept this deception of yours as a gift and a blessing.'

The Seth needed a pretext to emerge in his true colours. His daughter-in-law's words immediately brought out his real self. His eyes turned red with anger as he said, 'In this house my wish is law. If you want to do as you wish, there is no place for you here.'

At this, his daughter spoke. 'This house doesn't suit us either. That is what we came to tell you, but we got distracted by nonsensical nothings. If you feel like it, you can give us your blessing. We are leaving now. We do not want to breathe the air of this house.'

The Seth was now in magnificent form. 'You are welcome to leave, but I won't give you a single paisa from the dowry given by her family or the gifts given by ours. Don't rely on that.'

The father was in a rage, but the daughter couldn't help laughing. Still laughing, she said, 'We'll rely on no one but ourselves. We don't care a straw for your dowry or gifts. If you don't blush at the idea, we are ready to go naked.'

Throwing off the pretence of a father–daughter relationship, the Seth said, 'I knew this would happen. Of course, you will now dance naked everywhere. You can do as you please, but these jewels are mine. If I hadn't brought you up, could you ever have dreamt of such dowry or gifts?'

'These dreams suit people like you, not us.' So saying, his daughter and daughter-in-law began to take off their jewels. They had so enjoyed the pleasure of dressing up that they had given no thought to the monetary value of the jewels. When the daughter-in-law had taken off all her jewels, one by one, and finally began to remove her head-ornament, the mother's heart overflowed.

Through tears, she said, 'Fortunate one, don't remove this symbol of marriage.'

There was no limit to the Seth's greed, but today he was tortured more by the challenge to his honour as master of the house than by his greed. He was almost out of his mind with rage at the sight of his daughter making light of the honour that had endured for generations. It was as though ghee was gradually being poured into his flaming indignation and obstinacy. The Sethani's senseless remark infuriated him once more. Grinding his teeth, he said, 'What has marriage got to do with a head ornament? Poor women can't afford to wear gold head ornaments. Does that mean they are not married? Whatever happens, I won't give them a single pin.'

Smiling, the two girls took off their head ornaments and handed them over. For the first time in her life, the Sethani rebuked her husband. She said, 'Has a mad dog bitten you or what?'

The Seth growled back, 'A mad dog has bitten these two. But, of course, why would you see that? Catch me trying to appease them. If they want to trample on lakhs of rupees and walk off, let them.'

Unable to draw another breath in that polluted atmosphere, the two of them walked quietly away. But the mother's heart was not yet free of illusion. She asked tearfully, 'Daughter, where will you go?'

'Wherever destiny leads us,' Beeja replied softly as she walked away.

Such matters cannot remain hidden. So far, the villagers had knowingly pretended not to know. They had turned a deaf ear to whispered rumours. Under our clothes, which one of us is not naked? And then, who would dare step forward to bell the cat? The powerful can make stones float on water. One can survive without the sun, but without the moneylender one cannot survive even for a moment. They had bowed their heads and scratched their necks. Who would take the lead in speaking up? Though such outrageous behaviour had never been seen or heard of, no one dared break the silence. To open one's lips would be to get a drubbing, so everyone feigned ignorance.

But when the Seth's son was seen emerging from his house, dressed as a woman, accompanied by his bride, the people got the shock of their lives. Though no one spoke, the wind began to crackle with whispers, which made the air boil. How was it possible to swallow this rock? Can an elephant pass through the eye of a needle? People ran out of their houses and gathered together. It was as if someone had disturbed a nest of hornets. Marriage between two women! Oh no, two girls have got married to each other! What a slap on the face of manhood! This new way of living will destroy both kinship and community! It will blacken the face of the sun! How did the Seth manage to suppress reality all these years? Can there be any greater deception than this? If this matter is not settled, it will be the end of the panchayat's authority. This python cannot stay hidden in anyone's pocket.

In the twinkling of an eye, all the advisers and elders, big and small, surrounded the girls. A cry arose from all sides, 'Don't you dare take another step till this matter is settled. If a woman marries another woman, what is a man to do—go and find a mousehole for himself?'

The bride retorted sharply, but her words were lost in the din created by the judges. The air echoed and re-echoed with shouts of 'Justice, justice!' Then, the Seth's daughter raised her hand and made a sign asking for silence. When silence fell, she said in a loud voice, 'We don't need justice, but if you are so eager for justice, wait while I go home and return.'

So saying, she went towards her house. People made way for her and waited. When she returned, she was holding a scarecrow in one hand. The same turban, the same angarkhi and the same dhoti. She walked up to Teeja and sat down to dig a hole in the ground. People watched in silence as she planted the scarecrow at the edge of the village square. The fringe of the turban brushed the ground. The moustaches under the flat nose were intimidating in appearance. Then she stood up and said loudly, 'Do you think we are afraid of you moustached men? We might as well be afraid of this scarecrow! You men are worse than the scarecrow. Look your fill. We are moving on now, and we challenge you to stop us. Let us see which son of a man dares try!'

These words cast such a spell on the men that each of them began to see his own face reflected in that of the scarecrow. All the judges stared at their faces mirrored in the pot that served as the scarecrow's head, and the two women partners walked away. No one even looked at them. As soon as they disappeared, everyone felt as if the scarecrow was laughing. What was there to laugh at? How dare a scarecrow laugh at living human beings and deride them? Everybody felt disgusted by the scarecrow, and as one man they fell on it and tore it to pieces. Some fortunate ones were able to lay their hands on a scrap of turban, dhoti or angarkhi. They were relieved when the scarecrow was torn to bits. Then they quietly dispersed, and as soon as they got their heads under their own roofs, each man began roaring like a lion at the women of his house.

The two female partners, arms around each other's necks, went out of the village. The earth was green as far as the eye could see. In the fields millet stood head-high, waving in the breeze. Flowering creepers lay across the borders between the fields. Small bushes and trees stood buried in webs of greenery. Clouds wobbled drunkenly in the sky. The beauty of earth lay before them, limitless, stretching out in every direction. For the first time, these beloved daughters of nature met with nature. Leaping like does, they climbed a hill. Mad with joy, they chased each other to the highest peak and began to whirl round and round, holding hands. Far away, they could see the houses in the village looking like pockmarks.

A group of clouds touched the hill. Rain fell in torrents. The air vibrated as though with drumbeats of joy. Flashing around them, the lightning throbbed with eagerness to see the beauty of the two friends.

Wiping Beeja's face, Teeja said, 'The lightning is thirsting to see us. Perhaps its thirst cannot be quenched through these veiling clothes . . .'

Beeja answered, 'What use have we for veils? Why keep the poor lightning thirsty?'

As the blouses fell open, the lightning flashed. As if it too, hidden in clouds, had been thirsting for centuries. A glimpse of these pairs of lotuses quenched its thirst. Once more the joyful drumbeats burst forth.

After a while, the lightning flashed again. This was a more prolonged wave of lightning. Like red velvet mites,* the two stood, embracing, losing consciousness in union with one another. Their breath almost stopped as they drank nectar from each other's lips.

Like the clouds, they discharged their passion and slackened their embrace. The inanimate life of the hill was infused with new meaning, and a new lustre dissolved into the lightning. When consciousness returned, they put on their clothes. The lightning growled and flashed once more, as if it bore a peculiar grudge against clothing. As the growls echoed, they again fell into each other's arms.

Gambolling in the rain, they descended the hill, feeling light and fresh like the flowers that grew around. Streams of joy flowed around them. With relaxed limbs the soaked earth was blessed by the pure love of the clouds.

It was only when they reached the foot of the hill that they fully realized the heights of their love. If there was anything in

---

* Red velvet mites, known as *mamolya* (the word used in the story) in Western Rajasthan and as *veerbahuti* in Hindi, are tiny, beautiful, bright-red arthropods that live in the earth and appear on the surface after rain. They are found in many regions, including deserts. Giant mites are found in north India. They are also known as *teej* because they appear in the rainy season. They do not mate. The male leaves his seed on vegetation, and the female sits on it to absorb it.

the world clearer and purer than the untouched water shed by the clouds, surely it was the deep love between them!

But in this human world one cannot live by love alone, and, in addition, they were two girls. They wanted to set up house together in a new way of their own, making enemies of the village men.* This was as difficult as trying to overturn the hill. If they could have their way, they would have preferred never to look again at any human habitation.

Unthinkingly, busy talking to each other, they went straight to the haunted tank. Darkness was gathering on the face of the earth. As the rain ceased, they wrung the water out of their clothes.

The forest sighed in the wind. The deserted tank. A hundred and twenty-eight ghosts had their dwelling here. Not even a bird could flap a wing here after dark. Whoever ventured here never returned home alive. In broad daylight men trembled when they had to pass within a couple of miles of the place.

The two female companions sat on the brink of the tank, talking away fearlessly. Above, the moon played hide-and-seek with the clouds. Suddenly, Beeja said, 'The moon just whispered a mantra in my ear. If you give me a kiss, I'll tell it to you.'

Teeja answered, 'If you give me a kiss, I won't ask for the mantra.'

'No, the mantra is worth knowing,' replied Beeja.

'Tell me then, without my asking.'

'The moon keeps asking me why I look at its plain face instead of looking at the moon who's sitting next to me.'

'Nonsense, the moon whispered that mantra to me, not to you.'

---

* The words translated as 'set up house together in a new way' are *naya gharvās*; these words appear several times in the story. *Gharvās* refers to *grihasthāshrama*, the householder stage in the Hindu understanding of life. This stage includes marriage, sexual relations, domesticity and companionship. Detha plays on the word several times in the story.

The two moons had just begun to drink each other's nectar when, suddenly, a voice echoed near them. 'I knew the two of you would come here.'

Startled, they came out of their embrace. They looked around. A dazzling white man was standing nearby, smiling at them. He looked as if he was moulded of moonlight.

Smiling, he said, 'Today, our deserted tank has been purified. But I'm astonished that you were not afraid to come to this tank of ghosts.'

Taken aback, they both stood up. Beeja replied softly, 'There's reason to feel afraid of human beings. What is there to fear from ghosts?'

'You are absolutely right,' said the ghost chieftain, smiling. 'We endure this existence because of the actions of dishonest humans. We revenge ourselves on the fearful ones by frightening them even more. We hate to see any sign of humans. Today, those hypocritical villagers tried their best to harass you!'

Surprised, Teeja asked, 'How do you know about that?'

The ghost explained, 'We heard the humans whispering about your marriage. We love to have fun so, invisible to human eyes, our whole tribe went down to watch the hubbub. Our hearts were delighted by the two of you. To save you, we arranged the scarecrow episode. Otherwise, do you think those wicked ones would have let you escape? To defend you from anyone who tried to harm you, I stayed with you right up to the hilltop.'

At this, the girls were suffused with shyness. The ghost chieftain began to laugh and said, 'You were not shy before the lightning, so why should you feel shy at my words? The sight of your love made me feel that this life is worth living. I'm the chieftain of our tribe. You can set up house here without fear.* Near this lake I will erect a palace which a king might envy. The state treasury may run dry, but you will never be in want. All the

---

* *Gharvās karau*: live here as householders.

wishes of your heart, small and big, will be fulfilled. I can never repay you for the joy I've found in the sight of your pure love. Women can come here, but no son of a woman will be able to cast a sharp glance at you. You can now disport yourselves to your hearts' content in this palace.'

Looking in the direction indicated by the chieftain, the two women saw a snow-white palace gleaming before them. What unmatched carving and what wonderful windows! Inside, the palace glowed with light. Outside, the moonlight waved its white fan.

They had not realized that their love was such a blessing. When they entered the palace, they were struck speechless with wonder. Saffron courtyards. Crimson walls. Vermillion ceilings. A lotus swing seat. A bed of roses. When they began to swing in the swings of joy, they could not stop swinging. Brighter than saffron, those two birds so lost themselves in the joys of togetherness that they became altogether oblivious to the world and themselves. After all, what can compare in bliss with that primeval trance of the bodiless Kamadeva?

Finally, they emerged from the trance, returning to consciousness. Looking into each other's eyes, they smiled. Mingling her tuneful voice with that pure smile, Beeja said, 'The ghost chieftain must have once more felt that his life is worth living!'

The words slipped out of Teeja's mouth, 'The Gods in Indra's world, too, must have felt that immortality is worth having.'

At dawn, when they came out of the palace and saw the sun rise, they felt as if he was rising from the pure petals between their thighs. Ever since that night, the sun has forsaken its former dwelling and has begun to rise from this new abode, whence he rises even today. All the joys of the world throbbed with eagerness to dwell in the bed of that palace. The thirst of the whole universe was encompassed in that one thirst of theirs.

A fortnight flew by on wings of rapture. Nothing was lacking in the solicitude of the ghost chieftain. One day he said to them,

'In your happiness you have forgotten the world, but the world has not forgotten you, even for a moment. You can visit the village if you like. There is nothing to fear, since I will be ready to protect you from danger. The village women are free to come here. Even the sun gets tired of being alone. So does the moon.'

The words escaped them both simultaneously, 'But we are two.'

Smiling, the ghost chieftain replied, 'But you are one life and being—in fact, even less than one at the moment of union.'

They had got over their shyness now. At the chieftain's words they burst out laughing. The chieftain's smile paled before their unrestrained laughter.

Then, flying and fluttering in circles like a couple of butterflies, they reached the village of the humans. The same encirclement of walls and barriers. The same huts and roofs. Each with its own limits and boundaries. Each with its own kitchen and stove. Each with its own fire and smoke. The squabbles of thine and mine. Heaps of rubbish lying here and there. Amid all the squabbling to secure peace and happiness, bankruptcy showed its face. Worries and anxieties over children. Stinking baby clothes. Filth everywhere. Conflicts and quarrels in every house.

How had they lived in this hell for so many years? How had they grown up here? Today, remembering that past life, they were filled with disgust. How dreadful! But the villagers remain immersed in their life. They decorate the courtyards with red-and-yellow patterns. They draw pictures on the walls. They sing songs on special occasions. They cook special dishes at festival time. They swing. They dance and sing. No one sees filth anywhere!

Today, seeing the couple for the second time, nobody made any attempt to secure justice. Instead, they hurriedly closed their doors. Everyone was terrified of the ghosts from the tank. The ghosts could waylay you and wring your neck. One's own neck is dear to everyone. As for these two highly fortunate ladies, they were fit only to live with ghosts. They had procured the right company for themselves. Well, it would take someone of their own nature to deal with them. Whoever met them passed on with eyes downcast. Even the star-carved cudgels betrayed signs of trembling.

Beeja's father was sitting in the courtyard, busy drawing up his accounts, when he suddenly saw his daughter and daughter-in-law approaching. At first he nearly swooned. Then he managed to stand up, though he was trembling like a leaf. His dhoti came undone. Folding his hands, he said, 'I'm ready to give back all the gifts and dowry with interest, only be gracious to this poor man.'

Irritated, Beeja stepped forward and said, shaking her head, 'We don't want your gifts or dowry. We have come just to meet you. We don't want even a straw from this house.'

Swallowing his spittle, the Seth replied, 'Why not? Aren't you the daughter born to me?'

'I know well enough that I'm your daughter. I know what a father's love is, too! But if in future you ever mention giving and taking, I'll never set foot here again.'

The father was at a loss for an immediate answer. Trying to master his agitation, he again folded his hands and said, 'Now that you're living in royal style it's not possible for you to keep coming here. Whenever you send word I'll be only too happy to attend on you.'

He deliberately did not mention his fear of the ghosts. The daughter was filled with disgust. She felt as if she had slipped into a pit of excrement. She immediately prepared to leave. Teeja, in any case, had not the slightest desire to step into her in-laws' house. She also turned away.

Holding up his dhoti with both hands, the father stumbled along behind them, saying, 'Daughter, are you going away without meeting your mother? The poor thing is half blind with constant weeping.'

As she walked away, Beeja said, 'Ask mother to come to our house. She'll be quite safe.'

With that, Beeja strode off, and Teeja hurried to keep pace with her. She understood the turmoil in Beeja's heart, although

Beeja did not speak of it. When they were well beyond the village boundaries, Beeja screwed up her face and said, 'I'll need to bathe in perfumes to get rid of that stink!'

Laughing, Teeja replied, 'Isn't our breath perfume enough for you?' and took Beeja in her arms. The screaming peacocks bent and bowed in dance. Frogs mingled their sweet music with the breezes. Leaping does stood still to gaze at that union. Full of joy, pigeons cooed and danced. Crickets spread magic waves of sound through the forest. It was as if that uniquely uniting embrace had blessed all nature with liberty.

In a short while, they began to yearn for the solitude of their palace, so they raced towards the tank. Far behind them indeed was that hell of a village.

Early next morning, a loud knocking on the door woke Beeja up with a start. She hastily awakened Teeja. Both of them hurriedly put on their clothes and raced down the stairs to open the sandalwood door. There stood her mother with that friend of Beeja's. Before Beeja could speak, her friend said, with a teasing smile, 'Even newly wed brides don't get up so late!'

Beeja was still not quite awake. Forgetful of her mother's presence, she said, rubbing her eyes, 'We are no less than newly wed brides.'

When they set foot in the palace, those two forgot themselves in wonder. Now they saw what they had only heard about. Who but those who had control over the tribe of ghosts could create such a marvel? How had such unheard-of skills come about? So stunned were they that the splendour of the palace appeared four times as dazzling as it actually was. They had come prepared to say a great deal but found themselves unable to utter a word. They felt like two crickets suddenly introduced into a golden castle.

After gazing around to her heart's content, the Sethani stared in wonder at Beeja and muttered, as if in a trance, 'Did I really give birth to you from my own womb?'

Smiling, Beeja answered, 'Well, you or the midwife should know. How am I to answer that question?'

Beeja's friend was irritated by the Sethani's tactless question. In a warning whisper she said to her, 'Is this what you came to ask?'

'Don't tell me you regret having come,' Teeja said.

Meanwhile, Beeja was busy serving up a number of delicacies. After they had eaten their fill, she asked them to rest on the golden bed while she and Teeja ate together.

After eating, Beeja went to her mother. She found both women fast asleep, their backs to each other. They had tried their best to resist sleep, but even a person kept awake by agonizing wounds would have fallen asleep on that velvet-covered golden bed. These, after all, were healthy women worn out by work.

Some hours later, they woke with a start, sat up and looked around. A king would have envied that splendour. How painful it is to see such a dream when one is wide awake! The mother nudged Beeja's friend. 'Why don't you speak out? If you keep quiet, how will they know why we came?'

The niece sighed deeply and replied, 'The wealthiest person would go into a daze at the sight of this glorious palace. I don't know what to think or what to say.'

The four sat together and chatted for a while. Then, Beeja's friend mustered up courage and said, 'On the third day after you left the village, the news about this palace broke. No one needs to talk about such a thing—the wind blows it to all ears. Were they not restrained by fear of the ghosts, men competing to marry you would have waged a second Mahabharata. The king himself set out for the conquest, but when he was halfway here, he took to his heels. Once the lord of the country admits defeat, who would dare make the attempt? But all of them— young and old, great and small—are writhing with the same inner torment.'

Teeja interrupted, 'Why, what harm have we done to anyone?'

This time, the mother answered, 'What greater harm could there be? Your household has made men lose face altogether.'*

To this, Beeja replied, addressing her friend, 'Well, we have no remedy for that.'

This gave the friend her chance. In grave tones she said, 'You do have a remedy. In fact, that's why we plucked up the courage to come here today.'

The two lovers began to pay attention. The friend went on with her sermon, 'Your marriage was a farce. The sweat of a man has not touched even your shadows.'

'Nor will we let it,' retorted Beeja at once.

'No, daughter, that's not possible, not even in a dream. A woman can survive without water but not without a man's sweat. Your father has received a great many offers. The finest and wealthiest young men of the province are willing to marry the two of you—separately, of course. Give up this false pride now. Settle down and be happy. Start a family. Bathe in milk, have many sons and prolong a lineage like a creeper with many leaves. Your father is only too eager to give each of you a double dowry.'

Smiling faintly, Teeja said, 'We've already tasted the fruits of the endeavour to prolong the lineage through us! Now this creeper has to be pulled up by the roots. As for happiness, our present state is the greatest happiness for us. We have no answer to your proposal except to clap our hands and laugh heartily.'

The mother's face fell. Turning to Beeja, she asked, 'What do you say, daughter?'

'Why would I say anything different? Please don't bother to come here with such advice.'

The mother's heart began to sink when she saw the anger in her daughter's eyes. She remembered the troop of ghosts, and her

---

* Your *gharvās*, meaning their marriage and household.

hair stood on end. Looking at Beeja's friend, she said softly, 'It's getting late, we'd better go now.'

The friend stood up quietly. Enough that they had seen life inside the palace, as though in a dream. Beeja did not even go to the door with them.

The next morning, there came the same knock on the door. A startled Beeja opened it. On the threshold stood her friend with bowed head.

Surprised, Beeja said, 'Do you know, last night I dreamt that you were standing at the door, exactly like this. As soon as I kissed you, you ran away. I called and called after you, but you didn't even look back. Well, now I'll kiss you again, and let's see how you run away from me!'

Smiling, she quickly kissed her friend's left cheek. As she kissed her, tears began to flow from her friend's eyes. Beeja's smile vanished. Pulling her inside, she said, 'Are you upset because I kissed you? I only . . .'

'How can I possibly be upset by your kiss?' broke in her friend tearfully. 'These tears have been stored up for a long time, and your kiss opened the floodgates. I've thought and thought about it, but I still can't understand how you two had the courage to do what you did. I'm not even worthy to look at your union. Yesterday I didn't get a chance to say this in front of Mother, so today I came on my own.'

When she saw Teeja, her tears began to flow once more. She kept looking from one to the other of the two lovers' faces and crying helplessly. Her pain could express itself only through tears, so they did not try to stop her. Each tear contained the bitterness of a whole ocean.

When the tears stopped flowing, she began to reveal the bitterness in words. She told them that when she had married, she had felt sad to leave her parents yet also happy about going to her in-laws. But the first night with her husband marked the beginning of all her woes. Though he was a male, the husband who had taken her hand had not an ounce of maleness in him. Her in-laws knew this, yet they had cheerfully conducted the wedding with much pomp and show. They had thought that the touch of a youthful virgin bride might stir up his youth and heat his blood. But they were mistaken, and the innocent girl had to suffer for their mistake. When all his force was of no avail, the husband appeased his wounded pride by biting her all over her body.

She showed them her body. Her back, chest, arms, buttocks, thighs—all were covered with blue scars. She had told her parents the truth, but they had not come to her rescue. The honour of great families must be protected in public. Who would dare expose all that goes on in secret? How long could she escape her father-in-law's and brother-in-law's lust? She was forced to give in. Can a sheep save its life while living in a cheetah's den? Though her husband knew what was happening, he did not object. He began to immerse himself more and more in the family business. The business prospered immensely after his marriage. The family assets and property increased. Everyone was happy with the bride who had brought good fortune.

Beeja broke her silence and said with a sigh, 'And you had to be happy in their happiness!'

'What else could I do?'

'Are you still happy?' asked Teeja.

'Well, I was happy enough so far, but when I saw your life, all my sorrow came welling up again.'

Beeja immediately said, 'Now you need not go back. Who will dare take on the three of us together?'

'No,' replied her friend, shaking her head. 'I haven't come to stay here. I have lightened the burden of my heart by weeping and telling you my woes. Only death can save me from my in-laws. They have lakhs' worth of property, sheep and cattle, and seven three-storey houses. It's not so easy to shake off those attachments. And I have not yet had a child. I will be at rest only after producing an heir to all that wealth. My brother-in-law has come to fetch me. I'll have to leave the day after tomorrow. But I won't forget your kindness until my dying day. Your courage and happiness have consoled me, but I don't have the kind of strength required to live like you.'

She had much more to say, but her eyes filled with tears, and she could not speak further. After a while, she wiped them and said, 'Yesterday you made me eat separately. Today I'll eat with you. Perhaps I'll get some good sense by eating your leftovers.'

'You have good sense already,' said Teeja. 'But you can't get rid of the ghosts of your ingrained ways of living.'

As soon as she uttered the word 'ghost,' the ghost chieftain appeared on the scene, but the friend did not get scared. She gazed in wonder at that dazzling sheen. 'Why did you think of me?' asked the chieftain.

Teeja burst out laughing and said, 'You are not the ghost I thought of. You are the invisible, living flame of that which is to be. Anyway, we are always glad to see you. We can struggle on only because of you.'

Embarrassed, the ghost chieftain said, 'Better not praise me too much, or I'll get a swollen head.'

Then he looked at Beeja's friend and said, 'I heard your sad story. Now you can happily return to your in-laws. You will find that your husband has become potent. Your father-in-law and brother-in-law won't dare to raise their eyes in your presence. You will conceive by your husband and will give birth to five Pandavas.'

The woman was overcome with joy. 'Take care that you don't go out of your mind with joy,' said Teeja playfully.

Beeja turned to the ghost chieftain and asked, 'Do you really know how to do this?'

The ghost chieftain answered proudly, 'There is nothing that we do not know or cannot do.'

The three women sat down and ate together in celebration of the unexpected boon. After chatting for a while, Beeja and

Teeja walked down with Beeja's friend to the village. They kept reminding her to keep them informed of her happiness once she reached her in-laws' house.

On the way back, Beeja seemed lost in thought. 'What are you thinking?' asked Teeja. 'Is it something you have to hide from me?'

'Can I hide anything from you?' replied Beeja, hesitantly, 'It's really something worth thinking about. If you pay attention, I'll tell you.'

Teeja blinked. 'You silly girl, do I need to pay attention to hear what you say?'

Looking into her eyes, Beeja said, 'Didn't anything occur to you when you saw this boon being conferred?'

Teeja took her in her arms and replied, 'What occurred to you occurred to me as well, but it's useless to think of it. There's nothing lacking in our happiness, is there?'

'No, nothing is lacking, but this boon has revived the regret in my heart. If you're willing, the deception inflicted on you can be undone.'

'I've never considered it an infliction.'

'That may be so. But how can I close my eyes to the blackness of that misdoing? Such blackness can't be erased by shutting one's eyes to it. On the contrary, it spreads even faster. Won't you give in to this small desire of mine?'

Moaning softly in the tightening embrace, Teeja said, 'If I hadn't given in, could this joy have been ours?'

'Why do you think this is the farthest our joy can go?'

'I think so because it is so.'

'Oh no, the farthest is still a long way off.'

'That's nothing but an illusion, a mirage. Anyway, if you think there's still more joy to be had, ask for your boon.'

Freeing herself from the embrace, Beeja said in mock anger, 'Why don't you understand? Only if you ask for the boon will my misdeed be erased.'

'But I don't want to be a man, in any incarnation. You were brought up like a boy. If you still want to be one, I won't stop you. Let's see what the syrup of that domesticity tastes like.'

Since Teeja absolutely refused to yield, Beeja had to agree. Once again, her upper lip began to itch for a moustache. Now she would be a real man in men's clothing.

As they neared the palace, they saw the ghost chieftain standing at the door. Beeja could not hold herself back a moment longer. She ran ahead of Teeja and approached the chieftain. Uninhibitedly, she asked, 'Will the boon you gave my friend's husband work for me?'

The ghost chieftain replied in a loud voice so that Teeja could also hear, 'Why not? I was embarrassed to ask. If that is what you want, I have no shortage of boons.'

A delicate shade of shyness appeared on Teeja's face. Looking down, she said, 'What's the hurry? Let's enjoy the pleasure of this togetherness for the last time.'*

The ghost chieftain smiled and said, 'Since you are so enamoured of this togetherness, I'll leave one option open for you. Should Beeja ever feel that she has had enough of being a man, she has only to acknowledge her wish in her heart and she will become a woman once more.'

Beeja, who was lost in her dreams of maleness, reproved the ghost chieftain, saying, 'Once I get what I have so long desired, why would I want to reverse it?'

'That's as you wish,' said the chieftain.

The stars had just begun to gleam in the darkening sky. Looking up at them, Teeja said, 'Anyway, tonight at least is my night. I won't let you sleep a wink.'

Beeja was not to be outdone. 'Well then, after tonight, you will have to stay awake every night,' she said, turning her face away. 'So think again.'

---

* She refers here to sexual togetherness as *gharvās*.

'After tonight, I will never have to think again.'

Even though she clearly heard Teeja say these words, Beeja did not grasp their import. Closing the door, the two of them walked, anklets tinkling, to their bedroom. Teeja was in a great hurry today. She flung off all her clothes in the time Beeja took just to untie her blouse. Pulling Beeja's hand, she cried, 'Why are you so slow today? Usually, you're so impatient.'

After that, the two wet, pink *saras* cranes fluttered, entwined and took not a moment's rest all night.* Teeja kept wishing that the night would never end, but Beeja was longing for dawn to come before its time. Indifferent to their wishes, night ran its course and came to its accustomed end. The mild warmth of morning fell like a scorching fire on Teeja's eyelids.

As the sun rose, Beeja felt a tremor run through her body. All at once, her breasts flattened out and hair sprouted on her cheeks and upper lip. She scratched herself and felt her groin. Yes, indeed, she was now a fully developed young man. Her body was covered with curly black hair. Bubbling over with joy, he looked at his face in the mirror. For a moment, he felt scared of those huge curling moustaches. But how could he allow himself to feel scared? The honour of curling moustaches lies in their ability to scare others!

Seeing a turban, angarkhi and dhoti hanging on a peg, he leapt forward. For years he had dressed himself in these manly garments. Hastily, he wore the dhoti and angarkhi, and tied on the turban. The fringe of the turban, reaching his knees, waved proudly. Attired in full glory, he looked around. Teeja was nowhere to be

---

* The saras crane or *krauncha*, the tallest flying bird in the world, widely found in north India (now declining due to loss of habitat), mates for life and in Rajasthan and Gujarat is considered a symbol of fidelity. The Valmiki Ramayana begins with sage Valmiki's lament for a krauncha bird that is killed by a hunter, leaving its mate crying in desolation.

seen. She should have been here at this moment. Calling loudly for
Teeja, he strode through the palace. Then he heard Teeja's voice.
'I'm bathing, don't come in here.'

Where had this new modesty come from? The husband went
straight towards the bathing room from where the voice had
issued. Drawing aside the special red curtain, he went in. Doubling
up with shyness, Teeja said, 'Look the other way. I'll put on my
clothes and come out.'

The husband went out, surprised. 'You were never so shy
before,' he remarked.

'Things were different before.'

'But we are the same. Just have a look at my new form. Look
at these moustaches, this turban!'

'The turban was there to begin with.'

The husband grew irritated and said crossly, 'Why are you
standing inside there, chattering away? Why don't you come out
quickly?'

Teeja stepped out, dazzlingly dressed. She looked at her
husband from head to foot. What an attractive figure! Curled
moustaches! A muscular frame! Hair curly and black as a snake!
Teeja said, 'May the evil eye not fall on you. Come, let me tie a
black cord on your wrist for good luck.'

When Teeja's fingers touched his wrist as she tied on the
black cord, he had great difficulty restraining himself. Lightning
darted through his body from head to foot. Catching hold of
Teeja's arm, he said, 'Today I will settle all the old accounts
with you.'

Teeja listened silently, with bent head, wondering what made
her husband use such language. To tease his wife further, he added,
'Today no candle will be needed in the bedroom. I'll engender
such light and heat as you'll never be able to forget.'

'That's enough,' Teeja replied, rebuking her husband. 'You've
barely become a man, but you've already learnt all their ways.'

'It seems as if the sun will never set today.'

'It will set soon enough, be patient. You must be sleepy, after staying awake last night. Why don't you eat and have a nap while I take a walk down to the village?'

'You stayed awake as well. But what's this new idea? You'll go alone and leave me here?'

'Do you expect me to go with you? It seems you have no shame at all. But I'm not out of my senses. How do you expect to survive if you ignore the ways of the world?'

Smiling, her husband said, 'It looks as if I'll have to teach you the ways of the world, after all.'

And with that, he picked Teeja up in his arms. All her struggles were of no avail. Laying her down on the bed of roses, he fell on top of her.

As darkness swam before their eyes, a new light spread. The petals of the lotus seemed about to break asunder but did not. Teeja felt as if the whole universe had entered her body. When they separated, it took a while for them to return to consciousness.

Then the husband, his eyes still closed, remarked, 'How many days we wasted, just fooling around.'

Turning away, Teeja replied, 'Wasted? What do you mean, wasted? The joys of that play can never be forgotten, not even after death.'

The same circuit again at night! While going through that circuit, the new idea gradually began to dawn in the husband's mind that a man is much stronger than a woman. In fact, a frail woman is of no account at all in the face of a man's unlimited strength. A man is indeed tremendously powerful.

That night, Teeja received the seed of her husband into her womb. In the last hour before dawn, both of them, exhausted, fell into a deep sleep. When the husband's eyes opened the next morning the sun had already climbed high into the sky, and his rays shone into the room. At the sight of the rays, a delusion awoke in the husband's heart, telling him that it is man's heat and power which rise in the heavens in the form of the sun. Woman is merely his shadow.

Earlier, the two of them owned the palace together. Both of them had the same rights and the same importance. Perhaps Teeja still thought of ownership in those terms! That would never do. The matter must be settled once and for all. Wonder of wonders, he did not wait for Teeja to awaken. Instead, he began to shake her and call loudly, 'Teeja, Teeja!'

Teeja sat up with a start. 'Why did you wake me so abruptly?' she asked, rubbing her eyes.

The husband's ears were not pleased by his wife's question.

'You can sleep whenever you like,' he replied dryly. 'Right now, I want an answer to one question. Who's the owner of this palace? You or I?'

Teeja could not grasp this right away. She did not answer but sat in silence. Her husband impatiently repeated his question. Looking at his curled moustaches, Teeja answered, 'Why are you worried about who owns it and who doesn't? The two of us live together in this palace. Isn't that good enough?'

'I'm not asking who lives or doesn't live together. Give me a definite answer to my question. Who is the real owner of this property?'

'The ghost chieftain,' said Teeja in a low voice.

This answer disconcerted him at first, but he soon recovered and said crossly, 'Why are you beating about the bush? Now that it has been given into our possession, who is the owner? Answer me. To whom does this invaluable wealth belong? To you or to me?'

Teeja's brain felt numb. Such a change of colour in one night! Beeja had never asked such questions or sought such answers. As soon as a man took over, everything went topsy-turvy. To prevaricate now would be fatal. She said, 'We have equal rights over this property, but if you still have doubts, you can ask the ghost chieftain to clarify the matter.'

The husband felt every nerve in his body grow tense. 'Don't you try to frighten me with your talk of the ghost chieftain,' he said tauntingly. 'Why should he take my side against you? What will he gain by favouring me, pray? But I never realized that you could harbour such deceit in your heart.'

'You've realized it now!'

This infuriated the man with the curled moustaches, and he grew mad with anger. 'Don't think I'll be cowed down by this lover of yours,' he shouted. 'I'll establish my own kingdom. I'll collect unlimited hoards of treasure and prepare a huge army. I'll build a mighty fortress, and hundreds of queens like you will wait on me in the women's quarters.'

Teeja interrupted, 'How can you talk such nonsense so early in the morning?'

So saying, she left the bed of roses and went out of the room. This palace was hateful to her now. Such a wicked change of heart in just one night! This was the same base path that their clan had trodden. If they followed this path, they could not escape falling into the same swamp. Just as darkness envelops the sky the moment the sun sets, so had blackness filled Beeja's pure consciousness the moment she became a man.

Teeja found no peace even after she had bathed in the spring of nectar. The sun and the moon are powerless before an eclipse. If she stayed here, squabbles and arguments would add to the bitterness. It would be better to go and pay a visit to Beeja's friend at her in-laws' house and find out how she was doing. Why not visit her instead of waiting for news of her? Perhaps a few days' separation would help the conflict to subside.

She dressed in simple clothes and opened the door to leave the palace. Enraged, her husband caught hold of her veil and demanded, 'Where are you off to now after setting my heart on fire?'

'You won't believe me if I tell you the truth,' replied Teeja quietly. 'So what's the use of telling you?'

'I'll figure out what the use is, but you can't go anywhere without asking my permission.'

What an impassable gulf had opened between them in this one day! Trying her best to keep the peace, Teeja answered, 'You're not in your senses today. I will go and see how your friend is doing at her in-laws' house. In twenty or twenty-five days, you are bound to come back to your senses. Then you can send me a message, and I'll return immediately.'

'Don't you give me any of your sauce! As if I don't know that you want to gang up with the troop of ghosts and make an end of me! I know the ways of sluts and whores like you! Get inside this minute, or else . . .'

'What will you do if I don't?' said Teeja, smiling.

The smile on her lips made him lose the little self-restraint he had. Dropping her veil, he grabbed her braid. One yank and Teeja fell to the ground. Dragging her by the braid, he proclaimed, 'I am not one of those fools who become enslaved to their wives and put up with women's nonsense.'

He dragged Teeja in and threw her on the bed. She clenched her teeth and shut her eyes. Not a sound escaped her lips. She felt it would be a degradation even to cry out in front of a husband who was so devoid of dharma. She felt as if she was suffocating. In a little while she sank into a deep well of unconsciousness.

Leaving the unconscious Teeja alone, he went out of the palace. He bolted the door from outside and began to wander about in the forest like a madman. In the course of his wanderings he came to the same hill and began to climb it. That hill, which was nothing but a heap of dry stones, seemed unshapely and colourless to him. Nature, steeped in sorrow, seemed to be mourning a death.

As soon as he reached the peak, the vision of that earlier day swam before his eyes. He closed his eyes for a while, but the vision did not disappear, so he opened them with a start. Where were those showers pouring from the clouds! Where was that song of the clouds! Where those lips! Where those unclothed embraces!

Where that immeasurable union of love!* Every pore of his body
throbbed with the yearning to become Beeja once more. And with
that heartfelt yearning his form changed. The same smooth cheeks
as before. The two lotuses blooming in the blouse. Eager for the
touch of Teeja's hands!

Running and leaping down the hill, Beeja unbolted the door
of the palace and rushed in. Shaking the unconscious Teeja, she
cried out, 'Teeja! Teeja! I've sloughed off that form of a man.† Open
your eyes and recognize your own Beeja.'

After much shaking, Teeja came back to consciousness. Her
eyes opened to see Beeja leaning like a creeper over her. The same
tender affection spilling over from the eyes! The same soft-as-
saffron body! The two fell into each other's arms, and that is where
they still are today.

Thanks to the ghost chieftain's miraculous powers, not only
the filthy seed of man but Teeja's womb burnt up forever. The bird
called man dare not venture within a distance of twenty-four and
twenty-four, a total of forty-eight, kos around that place. However,
just once I visited them, on Teeja's invitation. I saw that wonderful
palace with my own eyes, and I wrote this story at Teeja's dictation,
in her words. Would the ghost chieftain have spared me if I had
dared add a word to her account?

---

* The words translated as 'immeasurable union' are *anhad samādh*.
In yoga, this is a term for the final stage of union with the universal,
immeasurable Self. Here, merging in love becomes an image for merging
with the universe.

† The words translated as 'form of a man' are *marad rau kholiyau*. A *kholi*
is an outer covering, shell or sheath.

I Want the Moon[*]

Surendra Verma

[*Set in the 1980s, this novel recounts the life of Varsha Vashisht (the name she chooses, discarding her given name, Yashoda Sharma). She is a college student in a small UP town, Shahjahanpur. Her family is lower-middle-class, struggling with financial problems. She has a younger sister, an unsympathetic older brother who is married and a younger brother, Kishore, who is supportive. Her teacher, Divya Katyal, inspires her to make a life for herself. She acts in plays directed by Divya and works as a model for a local sari shop, facing violence from her father and brother. She applies to the National School of Drama, Delhi, against her family's wishes. Divya reluctantly marries and has a daughter, Priya, and Varsha has several male lovers. Divya and Varsha keep visiting each other. Divya brings all the furnishings for Varsha's first apartment. Varsha becomes a successful stage actor and then a major film star, and wins the Padma Shri. Varsha finally becomes pregnant by her upper-class, politically radical lover, Harsh, and keeps the child, though Harsh dies. The child is a boy. Varsha and Divya's relationship is the primary one throughout the novel.*]

---

[*] Extracts from the novel *Mujhe Chand Chahiye*, published by Bharatiya Jnanpith in 1993.

[. . .] Had Miss Divya Katyal not come into her life, she would
either have committed suicide or else become the harsh, depressed
life partner of some clerk, and the mother of four or five children.

When Varsha was in the intermediate, Miss Katyal came to
the college—from Lucknow. [. . .] She was fair and attractive.
Sometimes, in a *churidar–kamiz*, she would appear an alluring girl,
and at other times, in a sari, a dignified lady.

[*Divya invites Varsha to her house.*] A simple but attractive
sitting room. Comfortable furniture and soothing colours. There
were three oil paintings on the walls. As the strains of 'Abhi to
Main Jawan Hoon' faded away, the record slipped down and the
words of 'Hard Day's Night' emerged. What a colourful world this
was [. . .]

A mild scent wafted from Divya's body; she wondered what
its name was.

'Have you seen a soda bottle being opened?' Divya asked with
a faint smile. 'The cork needs to be pulled out for the flood in you
to flow. You need a medium of expression—try the stage.'

[*Before the play.*] Varsha bowed low before her. 'Goddess!
Accept your servant's greetings.'

Miss Katyal smiled at her, then lightly took her in her arms
and kissed her forehead.

[. . .] As if floating along, she ran into Miss Katyal in the wings,
who hugged her tight and kissed her cheek. These two kisses were
much discussed in the college staffroom. Professor Upreti, the
philosophy teacher, said, 'When women teachers from the big city
come here, they always bring germs of some dangerous disease
with them.'

[. . .]

'Who is this Miss Katyal?' her brother asked, in a tone so
insulting that she could not restrain herself.

'My teacher, my friend [*saheli*], my everything.' She met her
brother's eyes.

'You go to her house often, and even stay the night there?'

'Yes, I love her company.'

[. . .] Sunday was now her favourite day. From Monday morning, a part of her started waiting for Sunday.

Sometimes they would stay at home and listen to music. Sometimes they would go to the market with a long shopping list. Sometimes Miss Katyal would make notes for her research and Varsha would study. Sometimes they would make paneer parathas or egg curry [. . .] Sometimes they would take sandwiches and a thermos of coffee, and visit a ruin fifty miles from town or walk in a mango orchard. If Miss Katyal was invited to Dr Singhal's, Professor Chaudhari's or anyone else's house, Varsha would accompany her.

[. . .] Professor Upreti would be heard whispering in the staffroom, 'Immoral conduct right on the college campus.'

[*Varsha hears that Miss Katyal is returning to Lucknow, because her mother insists that she get married.*]

Varsha flung herself on her and wept. 'Don't leave me. I'll suffocate to death.' Madly, she showered kisses on her forehead, eyes, cheeks and lips, and wailed, 'I can't live without you. Don't leave me midstream . . .'

Supporting her with one arm, Miss Katyal brought her into the bedroom, sat her down on the bed and said, 'Listen, I'll explain it to you.'

She was about to sit next to her when Varsha got up, knelt on the floor, took her feet in her lap and showered them with kisses. 'I can't live here for a single day without you.'

[*Varsha goes home, takes poison and is hospitalized. Miss Divya takes another year's leave and remains in town. Most people think Varsha attempted suicide because her family was arranging her marriage to a widower.*]

Divya put her hand on hers and said tenderly, 'No other same-sex [*samlingi*] person has ever become as intimate with me as you have, so this one year is dedicated to our unique relationship.' [. . .] No one besides the two of them knew that this episode had anything to do with Divya; if they had, Mr Upreti's whispering in the college staffroom would have created a storm.

[*Varsha visits Divya in Lucknow.*]

She was given a separate room in Divya's house, but she always slept with her. [. . .] They came home late one night and prepared for bed. Divya emerged from the bathroom in a silk lungi-kurta, tying up her hair with a ribbon.

She gazed at her and said, 'You're looking very beautiful.'

'I'll give you one to wear at night.'

How could she dare wear this at home? [. . .] The dam broke, Divya's bosom was soaked in her tears, but the upsurge would not stop. Then suddenly she separated herself with a jerk and wiped her tears.

Mummy [Divya's mother] found the pair of them amusing. 'They separate only to go to the bathroom,' she told Rohan.

[*Divya unhappily agrees to marry Rohan. When Rohan leaves, the two women are left alone and Divya speaks.*]

'Don't go, darling. My heart is sinking.' They sat under the mango tree. [. . .] The cuckoo called. Whenever they spoke of their emotions, the cuckoo always called, Varsha thought. [. . .] It was Divya's last night in the bungalow. Varsha spent it with her. Both were silent. [. . .] Whenever Varsha woke, she kept looking at Divya. Divya put her hand on hers.

[*At the wedding, Divya is sad.*]

'I am compromising for Ma's sake. I respect Rohan but feel nothing else for him. Varsha, you've been my emotional support in recent years. I cannot share with anyone, even my husband-to-be, what I've shared with you. Don't forget me when your life begins.'

Rohan was cheerful. Laughing, he said, 'I told Mummy, I want Varsha as dowry. Without her, I can't make your daughter happy.'

[. . .] Next year, when Varsha came at Holi, she hugged and enthusiastically kissed Divya.

'Varsha, I didn't see anything,' Rohan teased.

[*In Delhi, Varsha has a friend and roommate, Anupama. Harsh's ex-lover Shivani also becomes Varsha's friend. Divya visits Varsha in Delhi. Harsh goes to see his family.*]

'I'll have to take leave of you. In any case, I don't want to be a third wheel between two intimate friends,' Harsh said, smiling.

'Look, Divya.' Varsha's eyes danced. 'He's talking exactly like Rohan.'

'Who's this Mr Rohan?' Harsh asked.

Divya laughed. 'Another third wheel!'

[. . .] There was a sound behind her. [. . .] Divya was standing there, smiling mischievously. 'Divya!' She threw herself on her, put her head on her shoulder and held her close. The same familiar touch, the same familiar smell.

'Didi has been here for an hour,' Jhumki [the maid] said. 'I wanted to wake you, but she wouldn't let me.'

She knew that sleep was sacred to Divya. She didn't like waking up anyone, especially a beloved person.

[*After she becomes a film star.*]

Varsha looked at the first page of *Tinsel Town*. [. . .] The investigative journalist had titled the story 'Bold Varsha's *Night*

Games' and declared Divya her first lover. 'From her teenage years, Varsha has been inclined towards unnatural love, an old fellow student of hers said. Her *lesbian* desires blossomed when she grew close to Divya Katyal in college. Who initiated whom we will leave to our dear readers' imagination. When she came to Delhi Varsha became *bisexual*. Along with male lovers, Anupama and Shivani became her friends on love's bed. Our enchanting heroine lived for a long time with Anupama in Jor Bagh. According to a neighbour, they shared a bedroom; fed up with their love sports, the poor neighbour now suffers from insomnia. Informants close to her report that Anupama's marriage ended due to this relationship. Readers will remember that two women recently got married in Madhya Pradesh.* [. . .]

'Your fame has reached me in forms that bewilder and stun me,' her father wrote. '[. . .] What can I write? We already had no control over you. [. . .] The community is spitting on us, and our very identity is threatened. [. . .] We don't know what you want to do with your life. All we know is that what gets into print becomes true. Tomorrow, when we try to arrange your younger sister's marriage, who will let us stand on their threshold?'

[*Varsha apologizes, denies the allegations and promises to get her sister married, which she later does. Her father, sister and sister-in-law all come and stay with her in her own house in Bombay.*]

'Your worries are baseless,' Divya wrote. 'Rohan simply said, if Varsha has had enough of the tinsel torture chamber, invite her here to relax.'

'You've earned enough,' Anupama wrote. 'Come back to your room in Jor Bagh. I have arranged *tranquillizers* for my neighbour's insomnia.'

---

* A reference to the marriage of policewomen Leela Namdeo and Urmila Srivastava in Bhopal in 1987.

'Darling!' Shivani wrote. 'My father and brother are proud of my friendship with you. As soon as you can, come to me at Greater Kailash so that we can do everything that *Tinsel Town* says we do! We'll send them explosive pictures of ourselves. With hugs and kisses . . .'

[*The novel ends with Divya being diagnosed with cancer. The doctors are not sure if it is curable. Varsha, Divya and Divya's daughter, Priya, lie on the grass, looking up at the stars.*]

On the Edge[*]

Sara Rai

At around eight o'clock on a foggy January evening, two blurry shapes stood under the light on the narrow street that ran alongside the church towards Hauz Khas Village. It was blisteringly cold. This month was always a cold one, but the air was unusually moist. So dense a fog was unusual too. A little away from the light, spheres of fog danced, like large white elephants made of steam colliding repeatedly with one another. Because of the fog, there was little traffic on the road. Off and on, a vehicle would approach, moving slowly, its headlights shining like ghostly yellow eyes. Acrid fumes of carbon monoxide hung suspended in the wet fog.

The dim shapes became clear under the light, as if standing in the spotlight on a stage. Two men—one very young, a boy; the other at that peak from which decline begins. Both were very cold and wore many layers of warm clothing.

'I thought I was late, but you have just arrived,' said Manoranjan. As he spoke, a circlet of steam emerged from his mouth, his words taking on shape as well as sound.

'Have you brought the money?' Javed asked. His young face was creased with worry. His cheekbones protruded, and the heavy

* First published as 'Kagaar Par' in *Purvagrah*, September–November 1999; reprinted in Rai's collection *Biyabaan Mein* (Rajkamal Prakashan, 2005).

fringe of his eyelashes looked as if he were wearing mascara. His voice was knife-sharp.

Manoranjan took a bundle of notes out of his windcheater and handed it to him.

'I got it with great difficulty. I told Akhilesh I would return it within a week.'

'Return it then.' Javed began counting the notes, then impatiently gave up and put the bundle in his pocket.

Looking at Manoranjan's face, he said with assumed indifference, 'I told you I'll send you the money as soon as I reach there.'

'So you're actually going?'

'I'll leave for Bombay tomorrow.'

'What's the hurry?'

'You ask that even though you know with what great difficulty I escaped after the police investigation?'

'Then you and the girl . . .'

'So you too suspect me? I've told you many times that I never look at girls, and this was such a disgusting business . . .' Anger suddenly flared in his eyes, like lightning, but he immediately controlled himself.

After a moment's pause, he added, 'I just want to get away from here for a while.'

'Then swear by me.' Manoranjan's face was burning.

'You are the only one I love.' Javed stepped forward and firmly clasped Manoranjan's hands in his own. Despite the cold, Manoranjan felt the stickiness of sweat. He bent and kissed Javed's head, feeling the prickliness of short hairs on his warm, soft lips.

'All right, I'm off,' said Javed. 'I'll be back soon. You'll see, the fuss will die down in a few days. And why should I be afraid when I've done nothing?'

'But what will you do in Bombay, how will you manage? Where will you stay?' said Manoranjan anxiously.

'I'll work out something. It's a matter of just a few days.' Lightly pressing Manoranjan's hand, he disappeared into the fog.

He was there one moment and gone the next, as if the fog were a demon that had swallowed him whole.

* * *

Nine months had passed since that evening, and there was no news of Javed. Nine months and six days, which Manoranjan had counted, first with hope, then with astonishment and disbelief, and in which the memory of Javed grew within him like a new creature. He constantly found himself thinking of Javed. Far from returning the money, he hadn't even written a letter; nothing at all. What had become of him? Manoranjan was in a quandary. Again and again, he dwelt upon little things associated with Javed and thought about his behaviour. He knew that these were just his thoughts and might have nothing to do with the real Javed, but he felt that he might be able to wring some happiness, some relief, from these thoughts.

Then suddenly, one day, he called up. 'Can you meet me tomorrow evening?' As if they had met just yesterday. Manoranjan's hope of meeting him again had dwindled. Who knew when he had returned and where he had been all this time? It was hard to be sure of anything about him. That same voice—slippery as silk, hiding the edge of an opportunistic mercilessness behind its slipperiness, hearing which Manoranjan's knees turned to water. What was this effect that he had on Manoranjan? Thinking of their wordless language of looks, gestures and smiles sent a tremor racing through his body.

He was awake most of the night. When he dozed briefly, he felt that leaves were falling all around him—leaves and more leaves from overhanging trees, leaves swimming, floating, rustling, covering him completely, and he woke, burning with the heat of desire for those radiant leaves. It was still dark. Far away in the silence, a dog was howling. A full moon swam into his imagination, caught in the bare boughs of a silk-cotton tree, and under it a dog with raised head, howling. Suddenly, he felt afraid and turned on

the lamp that stood on the bedside table. A consoling light filled
the room, and the dog's howling shrank into that other dark world
outside. He looked at the clock and found that it was only two
thirty. A wave of exhaustion washed over him, as if he had been
watching the clock all his life.

In the moment of waking—he had not slept, so in the journey
from being half-awake to waking up—he remembered that he was
to meet Javed that evening, and a fever of excitement took hold of
him. Evening, like an enchantress in glittering clothing, beckoned
him, and he drew the idea of the evening from his breast, where it
lay safely locked, and examined it as if it were a card, on the correct
or incorrect playing of which his life depended. He put out the
light and fell into an uneasy sleep that was broken by the groaning
of the first bus's wheels on the road, and found that dawn had
entered the room.

He got up and went out on the terrace of his third-floor studio
flat. He had stayed up late the previous night and had slept here
instead of going home. He had planned to finish the study of Baul
singers, on which he had been working for a long time, but his heart
was troubled, and he had been unable to work. A strong wind blew
on the terrace. He stood by the railing that bordered the terrace.
His heart was afloat on the breeze. His gaze surveyed the scene,
like a king surveying his kingdom from the safety of his fortress.
Delhi lay spread out before him. In the midst of the countless
squares of houses, like empty boxes piled higgledy-piggledy, were
familiar buildings asleep in the mist—Ashoka Hotel, India Gate,
Rashtrapati Bhavan. His soft hair stood up in the breeze, and the
white rag hanging on the wire fluttered wildly, like an unquiet
spirit desperate to escape the net of maya. His heart began to hum
a film tune, and it emerged as a whistle from his lips to float over
Delhi: 'Keep singing, O restless heart.'*

---

* A popular film song, 'Beqaraar Dil Tu Gaaye Ja', from the 1971 Hindi
film *Door Ka Rahi*.

Impatiently, he came back into the room and took from the cupboard the big white polythene bag in which he had kept the long skirt and matching top that he had got stitched by Banne Master the tailor. He took the skirt out carefully, examined it, slid it over his head and tied the cords at his waist in a flower-like shape. Then, with some difficulty, he pulled the top over his head. Banne Master had made the neck somewhat small. Although Manoranjan had stood for a long time in his box-like little shop that reeked of kerosene oil and explained to him that the outfit was for a friend who lived abroad and was quite 'healthy,' he had still made the neck small. When the friend was mentioned, Manoranjan had noticed the tailor trying to suppress an obscene laugh. These vulgarities no longer affect Manoranjan. To begin with, he used to burn with anger and hurt, but now such emotions seem futile to him; expending time on them is folly.

Long ago, when he was a student in class nine or ten, he had realized that, unlike other boys in his class, he was not interested in cricket or football but in girls' clothes and make-up. This unchangeable truth about himself had risen in him like a large sun. Since then, he had been hiding the girl in him, as if she were fragile and breakable as glass. Despite this, his mother suspected the truth, and when he came home from hostel during the vacations, she would say, 'Go and see, Manu, your friends are playing cricket. Go and play—someone will come to call you.' But no one ever came to call him. For one thing, he was no good at sports; he had played cricket only a couple of times, that too under compulsion. Any team he joined was likely to lose. Some people thought him inauspicious, and the boys of the neighbourhood considered him a queer fish.

No one showed any interest in the new red ball and willow bat which his mother had insisted on buying him, in the hope that they might help him participate in boys' games. No, he was interested not in boys' games but in boys themselves. When they played he would sit far away, on the stone bench at the edge of the playground, and watch them. Their young, strong bodies attracted him powerfully. The glowing, symmetrical lines of arms and legs and the sticky hair shining in the declining afternoon light delighted him.

This chain of thought took him back to his hostel days, which now seemed as distant as days of another birth. One by one, he remembered his fellow students—Rajat, Bilu, Tanvir of the beautiful fingers who drew beautiful pictures, Mukesh and the boy with the big mole on his cheek whose name now eluded him. Then Mohsin's carefree face appeared before his eyes—Mohsin, who fell prey to cancer in his youth. He remembered that night in his hostel room, when, to disprove the allegation of being a coward, he had lain on his bed with his stomach bared, and after all these years, the edge of the blade in Mohsin's hand flashed before his eyes.

The blade cut his abdominal skin and, with a kind of fascinated fear, Manoranjan saw a ruby-coloured line appear there. All the boys scattered, and the *sergeant* caned Mohsin. For some reason, instead of fearing Mohsin or being annoyed with him after this incident, Manoranjan was even more drawn to him. As if Mohsin were a magnet. Those nights of adolescence—hands, arms, skin, bodies sticky with sweat feeling each other in the dark. Thinking of Mohsin after all these years, he felt there was surely some similarity between Mohsin and Javed—the same amalgam of carelessness and cruelty, the same cutting edge?

Wandering and finding his way through the mists of the past, he emerged. Still wearing the skirt and top, he covered his head with a gold-embroidered brocade scarf and spread it over his shoulders. He luxuriated in the gold slipping and flowing over him. His long, slender fingers stroked the silk skirt with love and some surprise, enjoying its cool, tender touch. Then he took two steps back and looked at himself in the full-length mirror on the door. In the hazy mirror a flame leapt before his eyes. For a moment, he felt the flame-coloured skirt emit heat, yet it was cool as velvet to the touch.

Embers smouldered in the eyes of his mirrored reflection. Would this fire ever be satisfied? Manoranjan's heart beat fast. When he thought of Javed and looked at himself through his eyes, his lashes drooped and a smile played on his full lips, causing two dimples to briefly appear on his cheeks. He carefully took off the swaying skirt, folded the scarf, put them in the plastic bag and locked them in the cupboard. Had he left them at home, his mother would definitely have come across them, and that unaccepted truth would have hung between her and him like a half-told story, triggering for the nth time the game of pretending not to know.

He sat down at the table and wrote his name many times in many types of lettering on a piece of paper—Manoranjan Kumar Gupt. Some of the beautiful, round, full letters seemed eager to embrace each other, others sloped to the right, one behind the other, and inscribed themselves on his heart. Again, the same question popped into his head: is his name written on Javed's heart? Yes, no, yes, no, yes. Hurriedly counting on his fingers, he stopped at 'yes' as if unwittingly, and restlessness flooded him.

He drew from his kurta pocket the torn letter he had written a few days after Javed left, knowing well that he would never send it. Why had he written this letter? For himself? He had read it many times. Manoranjan read it yet again.

My beloved Javed,

At this time, when you may be strolling down Marine Drive, and when the lights must have come on along the shore, I want to tell you that there is complete darkness in my heart. You didn't come nor did a letter from you. I think of you constantly. I know you won't write to me. That is why I have written your name on this paper so that I can keep it close to my breast. If I have even a small place in your heart, you will come. I wait for you every day.

Your own
Manoranjan

As he read the letter, his eyes fell on his arm—a man's strong arm, strong-muscled, covered with fine golden-brown hair. The woman's heart in him sank, and a familiar despair tightened its hold on him. As had happened before on occasions when he focused on his being a man, he first cursed his fate and then castigated nature for this extreme injustice that had imprisoned his throbbing woman's heart in the strong body of a young man. He was imprisoned forever. In the context of his life, this 'forever' seemed endless, boundless, extending beyond the horizon. The thought of imprisonment made him feel the cold grip of the bars around him—the untender touch of iron and its smell that was like the smell of blood. Was his blood different from that of others? Why had nature picked him out to be different from others, to walk on the lonely road of his desires that were so hard to fulfil? Why? To desire not a woman but a man like himself—this was his destiny, this was his prison. He could express his feelings, he could love, only hidden from the gaze of others. Imprisoned in his own being, observing the outside world through the windows of his eyes. The terrible effort to recover from the deep wound within him shook him to the core.

No girl had been born in Manoranjan's family for several generations, and his mother had prayed for a daughter. He was born of the struggle between nature and prayer. The heart of a girl and the body of a man. Was this simply nature's mistake? No, he had come as a special response to prayer. Special, he insisted to himself. He stood up with a jerk, on the verge of anger, tore the letter to bits, threw them from the roof and watched them float down.

These days, he spent most of his time painting. At eight in the morning he would arrive at this Green Park *barsati* that Akhilesh had rented as a studio for him and would get to work. Akhilesh was his younger brother who worked for Larsen & Toubro. Conscious of Manoranjan's unstable financial situation, he often helped him out. Papa, too, supported him from time to time. Akhilesh had always said that Manu's brain was not suited to service or business.

In fact, he did not seem to have much of a talent for living. As soon as difficulties arose, he would accept defeat. Shopkeepers would pass off their old and overpriced goods to him, vegetable and fruit vendors would cheat him, and his university friends would make a fool of him and laugh at him. He was not a fool, but his shyness and simplicity made him seem like one. He lacked the ability to take up employment. When he tried to learn driving, it would seem to him that all the electric poles at the edge of the road were running towards him, and he would freeze.

His parents worried about him. Even as a child, he stayed away from other children. When he came home from boarding school during the vacations, he would sit all day in the small ground behind the house, which was dusty and overgrown with wild dry grasses, and keep drawing in his dog-eared sketchbook. There was no particular theme in his drawings. Once, when his mother, Mrs Gupta, flipped through the sketchbook in his absence, she did notice that there was not a single drawing of a woman among his many sketches. On every page there were men of different types, with neatly drawn arms and legs, and often the inner parts of their bodies, bones, nerves, and muscles, were also drawn in great detail. In some pictures, Superman or Batman, dressed in iron clothing, waged terrible battles. Here and there, something was written in a bubble next to the pictures. Mrs Gupta reached the conclusion that these days her son was reading a lot of comics. Several sketchbooks had been filled, and in the interval between finishing one sketchbook and getting another, he would use scraps of paper, or else draw on old newspapers or on the backs of calendars. He was so obsessed that he did nothing but draw.

When he grew up, more or less the same thing continued, and it rapidly became clear that he was not suited to any kind of job. He would go to sleep late, wake up late and then get back to his sketchbook and chewed-upon pencil. The medium of his pictures had changed. He had gotten hold of books on oil painting, studied them and begun to paint in oils, first on oil paper and then on

canvases bought with Akhilesh's help. As the paintings piled up in
Mrs Gupta's small flat, Akhilesh got him a studio, and Manoranjan
shifted his activities there.

There were still male figures in his paintings, but for some
time now, he had developed a passion for drawing trees. Vast, old,
leafless trees whose branches filtered the sky. Sometimes a man sat
with bowed head beneath a tree. In one picture, two yellow, heart-
shaped leaves had fallen from a tree and were floating in the air.
This painting exuded a sense of deep silence. Its title was *Thought*.
It was as if a tree growing in his imagination overshadowed every
picture. One day, he read about the *kalpavriksha*, the wish-fulfilling
tree, and for many days thereafter kept trying to picture it.

As he reached adulthood, he developed another habit of
which his family disapproved. Often, when he went out, he would
return home with some boy or other, whom he would introduce
as his friend. In itself, this was not a problem. It was good that he
was making friends. But Manoranjan's respectable, middle-class
parents noticed with dismay that these friends were always lower-
class and would quickly go into his room after hastily greeting
them or with their heads bent in embarrassment, as if they were
hiding something. Then they would hear whispering and giggles,
which puzzled them greatly. Manoranjan never laughed in this way
with his family. Perhaps this made them feel somewhat jealous.

His mother would ask, 'You were very happy today, laughing a
lot. What was it about?'

'Oh, nothing much. This Manoj is a joker. He makes me laugh.'

'Who is this Manoj?'

'His father owns the Chaurasia Paan Bhandar.'

This was enough to make his mother press her lips together in
a thin line of disapproval. Couldn't he have found anyone else to
make friends with? Was his tendency to roam around with street
boys a sign of low self-esteem? One day, it seemed to Mrs Gupta
that water was continuously flowing in Manoranjan's bathroom, as
if somebody was taking a really long bath, then there was subdued

giggling and then absolute silence . . . could they both be . . .? But
when she knocked at his door, Manoranjan opened it immediately
and seeing them both sitting there, she was reassured.

Around that time, Javed too began coming home with
Manoranjan. A thin but muscular body and very short hair cropped
close to the scalp, in military style.

'What does Javed do?' Mrs Gupta asked her usual question.

'He works at the PCO in the market.'

'Well, at least he does something.' But his mother still looked
displeased.

'Why do you think badly of my friends without knowing
them?' Manoranjan said, somewhat annoyed.

'He dresses like a big *sahib*, always suited and booted.' Akhilesh
smiled. This was true. Javed's shirt was always freshly ironed, his
trousers expensive and his shoes gleaming. His taste for fine things
was evident. He was much better dressed than Manoranjan in his
shabby T-shirts and worn jeans.

He had first met Javed when the telephone at home went on
the blink. He had to go to the PCO in the market to make a call.
There were many people in the line ahead of him, and he waited
three-quarters of an hour for his turn. Sitting on a narrow bench,
he looked around the room but soon exhausted what there was
to be seen. The picture on the calendar hanging on the wall soon
registered itself in his painter's memory; there was nothing special
about the Jaico clock hanging next to it; and the man inside the
booth would not stop talking.

When there was nothing left to look at and his boredom began
to touch new heights, he fixed his eyes on Javed, who was sitting
at the counter. He saw with surprise that each of Javed's features
seemed in opposition to the others. Thick, somewhat cruel-looking
lips beneath a thin nose, a flat, finely carved forehead above thick,
wild eyebrows, protruding cheekbones. And deep black eyes, filled
with a strength that made one want to look at them again and
again. All told, it was an attractive face. He sat like an effigy at the

counter, doing absolutely nothing, as if he had completely accepted that his destiny was simply to wait.

Finally, it was Manoranjan's turn. When he finished his call and emerged, he found that he had no money in his pocket.

'I've forgotten the money at home,' he said, embarrassed. 'I live in the apartment block across the road. Shall I go and get the money now?'

'Never mind. You must be passing this way every day. Give it to me when you can,' Javed said without raising his eyes.

The next day, when Manoranjan went to make the payment, Javed said, 'I've lost your invoice. Pay whatever you like.'

'Do you live here?' Manoranjan asked.

'I live here now. I'm from Pratapgarh. I've often seen you pass by here.'

Another day, Manoranjan was passing by when he saw that there was no one in the PCO. Javed was sitting alone, smoking. On an impulse, Manoranjan opened the door and went in. Javed held out the phone to him, but Manoranjan said, 'I don't have to make a call. I may not have told you that I like to paint pictures. I keep looking for different types of faces. If you won't take it amiss . . .' He paused as if searching for words, then said in a rush, 'I really like your face. Will you come to my studio and let me paint you?'

Javed raised his head and looked straight at him. There was amusement as well as irony in his eyes as he said, 'Really?'

'If you don't mind, I can pay you.'

Javed was silent for a moment. Manoranjan was looking at him timidly and was about to speak from sheer anxiety when Javed said, 'All right, I'll come.'

Manoranjan explained to him where the studio was and left.

Javed began to come regularly to the studio. Since it had been decided that Javed would come to the studio when he closed the PCO during his lunch break, they would first go together to eat at the Madras Café, which was just ten steps away from the studio. Manoranjan was generally satisfied with two vadas and sambar, but Javed had a big appetite. He would break large portions of a dosa and eat heartily, and he never refused when Manoranjan asked if he would like some more. He would eat two or even three dosas. Manoranjan liked this. It showed that Javed was a man. Manoranjan always paid, in accordance with the unspoken agreement between them. Javed was an informal person, and he seemed to have no objection to Manoranjan always paying for their meals. After the meal he would smoke a cigarette, while Manoranjan studied his face. He felt that after eating, Javed's face was coated with satisfaction, and this pleased him. Then they would walk to the studio and begin work.

Gradually, they began to talk about many things. One day, Javed was sitting on a *morha*, and Manoranjan was busy with the portrait. They were both silent. Suddenly, Manoranjan said, 'Do you know, that day when I saw you sitting alone in the PCO, I was drawn to you, as if there was a cord between you and me, as if some external power was pushing me towards you. Did you feel that way too?'

'A cord? What kind of cord?'

'Perhaps of sympathy. Perhaps I felt that you are like me, searching for something to remove your incompleteness? That's how I felt,' Manoranjan completed his thought after a brief pause.

'I don't understand such ideas,' Javed said. 'But perhaps it was that way, otherwise why would I have agreed to come?' So saying, he fell into thought, and clouds of doubt overshadowed his face.

'I don't know much about myself, and I've never thought about such matters so how can I answer your question?' he said, and Manoranjan, seeing that he was uncomfortable, fell silent.

Within a few months, their friendship grew a good deal. Manoranjan was enchanted by Javed, but it was hard to know whether Javed returned his feelings, because Javed did not talk much about himself; sometimes, he would resort to irony, at other times he would evade Manoranjan's questions saying, 'I don't know.' One day they were strolling from the café to the studio. It was a strange day—clouds interspersed with sudden sunshine. A white cloud dragged across the blue sky like a long, torn sleeve.

Manoranjan said, 'When I was a child, I would lie in the open ground behind my house, gazing at the sky for hours—so much blueness. I felt there must be thousands of layers of blue and behind them God's house. God for me is that Shakti, that power which sustains the whole world, which must keep a record of my life too, which must have written my destiny in black letters in a large book beyond the sky. Do you believe in that power?'

After a pause, Javed began to speak. 'I spent my childhood in a small town. Our house was small too. Two rooms that were always dark. Behind the house flowed a large, dirty drain on the banks of which everyone threw their household rubbish. If we opened the window, the filthy odour of the drain entered the house, and if we shut the window the house became completely dark.

'My father worked for a scissors manufacturer. He was addicted to liquor. He generally drank up all his earnings. We were five siblings so to fulfil our needs, my mother worked as a seamstress for the people in our neighbourhood. At night, she would make us all lie on the only wooden bed in the house, close together, like so many pieces of meat. If the window was ever open, we could see a dirty slice of the sky, the colour of which kept changing, blue or pink but mostly a dull white. Like you, I too would sometimes gaze at this piece of sky. To me, the sky meant freedom, openness. Standing at the window, looking at the sky, I could breathe freely. I would draw deep breaths, fill my chest with many breaths. I felt as if the expanse of the sky had entered me for a short time. How I yearned to escape that small prison. A cry seemed to rise from my heart. Do you know what happened then?' He stopped, and a crooked smile appeared on his face.

'The force you call God or Shakti opened a way for me to get out of there. My mother used to do some sewing at an old woman's house. The old woman's son lived in Delhi. My mother pleaded with the son to get me a job. I was twenty then and had twice failed the intermediate exam. The old woman's son had many business enterprises in Delhi. He had just opened the PCO where I work and needed someone to man it, so I came to Delhi and have been here for two years. But I want to tell you that, for me, the name of that force is opportunity—the opportunity to escape the bitterness of one's life.'

Javed's eyes were shining, and, having spoken for so long, he fell silent. He looked at Manoranjan with deep excitement. Manoranjan had listened to him with bent head. His eyes were fixed on the ground, as if Javed's words were an essential part of some script written on the ground, without reading which it was impossible to understand him.

Finally, he asked, 'Have you been back home since then?'

'No,' said Javed. 'I've been released from prison. But I've noticed something. I've left Pratapgarh, but whenever I suddenly wake up at night I feel that I'm back in that dark room, and the stink of that drain that flows near our house settles in my nose.'

'Did you think you could escape the past so easily?' Manoranjan's voice was low. 'We all live in a prison of some kind. Not being able to love openly is my prison. I am attracted only to men. That's the way I'm made. What can I do about this? Is it my fault? I know that it's very hard for an ordinary man to understand my compulsions and to love a prisoner.' Manoranjan's face was distorted with bitterness.

'Why do you think of yourself like that, Manoranjan? I desire you.'*

'Is that true, Javed?'

Carried away by their conversation, they had not realized that they had reached the building where Manoranjan had his studio in a barsati. In front of its gate, at the edge of the road, was a laburnum tree that was in full bloom and festooned with flowers. Standing under the tree and looking up at it, Javed saw hundreds of

---

* '*Main tumhein chahta hoon.*' *Chah* can mean love or desire.

blossoms, like delicate, glowing bunches of golden grapes. Flowers lay scattered on the ground as well. When he leant against the tree trunk, he felt the shimmering heat of the yellow flowers enter him.

'Yes,' he said firmly. 'It's true, Manoranjan. I feel that love itself is a kind of imprisonment. I remember my mother, bending, in dim light, over a heap of clothes in our small room. Sometimes, my eyes would open, and I would see her embroidering a sari or a dupatta. "Go to sleep now, Ammi," I would say, but she wouldn't lie down until she had finished the work. What beautiful flowers and tendrils she made, without looking at any design or pattern. A garden would bloom on the sari and spring would dawn in the heart. Now I think that maybe the work gave her a chance to rise above her dull and poverty-stricken life, and I feel that she worked day and night for us, for her children. Wasn't she also imprisoned, in the prison of love for her children?'

Javed continued to visit Manoranjan even after the portrait was finished. One day, Manoranjan's mother was returning from the market when she noticed Javed's PCO. Javed was there and so were several other boys, chatting with each other. Through the glass door of the small phone booth, she saw that a girl was talking on the phone. The boys were all staring at that girl. One of them bent down and lit a match on his shining shoe with a practised hand. 'Good-for-nothings,' she muttered to herself.

Some days later, by chance, Mrs Gupta, who never normally read the newspaper because she didn't have time to do so, happened to pick it up and, resting her feet on a morha, began to flip through it. Her eye fell on an item on the local page, which was about the abduction of a girl. Some boys had been taken to the police station for questioning. Continuing to read, Mrs Gupta got a shock. Javed, an employee of a PCO, was listed among those taken for questioning. Without knowing the details, she was convinced that this was the same Javed who was her son's friend and often visited their house. She became terribly agitated and called out to Manoranjan in a tremulous voice.

When his mother asked, he evaded the question. Mrs Gupta felt that he was not so much agitated as embarrassed.

'No, no, it cannot be Javed. He's not that kind of boy.'

'How well do you know him, after all?'

'He's not interested in girls.'

After this remark of Manoranjan's, a weighty silence enveloped the room under whose surface Mrs Gupta detected a layer of guilt. She soon broke the silence. 'So the police took him in for no reason?'

'Oh, the police often go after people for no reason. And we don't even know for sure that it is the same Javed.'

But it was. And today, even after so much time had passed, Manoranjan had not been able to free his mind from the poison of suspicion that had taken up residence there. Javed had repeatedly declared his innocence and washed his hands of the matter. But his mother's opinion and Javed's having been absent for so long . . . had Javed really told him the whole truth? As Javed had predicted, now that many months had elapsed, the incident had been forgotten. But it was still present in Manoranjan's mind, even though he had made light of it when talking to his mother. He was determined to clarify everything when he met Javed today. He felt trapped between his suspicions and his attraction to Javed.

He came back into the room and lay down on the floor with his eyes closed. The light coming through the door was bright now and hurt his eyes while a distant clamour seemed to echo in his ears. When he listened carefully, he realized that the clamour was within him—the rush of blood in his temples which sounded like galloping horses approaching. Then he went to sleep on the edge of the night's exhaustion.

In the evening, he dressed, his heart doubtful, and emerged from the studio into the lobby outside. There was no one there. He entered the lift and pressed the button to descend. The lift was dark, and as it descended his heart sank. He felt as if he was going into the depths of himself. When he came out, he found that the air was still, and a light-green rain was falling—it had dyed the neem trees that flanked the road a deep emerald. A few vehicles formed a serpentine line on Aurobindo Marg's wet surface. People who had got caught in the rain without umbrellas moved towards shelter. Without worrying about getting drenched, he began to walk fast in the caressing rain. Soon he was almost running. He felt that the rain had given him the shining black wings of a bird.

Javed was there already and was pacing with long steps under the canvas awning in front of the café. Why was Manoranjan taking so long? The café was full, people were coming and going. The ground had become muddy due to the rain, and people's shoes had spread the mud around. The fragrance of hot dosas wafted from the café, and the smell of filter coffee was intoxicating. Two girls emerged from the café—one had long, open hair and the other short hair—both turned to look at Javed and then began to walk fast. Javed looked at them as if assessing them. His eyes seemed to embrace their waists and walk a long way with them.

As the girls grew more distant, he saw Manoranjan approaching. He was walking fast, his arms moving along with his legs. He was wearing a blue T-shirt, and, for the first time, Javed noticed how big his ears were. They stuck out from his head; Javed was surprised that he had never noticed this before. Not that he had ever found Manoranjan beautiful. He tried to gauge his convoluted feelings for Manoranjan and felt a wave of irritation. He had found Manoranjan's ears very strange, and this should have amused him but instead it ruined his mood. Embarrassed, he felt that his position was unseemly.

Manoranjan stood before him with his old shyness and said, 'I thought you were never coming back. Did you like Bombay that much?'

Javed stood for a while without speaking. His eyes went to Manoranjan's face and then hastily moved away. He said in a low voice, 'I didn't go to Bombay at all.' He tried to make his tone careless, but a weight of some sort dragged him down, and he stopped there.

'What? Then where were you all this time? Why didn't you write to me?' Manoranjan's voice was full of astonishment.

'I went home,' Javed said.

'Is everything all right?'

'I hadn't been home since I came to Delhi, and Ammi's yellow face kept appearing before my eyes, sad, bent over her never-ending needlework. My heart wanted to see her just once, to tell her . . .'

'Tell her what?' Manoranjan hastily asked.

'That I lost my job. They threw me out after that business with the girl.'

'But you said you had nothing to do with that case?'

'I didn't, but the girl was not found, and some of my friends were arrested and are still in jail. The owner of the PCO threw me out just on the basis of suspicion.'

'That's very bad. What will you do now?' For some reason, Manoranjan was not looking at Javed.

Javed, too, looked away and said, 'I'm going back home. I came to Delhi to get my stuff, and I wanted to speak to you as well.'

He stopped. They had entered the Madras Café and sat down in their usual places. The boy who worked there wiped the table with a dirty rag and brought them coffee. When the boy moved away, Javed spoke so hurriedly that the words almost came out all at the same time, as if a strong wind blowing within him had opened a door and thrust them out.

'I'm getting married.'

Manoranjan sat stunned, looking at his face. At first, he felt that he had misheard. During the time Javed had been away, it had never occurred to him that marriage could come between them. Finally, he said, 'You said that you were not at all interested in girls?'

'I'm not. I still desire only you,' Javed said in a sinking voice that was swallowed up by silence before it could convince Manoranjan.

'Why are you marrying then?' Manoranjan asked.

'This is what Ammi wants, and I don't want to hurt her by refusing. She has put her whole life at stake for us. How can I possibly refuse her? It was she who chose Mehru for me.'

'But what work will you do there?'

'Mehru's father is getting me a job.'

Dejection had settled on Manoranjan's face. He asked, 'So you'll go back to the prison from which you dreamt of escaping?'

With a deep sigh, Javed said, 'When I left Pratapgarh and came to Delhi, I felt as if I had escaped from prison. Everything here seemed new to me. My world suddenly expanded. I liked the feeling. But now I see that if life in Pratapgarh was a prison, that prison is inside me. I have failed to escape from it. I keep going back to those places, those narrow alleys, the tea and paan shops, the peepal and mahua trees, that sitting at night on a rug to eat with Ammi by the light of a lantern or, if the electricity is working, by the light of a bulb . . . that same feeling of life having come to a standstill. All of this is inside me, and I keep reliving the past, there's nothing new at all in my brain. I'm a stranger here . . .'

When he stopped to draw breath after this long speech, Manoranjan asked, 'What about you and me?'

'I've told you that I still love you. We'll keep meeting.'

'But how?'

'I'll keep coming to Delhi, and you come to Pratapgarh too. Ammi will entertain you very well.'

'Hmm.'

Manoranjan sat silent. His steady eyes were fixed on the café wall, which was painted a cheap turquoise blue. Suddenly a pattern appeared on it. A straight line of ants was proceeding upwards, in a disciplined manner. Where were they going? He concentrated on trying to discover their intentions. Javed was still speaking, but Manoranjan had ceased to listen. He was watching the ants. They moved on, in accordance with some law of nature, carrying in their tiny bodies the knowledge of where they were going. Outside, the rain had stopped and a watery sun was trying to emerge from behind the veil of clouds.

Under Wraps*

Geetanjali Shree

[*The first half of this novel is narrated by a young man who was raised by Om and Ambika, who were supposed to be his paternal uncle and aunt (Chacha and Chacho). The novel begins after Ambika's death. The narrator knows that he is the biological son of Lalna, a village woman whose antecedents are unclear, but he does not know who his father is. In her youth, Ambika would watch Lalna working as a maid at a neighbour's house. Ambika rescued her and brought her to her own home. Ambika's husband, Om, was an alcoholic who rejected his wife's sexual advances and spent much of his time working in Hong Kong. Due to a doctor's mistake, Om went into a coma and was nursed by Ambika and Lalna until he died. Lalna then left for a while. The family lives in a huge building called Laburnum House, where many conjoined houses share one rooftop. The neighbours think that Lalna is the maidservant (she addresses Ambika as Bahan-ji or older sister, which is what many maids call female employers), who had an affair with Om or some other man and produced the child. In fact, Lalna and Ambika were long-term lovers who briefly drew a doctor into their love games on the rooftop. Ambika did more work in the house than Lalna. The women raised the child together and addressed him as Bitwa (small son). After his aunt dies and Lalna returns to the house, he hates and mistrusts Lalna. He prefers to consider Ambika (Chacho) his mother.*]

---

* Excerpts from the novel *Tirohit* (Delhi: Rajkamal Prakashan, 2001).

Nephew's Narrative

I'm standing at the window where Chacho used to stand. Alone.

Not with me.

Like a beautiful picture framed by the window. As if looking at herself among the people who came and went at Laburnum House. Large eyes and a thin nose drawn with a pointed pencil. Big purple lips. A dark purple complexion like a rose apple.

'Uff,' Lalna would say. 'If you cut her, you'll find not blood but rose apple juice in this Chacho's body.'

Standing at the window, Chacho would idly raise one arm and untie the ribbon in her hair, releasing a curly, dark cloud. A gold-bordered sari, onion-pink or paddy-green or sky-blue, its end opening like a Japanese hand-fan below her left shoulder, seemed about to slip off her chest encased in a tight blouse with *maggie* sleeves.

She would rest her full, round arm on the window.

Like this.

'Uff, so beautiful,' Lalna would say. 'She fills it up with air from the cycle pump, this arm so tight and full.'

[. . .] No one had seen Chacho. A decent girl from a decent family, wife of a prosperous husband working in Hong Kong, quiet, well-behaved, self-restrained, she is never to be found outside the house at night and is not among those who wander around in darkness. She can never think of such things. So who would see her do them?

'Only the rooftop,' Chacho would say.

'The rooftop is ours,' Lalna would say.

The rooftop that lies spread under the two girls and wants to fill their hair with stars. The girls know the breeze that fans them. They open their hair. When the roof churns the sky with clouds, heaps of stars are shaken out on to the girls. The girls tell each other everything, all those things which only girls tell each other.

No one sees them together because everyone sees one with someone else and no one sees the other.

The girls take off their slippers. They walk barefoot on the roof, holding hands. They walk to the edge of the neighbourhood, homes left behind, sir and madam left behind.

This is their world. They hold each other tight lest one of them, delighting in this free kingdom which belongs only to them both, should fall off the roof.

[. . .]

When many shapes of a person keep rising and dissolving around you, be sure that she is gone. Being with so many shapes of her means not being with her. They arise and dissolve, and when they arise again someone else's shadow glimmers among them.

It is not possible to be with Chacho now without Lalna.

Not this present Lalna but that one whom the people of Laburnum House called Chacha's Kashmiri apple. Even to me. That was in my foolish childhood, and I would reply, 'Chacho is a rose apple.'

'And this Kashmiri apple . . .' I, too, would laugh when they, laughing, said this.

'She was an itty-bitty thing when she came,' Chacho would tease. 'And look what a fatty she is now.'

'I won't wear it,' Lalna would say, upset. 'You said I'm ugly.'

'I said you're beautiful,' Chacho cajoled her.

'But you have big eyes. Like two halves of a mango.'

'And you a big bottom. Like a drum.'

The two of them had a *programme* of acting plays. Chacho's silk saris are draped on the water tank on the roof. They tie their petticoats around their chests, then apply vermillion to each other's soles, draw flowers on their palms, put red dots on their foreheads.

I would happily hold the bowl of vermillion or wash and wipe their hands. Go put this downstairs, take this upstairs—this kept me happy in those days.

Fragrant night jasmine garlands on their wrists, waists, necks, ankles.

My garland got crushed and turned a moist orange.

Pleats are swiftly made in rustling saris—one, then another and another. The iron runs over them.

I am turned into a swami baba with two *chunnis*.

Two more gold-edged chunnis appear. Turning their backs to me, Chacho and Lalna remove their blouses and tie transparent muslin chunnis decorated with spangles around their chests, making a large flower-knot between their breasts. Damayanti and Shakuntala seem to have descended from the calendars, swaying plaits threaded with marigold garlands, taking me in their laps, kissing me. 'How sweet he looks. And we?'

'Let's sing,' they say, and they sing as if the roof is a stage and the roof a spectator.

[. . .]

I am retreating into the past, and I see the nephew that I was, invisibly hovering between the two young women. Obstinacy as well as tenderness.

Their intoxication attracts him unawares. He is a silent sharer of their whispers.

'Why do you have to walk between us?' Lalna teases.

Chacho lovingly strokes his head.

'There's no place between us.' Lalna sticks close to Chacho.

'There is.' The nephew pushes her.

'But I knew your Chacho when you didn't exist,' Lalna taunts.

'But ask her, didn't Chacho take you in her lap when you were so tiny?' Chacho picks up the nephew and grants him victory.*

'All right, I'm nothing to you.' Lalna is annoyed.

'You are,' the nephew assures her.

'She is?' Chacho tickles him.

'Less, less.' He leaps at her.

Like a creature pushing its head in, he burrows between them. To obtain a share of both or to separate them a bit?

---

* *God mein lena*, 'to take in one's lap', also means 'to adopt'.

*[His uncle would send him to call the women down from the roof,
asking what it was that could happen or be spoken of only on the roof.]*

The two women sit in smoke. They wrap the nephew in shawls
between them. He doesn't know why they laugh, why they cry. He
doesn't want to know either. Replete with their milk-and-butter-
like fragrance, he falls asleep amid their voices twinkling like stars.
[. . .]
'We talk of those things on the roof which only girls talk of,
which can only be talked of on the roof. Understand?'*
Whispers in dreams.
*[As young boys, he and his friend Paresh climbed up and looked
down into a ground-floor room through a skylight.]*
Chacho was sitting on a chair, and her body below her waist
was shaking with gentle but regular movements.
'Look at your uncle,' he said. 'How he has opened himself up.'
And he spread out his thighs on the roof.
I saw Lalna's back and head. She was bending in front of
Chacho's chair, moving her head fast, right and left, right and left,
her open hair throwing off sparks.
'Oho,' said Paresh greedily, 'look how Lalna is licking as if it's
chicken curry.' He pulled me down. 'Come on, get going,' he said
with youthful depravity.
It didn't occur to me to say that Chacha was in Hong Kong.

Lalna's Narrative

*[Lalna narrates the second half of the novel. She recounts, among
other things, how Ambika gave her many valuables and much money,
but balked at the idea of Lalna's buying the neighbour's house and*

---

* *Baatein karna* means to talk, converse, but is also a euphemism for
having sex.

living there on her own. When Lalna falls ill, she and her son start speaking again.]

Neither you nor your Chacho understood the mystery of the womb. She, too, feared that seeing you incline towards her, I might blurt it out, fearless as I am.

Listen, you two, to the profound mantra of motherhood—a mother is not she in whose womb the foetus grows but she whose womb calls out. If you can, look—motherhood is a wave that flows not out of the womb but into the womb from outside.

You are Bahan-ji's son.

Bahan-ji, you are Bitwa's mother.

Bahan-ji, I raise my head, look, your son has again stopped talking to me. Just as when Om Babu was in a coma. But I keep talking to him.

[. . .]

We will not be able to celebrate Diwali.* If we did, I would take Bahan-ji's diamond set from the bank locker and wear it. But I will light a lamp in that window which became the path that we traversed to each other. For us, Lakshmi came by that path, Saraswati too and Durga too.

If not for that, where would Lalna be? A shiver runs down my back when I think of it.

[. . .]

If you asked, I would tell you that passion is not what you think it is—man and woman, and woman and man, and *bodies, bodies, bodies!*† *Love affair, love affair!* Lalna with Om Babu, Lalna with so-and-so or so-and-so . . . Lalna with that doctor . . . someone else with that doctor . . .! If these are love affairs, they are negligible, if imagined, they are stereotypical.

---

* Festivals are not celebrated for a year following a death in the family.

† The word here is *bodiyaan*, a concocted Hindi plural of the English 'body'.

But when darkness sways in gusts of wind and the axis of the roof draws down the sky, something happens somehow! Our hearts leap to our mouths, and a flame dances before us. We run with the flame to catch it like a balloon.

Earth, water, fire, sky, space. Sometimes the five elements meet in a way that creates a universe.

We both would go to the roof again and again. To meet that flame. Sometimes in the golden redness spread on the roof. Sometimes in the silver moonlight like flying leaves. Sometimes in the green evenings of the roof, gradually growing ever more thickly knitted.

The doctor didn't understand this. We were loving the breeze when he came along by chance and some drops fell on him.

[. . .]

Bitwa doesn't come into this at all. And I don't want to speak of this to him, although I came and sat here, intending to do so. These are memories that surfaced on their own. What is there for you here, Bitwa—nothing, right? You are nowhere near their centre.

These are those things the source of whose vibration is deep within some people, from where an imperceptible tremor arises, gradually creates an uproar and encircles two girls who have grown together into young women, have been little girls together and grown old, and whom spectators have seen together yet have never managed to see.

Winged Boat[*]

Pankaj Bisht

[*Vikram, the narrator, is a married man with children and works as a
commercial artist in an ad agency in Delhi. In 1986, Anupam joins the
agency as a highly paid creative director. He is brilliant and arrogant,
insisting on his own way in projects. Gradually, the two become friends
and visit each other's homes. Anupam is a connoisseur of music of all
kinds. He has many books, a reproduction of a painting of a nude man
by Bhupen Khakhar and a photograph of Michelangelo's David. He
plays Freddie Mercury's 'Don't Stop Me Now' obsessively and gets so
drunk that Vikram has to put him to bed. Anupam's conversation is
scintillating; he recites his poetry and analyses Dracula as a symbol
of sexuality, who transmits his desires by biting people. He contests
Vikram's view of sex as the means to reproduction, saying that it is also
the medium of blissful mutuality. One evening, Anupam grows tearful
and begs Vikram to stay over, saying that he is consumed by loneliness,
but Vikram refuses. Anupam gives his diaries to Vikram to read and
tells him that he had once attempted suicide. The diaries describe how
he was bullied and raped in school in 1976, and when he was in college
in Dehradun, had an affair with a librarian, whose wife beat him up
in public, forcing him to leave town.*]

---

* Excerpts from the novel *Pankhvaali Naav*, serialized in *Hans* magazine
in 2007 and published by Rajkamal in 2009.

155

Bombay was a more *liberated* city. *Cruising* was easy there. Anupam
had joined a *gay* group. During his training he met Kulbhushan,
who was the news editor of *News Day*. Their friendship took off.
Kulbhushan was single, and his *orientation* was known in the
journalist community. Their relations heated up, and Anupam
moved into his flat. Now they were together all day. They came
to office together and went home together at midnight. Anupam
described this as the happiest phase of his life. 'Happiness is not
in my lot, and if ever it does come to me, by the time I realize its
presence, it has touched me and left.'

[*Kulbhushan becomes a regional editor and is posted in Delhi, where he
has to live in his mother's bungalow on Shamnath Marg. His family
insults Anupam, who asserts his rights and is unable to maintain an
appropriate distance from Kulbhushan. Finally, Kulbhushan refuses to
meet him because of the growing scandal at work and at home.*]

Anupam spent the night sitting outside the house, waiting to
meet Kulbhushan. A bone-chilling December night. Sustained by
cigarette smoke. Kulbhushan was aware of his presence but refused
to open the door or even glance outside. In anger and despair,
Anupam began to throw stones at the window. No one emerged,
but the police appeared and took him away. When he tried to
create a ruckus the ASI slapped him so hard that he almost fainted
[. . .] and said, 'Sit still. No need to talk nonsense.' [. . .] No doubt
all this happened at the editor's instigation.

The distress with which Anupam wrote of that editor in his
diary, calling him my lord, my beloved *sir*, told of his irrepressible
love, innocence and helplessness. [. . .] Kulbhushan could have met
him anywhere in the city but he didn't. Anupam believed (and
this drove him to distraction) that Kulbhushan had found another,
probably younger, companion.

Anupam's voice grew tearful when he said that *sir* had
tired of him. Perhaps four years was longer than usual for such

relationships, which the search for a *kick* and the burden of guilt
and shame prevent from remaining normal.

[*After Kulbhushan left him, Anupam did not return to work but
haunted the places where he could get a glimpse of Kulbhushan. Then he
gave up journalism and became a copy writer. One evening, Anupam
sadly tells Vikram that Freddie Mercury, who was an Indian Parsi,
died the previous year, and then reads to him a part of the poem 'Two
Loves' by Alfred Douglas, Oscar Wilde's lover, in which occurs the line,
'I am the love that dare not speak its name.' He reads out his own Hindi
translation of the lines, tells Vikram the context and then recites Wilde's
famous speech at his trial for sodomy, in which Wilde defended the love
that dare not speak its name as the noblest form of love.*]

Oh! That is why he had read the poem to me. Now I understood
what this second love was, which David, Jonathan, Plato,
Michelangelo and Shakespeare all experienced. The story upset
me. I suddenly began to feel unprotected. I was not sure what I
might have to do to save myself. [. . .] Terrified, I averted my eyes.
    He said, 'I want you to kiss me.'
    I felt as if a violent animal had pounced on me. Unwillingly,
my eyes rested on him. His eyes were closed. [. . .] Finally, he
opened his eyes and looked at me. A triple flame of desire, hope
and pleading lit up his eyes.
    I cleared my throat and said, 'Look, Anupam-ji, I have my
limits. This is very hard for me. I can only love a woman.' [. . .]
    'When did I ask you to give up women? I want to partake of
love with you as a woman does.'
    His left hand was stroking my right foot. The intensity of his
pleading raised a storm in me. My foot shrank away from him.
    I saw that his hand, in despair, was stroking the floor.
    I tried to explain, 'Look, I do not stray far even there. I can't
separate sex and love. I can't have a series of affairs.' [. . .]
    As I was leaving, he said, 'At least give me a hug.' [. . .]

Before I could speak, he had embraced me. I became lifeless like a statue. [...] His embrace filled me with a strange revulsion. The smell of his sweat nauseated me. Some foreign *deodorant* distorted it further. Never before had I been disgusted by the smell of a man's body. This was not the sweat of labour but the stink of lust and perversion. [The next day] he said, 'Vikram-ji, yesterday's chapter is closed. Forget it. You are a friend whom I cannot imagine losing.'

[*They continue to discuss sexuality. Vikram lectures Anupam about a book he has read which analyses homosexuality, both male and female, as the unnatural product of gender segregation and patriarchy. He also says homosexuality is not worth risking AIDS for, because 'it's a meaningless exercise.' He wonders if Anupam had a domineering mother. Anupam introduces Vikram to his friend Sharmishtha, a married artist. Vikram is attracted to her and wants to have an affair with her. Anupam has had a brief affair with Sharmishtha and shows Vikram pictures of them together, with him dressed as a woman and her as a man. Sharmishtha asks Anupam to live with her and her husband in a threesome, but he refuses, telling Vikram that women want constant attention and intimacy, leaving one no breathing space. Meanwhile, a male friend of Anupam's, who is a drug addict, moves in with him and financially exploits him. They have a violent fight, which creates a scandal, and Anupam has to leave his flat. Anupam tells Vikram about transsexuals and about his life as a gay man in Delhi.*]

The gay group had to leave the coffee house because the police kept harassing them and other customers complained. They began meeting at one another's homes. [...] Among their meeting places were Central Park in Connaught Place, Jantar Mantar and Nehru Garden. The search for partners went on everywhere—from cinemas, theatres and art galleries to cheap hotels in Paharganj and five-star hotels too. *Lesbians* did not have these opportunities. [...] They were considered nothing but so-called bad-charactered women from *elite* backgrounds, whose husbands were either impotent or licentious, as in Ismat Chughtai's story 'Lihaf', or who had been corrupted during their hostel days. [. . .] They had to hide their identity [. . .] and searched for companions with great caution in gay societies or in *Bombay Dost* or in underground newsletters.

[. . .] The truth was that Anupam had never tried to hide. In one sense, his attitude was, to hell with the world. He would say, the time to stay in the *closet* is over. This is natural, just as much as man–woman love is. It's nothing but a matter of sexual preference.

[*The boss warns Anupam about AIDS and tells Vikram that Freddie died of AIDS. People start shunning Anupam, and this escalates when the office peon accuses him of making passes at him. Anupam resigns his job and takes a post in the Gulf.*]

Whatever he was, he was my friend. All my sympathies were with him. I didn't dare openly stand up for him, but he was no ordinary man. [. . .] His departure was a relief for me but a bigger relief for him. It was no bad thing for him to distance himself from a society that could not absorb, understand or endure him, and where he was the target of rumours, insults, contempt and amusement. I would certainly *miss* him, but it was not an onerous trade-off for me, since his presence had become harder to take than his absence.

[*Anupam refuses an office farewell party, so Vikram takes him out for dinner.*]

Suddenly, Anupam stood up. 'Back in a minute,' he said and slowly walked to a gentleman sitting on a sofa. I saw that the man had salt-and-pepper hair, wore glasses and was fair and slim.

I suspected something.

He was smiling when he returned. Without my asking, he said, 'You guessed right. That's Kulbhushan.' I hadn't spoken. 'That was what you guessed, wasn't it?' I was taken aback.

[. . .] I couldn't help laughing. I turned and saw that he was looking at us. Perhaps at me.

'Want to meet him?'

'No.'

'Why not? Do you object to meeting rivals? He's not a bad fellow.'

I laughed. His joke was poisonous.

Our meal was ending when Anupam said laughingly, '*Look, the mountain is coming to Muhammad.*'

I looked around.

He was behind our table.

'All right, Anu, *all the best then*. We'll meet again, God willing.'

Still seated, Anupam shook hands with him. 'God won't be willing. *Anyway, thanks.*' His tone was bitter.

'When are you going?' Kulbhushan asked politely, ignoring his aggressiveness.

'Tomorrow! Meet my painter friend, Vikram.' I stood up, and shook hands with him. [. . .] He looked me up and down coldly for a few seconds, then suddenly removed his cold hand with a jerk. There was an odd intolerance and arrogance in his manner. [. . .]

Anupam's face blossomed with a strange joy. Kulbhushan looked tired and ill in comparison to me; I am athletic, and my height is five eleven. [. . .]

He said once more in a formal tone, '*OK, bye then.*'

Without looking at him, Anupam gathered pieces of chicken with his fork. After waiting a few moments Kulbhushan was turning to go, when Anupam stopped him. 'Listen, whose ghazal is this? *Kabhi ae haqiqat-e-manzar . . .*'

'Iqbal!'

'Are you sure? Not Firaq?'*

---

* The ghazal is by Iqbal. Anupam deliberately refers to Firaq Gorakhpuri (pen-name of Raghupati Sahay), 1896-1982, an Urdu poet known to be homosexual.

'Why?' he said with a start.

'Because there's a strange verse in it.

Na voh ishq mein rahi garmiyaan na vo husn mein rahi shokhiyaan
Na voh ghaznavi mein tarap rahi, na voh kham hai zulf-
e-ayaaz mein

Passion has lost its heat, beauty has lost its fire.
The Ghaznavi no longer yearns, Ayaz's hair no longer curls.'*

Then he laughed loudly. 'Look, there are exceptions everywhere.'

In the dim light I saw Kulbhushan's face turn ashen. Ignoring him, Anupam put the last morsel in his mouth and chewed it.

Kulbhushan pulled himself together and slowly walked to the door, without saying a word. [. . .]

[At the airport as Anupam leaves the country.]

Before Anupam joined the line for security check and went out of my reach, I embraced him. He hugged me as if he would break my bones. Slowly, he began to sob and kept sobbing. This unexpected emotion unsettled me. I patted him, separated myself, turned around without looking at him and walked away as fast as I could. My throat was choked, and tears dimmed my eyes. I went straight into the toilet. For a long time, I stood there, holding the washbasin, trying to control this upsurge.

[Anupam leaves as a gift for Vikram a commissioned portrait of himself.
Vikram is troubled by the idea that a man loves him like a woman, so
he puts the portrait away in an attic. Anupam returns after two years
and is now an alcoholic. He looked young until he was forty but is now

---

* Translation mine. Mahmud of Ghazni and his male slave Ayaz, who was his lover, were types of eternal passion in Urdu poetry.

ageing. He tells Vikram that he has turned the autobiography he was writing into a Hindi novel. He moves to Bombay.]

He had freed himself of me on an emotional level. It was a relief that I was now outside the bounds of his desire. Being relieved of the tension in which I had for so long continued to maintain my balance, as if walking on a tightrope while in constant fear of falling, felt joyful, like suddenly being cured of an old ailment.

But no, relationships of desire do not break thus, just as ailments that have become part of the bodily structure do not end in a miraculous way.

[*In 1995, Anupam sends from Goa a photo of the sea taken by someone called Rob.*]

On the back was written, with a black sketch pen in large letters:

> Society, as we have constituted it, will have no place for me, has none to offer; but Nature, whose sweet rains fall on unjust and just alike, will have clefts in the rocks where I may hide, and secret valleys in whose silence I may weep undisturbed. She will hang the night with stars so that I may walk abroad in the darkness without stumbling, and send the wind over my footprints so that none may track me to my hurt: she will cleanse me in great waters, and with bitter herbs make me whole.

It was a quotation, but I didn't know where it was from.* Below it he had written, 'With boundless love, for dear Vikram, Anupam'.

---

* The quotation (translated by Bisht into Hindi) is from *De Profundis*, Wilde's long letter to his lover, written in prison. This passage anticipates his release and exile from England. I use the original English words here. Two Hindi reviews of *Pankhvali Naav* quoted this passage but failed to identify it.

[*Vikram receives a letter telling him that Anupam has been murdered.
He goes to Bombay to look at Anupam's flat and searches for the
autobiography, but it is not there. Twelve years later, Vikram goes with
a colleague, Mehta, to meet Anupam's mother in Dehradun. He offers
her Anupam's portrait, but she refuses to accept it. She shows them a
letter that she says she received the previous week from Anupam, and
tells them that he has married Sharmishtha and lives in Bahrain,
where he is the editor of* Khaleej Times. *Vikram feels that some kind of
web of illusion is being spun. They leave and converse on the way back.*]

Mehta asked me, 'Who wrote the letter to you?'
    I couldn't speak.
    'Do you recognize the writing?'
    I said, 'Hmm.'
    'Who told you?'
    Before he completed the sentence, a wave of emotion drowned
my tearful voice in sobs. [...] I controlled myself but did not tell him
who had written that letter four years ago to say that Anupam had
drowned, had been murdered, and that it could not have been an
accident because he was not in swimming trunks but in underwear,
and the strange thing was that he was wearing socks. [...]
    I had gone to his house in Dadar, Mumbai, and had found that
his brother-in-law had taken away his things. [...] Wouldn't his
novel have been among those things?
    'So the writing...?' Mehta was trying to emerge from the fog.
I was surprised because he, too, had seen the writing.
    'I can't say,' I said in as impartial a tone as I could muster.
    He looked at me, trying to read my face. Perhaps he could not
be sure. I was back to normal.
    I certainly recognized his writing.

Girlfriend–Beloved[*]

Akanksha Pare

'This story is as true as nights spent awake when in love. It is as false as lovers' vows.'

This was the first entry in her *diary*. Her writing was beautiful. After this line, a whole page was practically blank. Here and there, she had drawn flowers, leaves and stars. A cottage, a path from the cottage, mountains, the rising sun and, yes, a tree and a bird sitting on it too. Throughout the diary she had written short sayings and verses, some in green and others in blue ink. The diary was tattooed everywhere with the same flowers, leaves and crooked lines.

Amongst these images, she had written about her pain in beautiful calligraphy. A pain inflicted on her by one of my own. A pain I could not imagine, yet the one who had inflicted it was quite at ease, oblivious of anything untoward.

So far, I had been reading the *diary* in a haphazard way. Sometimes the first part and then suddenly the last page. Sometimes a part in the middle. Half the time I was looking at her unique but untrained artistry. Then I would remember that I must read the *diary*. I must share her pain. Long ago, I had read somewhere that such scattered doodles reveal a person's state of mind. One does not doodle on page after page like this for nothing. The heart's turmoil spills on to paper in these colours. Only when one is in a

---

[*] 'Sakhi–Sajan', published in *Vak*, July–September 2014.

quandary do such pictures emerge. Pradeep once said that some
people have the habit of doodling whenever they come across pen
and paper.

I was trying to understand the drawings in this *diary* that
looked like a schoolchild's notebook. Pradeep enjoyed reading the
heart's emotions in such *doodles*. He often said to me, 'A person is
fully revealed in doodles, Kusum. If somebody makes five doodles
in my presence, I can tell you what is going on in their heart and
what their repressed desires are.' I tried to remember how he had
interpreted symbols. Stars stand for hope, hopes in one's life that
are hard to fulfil. Yes, she had cherished unlikely hopes in her
innocent heart.

I began to read.

'A piece of grey sky glanced into my balcony and told me it
was time for her to arrive. I thought I should settle myself and
adorn the room a bit. I could do the opposite too, adorn myself a
bit and settle the room, but I have never enjoyed adorning myself,
not even when I was the right age to do so. I like standing in front
of a mirror. Yet there is something about her that makes me want
to settle myself even if I have just returned from office and am
exhausted. Even if I would rather relax, I wash my hands and face,
make myself look brighter and wait for her to enter the room,
chirping, filling the room with her chirruping. At first, I found her
company very strange. She talks so much. She can't be silent for a
moment. I've been in this room for four years. Never has it been
so bright and cheerful. Now someone or other is always popping
in to see her. The room always seems full. She drags me into
conversation, willy-nilly. Is this how you do things in your family,
Sonali? Have you been there, Sonali? Do you like this, Sonali?
Whenever she's in the room, it's nothing but Sonali, Sonali. Before
her, I never knew what a home is and what family love is. She takes
care of me. I like it very much.'

Oh, so her name was Sonali. How strange—I've heard
the names of hundreds of her companions but never this name.

Do children hide so much from their parents, even from their mothers? Isn't a mother a friend? I asked myself. It's only in books that mothers and children are friends. This friendship is confined to the features pages of newspapers. Perhaps there are some fortunate mothers whose children are their friends.

But this is not something that can be shared even with a friend. Can anyone tell a friend that she has . . . that she . . .? I could not think further. Perhaps I could not gather the courage to think further. I have thought of myself as belonging to a new era. But this newness stuck in my throat. I could neither weep nor speak. This was disloyalty, a crime, exploitation of someone, taking advantage of someone—what was this after all? Even if I were able to figure it out, what difference would it make? There was no court to which this matter could now be appealed.

Feeling disturbed, I closed the *diary* gently and went out on to the balcony. This corner of the balcony was the only space of my own in this unfamiliar metropolis. Wherever I looked, tall buildings were all I could see. Three of us lived in this house, a five-room flat on the third storey. I say 'house' because there is a long way to go before it becomes a home. When I looked out of the balcony, I felt as if cement trees had sprouted all around. I saw small windows in these tall buildings, which were lit up in white or yellow as soon as darkness fell. Some windows remained lighted late into the night, and the lights in these windows often helped me pass the night.

If she caught me awake, she would scold me instead of asking affectionately why I could not sleep. 'Go to sleep or you'll fall ill. Then I'll have to take leave from the office to look after you.' Was it my fault that I couldn't sleep? I was tired of telling her that. I had long forgotten how to tell her that worrying about her kept me awake. That would have only led to her scolding me more. I knew she would fly into a rage and scream at me. Often, I wanted to search for my lost daughter in her anger and her shouting, but the more I tried to do so, the more I realized my own helplessness. She is right. I am here to help her. If I fall ill, where will she run—to her doctor or to mine?

But this was before I read her *diary*. After reading the *diary*, I wanted to shake her and ask what mistake we had made in her upbringing that had led her to behave like this. The fault was hers, but it was I who felt suffocated. Perhaps she does not even realize that she has taken a life. I didn't want to quarrel with her. With great difficulty, she had become capable of giving life. Her doctor had warned me that the slightest stress could become an obstacle in the path of the new life. She had to be very careful too. I was happy that this five-room house was going to become a home. After ten years of marriage, her body was finally expanding. This daily expansion awakened new hopes in me. Today, she had gone to the office after several days. As soon as she left, I took that lavender-coloured *diary* out of the cupboard. There was much more for me to know and try to understand.

She had written, 'Letters of the alphabet look beautiful in red. But Bela says red is used for enemies. I am writing for a friend. She is more than a friend. I like her. I want to be like her. Just as lively and just as cheerful. How easily she becomes intimate with others. She doesn't let me write in black ink either. She says writing in black ink brings about more struggles in life, and I already have enough struggles to deal with. She was the first girl whom I told that Papa does not live with us, that is, with Mama. I told everyone else in school that Papa works in the Gulf and comes home during vacations. The girls in my class were not fooled, though they never asked directly, "During which vacation? When does your Papa have a vacation?" With great ease, Bela told me that there was no need to lie. I should tell the truth. I should say that Papa has divorced Mama, married someone else and abandoned us. How can I tell Bela that neither I nor Mama have the courage to say this? That is why Mama sent me off to boarding school. And now that I have a job I am still staying in a hostel. Mama has taken a job in another city. We have no home. We meet at my grandmother's house. I go there and

Mama comes there to see me. She never invites me to the city where
she works. I think she probably hasn't told anyone that she has a
daughter. I want to tell Bela that I want to be like her, accepting
everyone with such openness, saying everything so openly.'

Any mother should be proud when her child is praised. That
Sonali was deeply influenced by Bela was evident in every word
she wrote. But I keep looking at the lines she has drawn to make
a cottage. She has drawn a path too, but the gate to that path is
closed. Pradeep said that people who draw a gate to a path find it
hard to let others into their lives. They do yearn for a family, but
they are so cautious that very few people manage to come close to
them. They are unable to reconcile their nature with their desires,
so they end up alone. Is that why Sonali . . .? Why do my thoughts
always stop when Bela seems to become associated with her?

There are flowers in her diary and bunches of flowers too. She
has drawn a butterfly on one flower. That was after Bela had been
living with her for a year. A butterfly on a flower is a sign of love
and of surrendering oneself to someone. Are the emotions the
same even when the surrender is unnatural? Does love not know
the differences between bodies? Does the heart not recognize the
difference between a male and a female body? Surely not. That
is why she drew so many symbols of love. The two of them must
certainly have had some happy days together. She has drawn many
stars. Some tender leaves. Some geometrical patterns. All these are
signs of beginning a new life.

'When she kisses me I feel that I am flying through the air.
When her soft hands touch my body I . . .' I squirm when I read
this. I feel nauseated. I don't want to read further. I can't believe
that my daughter and another girl . . . and then she left her and
calmly came away. That girl kept suffering the hell of missing her,
and my daughter calmly got married and became absorbed in her
new job. Once I saw in the newspaper a picture of people wearing
rainbow masks and asked her, 'What is this demonstration about?
They look very strange.'

'You won't understand, Ma. It's just something.'

When I remember that exchange, her voice seems to rise from a burrow. Somehow, I managed to ask her again.

'These are boys who marry other boys and girls who marry other girls.'

'Marry?' The surprise with which I said this was matched by the ease with which she replied, 'Yes. So what? Anything goes in cities. Many girls feel that they can only live with their girlfriends. There are some crazy girls of that kind.'

Before I could ask more questions, she got up and went into the next room. I don't know whether she did not want to face the past or whether memory was reopening her wounds. That tattered old diary was writhing under my mattress. Her weeping, her pleas to Bela to stay with her, her asking not to be forgotten. I can see it all so clearly.

I tried to remember Bela's face when she left the working women's hostel and came back to get married. I don't remember seeing any unrest or grief on her face. She had made friends with Vinit at her workplace and had got married to him. There was nothing unusual about her life. Nothing was written on the last pages of the diary. Just many pictures of eyes. Many, many eyes. Pairs of eyes that are symbols of waiting. No faces. Just big, black eyes full of sadness.

It feels as if she had no more words. Her desires ended. She suppressed her heart. No pictures, no doodles. Just two lines written in red ink:

Bhoole hain rafta-rafta muddaton mein unhein ham
Kiston mein khudkushi ka mazaa ham se poochhiye

Little by little, over a long time, I forgot you.
Ask me about the pleasure of suicide in instalments.[*]

---

[*] A *sher* from a ghazal by Khumar Barabankvi, the pen name of Mohammad Haider Khan (1919–99).

Lado*

Madhu Kankaria

An evening, inauspicious as a black *brahminy* kite flying in the sky, descended into our courtyard when she returned unannounced. Lado, I mean. All of a sudden, she was at our door, like a leaping flame, bringing with her all the shadows of time past. A bright red sari covered with gold embroidery, a furrowed forehead, uncombed hair, chapped lips. She carried just one attaché case and looked as exhausted as if she had been walking a whole day and night. All of us were startled, as if we had seen a snake.

'You?' stammered Bua.†

'Yes. The vacation is over, and I have to join college, but first I must meet Suhani.' Swallowing spittle, she somehow brought out the words.

I quickly made tea. She did not drink it and went to her room, her thundering footsteps making the earth shake. She closed the door from within, then emerged with her bag, ready to leave! Fortunately, at that moment the kind Kalidas sent clouds, and rain

---

* 'Lado' was published in *Naya Jnanoday* in 2019.

† *Bua* is a paternal aunt (father's sister). The narrator is visiting her paternal aunt, whose daughter, Lado, is the narrator's cousin.

came pelting down.* The rain saved us. We felt reassured. How could she go out in such rain?

Bua asked, 'Is all well at home? Why didn't Kunwar-sa come with you?'†

She stood silent for a moment like a statue, then responded in a harsh voice, 'He must be fine.' Then, like the gusts of wind on that evening of incessant storm and rain, she went out to meet Suhani, just as Tulsidas had once crossed the foaming Ganga on a dark rainy night to see Chandravati.‡

We were afraid to talk to that blazing flame, yet we wanted to talk to her. We understood that she had not returned home in the same way as she had left, when we had bid her farewell after her wedding. Much water had flowed out of her lake since then. Finally, Bua plucked up courage and caressingly said to her in a gentle voice, 'You could meet her tomorrow. Suhani is not running away. Why don't you rest today?'

Her silence fluttered like the wings of a wet bird. Some fresh drops fell on us. I had read somewhere that disaster strikes when a daughter gets angry. In those moments, the sight of her angry, throbbing eyes overshadowed our spirit with an unknown tender sorrow and fear, so that whenever she came before us our tongues turned to wood. We didn't dare tell her that she had been transferred to Baroda and that she therefore did not need to come to Jaipur to join college.

She returned very late at night. I took her favourite layered aloo parathas to her room, hoping to get a glimpse into her

---

* In the fourth-century Sanskrit poet Kalidas's famous poem *Meghaduta* (Cloud Messenger), a husband separated from his wife sends her a message of love through a wandering cloud.

† A polite way of referring to her son-in-law, Lado's husband.

‡ According to the life legend of the sixteenth-century Hindi poet Tulsidas, his wife visited her parents and he could not bear the separation, so he went to see her despite the weather.

restless heart. She was there yet not there. A sad poem looked out of her eyes.

The next day, when animated scenes of life appeared all around, she was walking on the drenched grass early in the morning. Perhaps the night was long and sleep short, or she was worn out from battling herself, or else her mental agitation had settled into equilibrium. Her sudden descent, without invitation and without ceremony, had created an unspoken tension between the two families. There was an acerbity in the air. Doubts and apprehensions raised their hooded heads in everyone.

Bua had taken a mental vow according to her Jain beliefs. The vow was that she would make a pilgrimage to Shikharji within a month of the wedding having successfully taken place.* Lado's sudden arrival had put that plan on ice. Bua, who was given to rituals and apprehensions, took this as a sign of misfortune and blamed Lado.

For the first time, Lado shrieked in response, 'Why did you get me transferred to Baroda without consulting me?'

'We did it for your own good.'

'My good? If you cared about what's good for me, you would never have separated me from Suhani. I'm incomplete without her. I'm cut into two halves. Getting me married was not enough for you? You had to get me transferred too. All of you want to get rid of me.' A desert was blazing in her. For some reason, she reminded me of Panchali burning with rage and humiliation after the attempt to strip her of her clothing.†

---

* Shikharji in central India is the most important Jain pilgrimage site, where most of the major Jain teachers attained liberation.

† In the Mahabharata, villainous kings attempt to strip Princess Draupadi (also known as Panchali) naked in public. Krishna saves her, but this insult is one of the main reasons for the ensuing war. In the Indian imagination, this event symbolizes injustice to women.

Shellfire continued on two fronts. The return of the daughter of the house turned the house into a cremation ground. Elections had been announced. Phupha-ji was absorbed in preparations for the public rally to be held the following week to drum up votes.* His opponent had got hold of the records of his illegally held properties. That was another misfortune hanging over his head. A press conference was being arranged. Lado's returning in this way had disrupted his single-minded involvement in plans for the impending verbal battle. Everyone was flustered when they saw at large the jinn that they had stoppered up in a bottle with great effort.

The house was submerged in waves of unrest and tension. It felt as if endless night had descended into the courtyard, and we all, eyes shut in terror, were watching the flow of an imminent cataclysm.

Oh Lord, bestow a little peace on this home! This was the prayer that arose in me.

Part of me wanted to stand up for Lado and support her. I wanted to wait for an explanation of that incomprehensible mystery, which prevented her from enjoying any of the world's pleasures. Even her recent marriage had not awakened life in her. She was broken, body, heart and soul. She was cut off from both her past and her future.

Another part of me adhered to the family that stood firmly against Lado. I took deep breaths and tried to relax my body in order to relieve some of this inner tension. When that proved futile, I broke the rope and returned to my own grinding mill in Kolkata, hoping that this would induce Lado not to see me as entirely united with the opposition.

But the story was still half told. It ended five days later.

Within five days of my leaving, in the last watches of the night, with the Lord of the universe as witness, she swung from a rope tied to the fan and was absorbed into the five elements.

---

* *Phupha* is a paternal aunt's husband.

Bua was not able to return to normality for a long time. Especially when rain poured from the sky and lightning crackled, Bua would keep chanting the *navkara mantra*—*Om namo arihantanam, Om namo siddhanam*—in order to deal with the sharp bite of memory.* When that did not calm her heart, she would dial my number. On the phone, Bua would keep repeating the same story as if to ensure that nothing remained unsaid or unheard. She would ramble wildly, but the essence of all her talk was that on the night of the hanging, too, it had rained, just as it was raining now; clouds had rumbled and lightning had flashed. Harsingar flowers had showered down on the ground.† Because the wind was so loud, rattling the doors, we all had closed the doors to our rooms. If only we had not closed our doors . . .

I would mentally complete what she was saying . . . one night would not have merged into another night in this unexpected, otherworldly way!

* * *

Five years later, I again had occasion to go to the Pink City, Jaipur. The occasion was the wedding of Bua's youngest son, Rajiv. Amid the hubbub and merriment of the wedding, I met Phupha-ji. Looking at Phupha-ji adorned in a milk-white shervani and a pink turban, I felt as if time had stood still. A few silver hairs had appeared at his temples. Although he had not managed to save his daughter, considerable contentment was visible in his countenance at having saved his government from a revolt hatched by rebellious legislators. Protected by smart-looking security guards and flanked by supportive ministers, he looked busy, as if in the posture of

---

* The *navkar mantra* is the most significant mantra in Jainism, with which meditation begins. The devotee bows to the five supreme selves, and to teachers and sages.

† Harsingar, literally the Lord's adornment, is a small white-and-orange flower (night jasmine) that is offered to Lord Shiva.

a Paramahamsa.* There was no shadow of the past on his face. In response to my salutation, he airily waved a hand over my head and, throwing a half-smile at me, went on his way. Lado's brothers, Rajiv and Sanju, were in the same state. All of them had washed their hands of the matter.

I embraced Lado's older sister, Bimla, in the usual way. The ghost of the past weighed down our hearts and minds. As soon as we were alone, our sleeping anguish awoke. Bimla opened her heart immediately.

'Jiji!† If only Lado were here today,' she said, and tears held back for years began to flow. When I put a hand on her shoulder she began to sob. 'Jiji, why did she do it? Perhaps there are truths in life that cannot be shared with everyone. Jiji, now I understand why Lado could not share her truth with us. She was a *lesbian*. If only we had been able to understand this at that time. Oh, why are humans so powerless?'

What? *Les-* . . . This was not a word but the design of her life that suddenly opened up.

'When did you realize she was that?'

'Oh, Jiji, it struck me for the first time when the newspapers regularly reported on the *gay* movement and so on. If this had not appeared in the newspapers, perhaps we would never have understood that whatever Lado was, she was not to blame for it.'

'But was Lado aware of the truth about herself?' The words burst from my lips.

Something shook her from within. Restraining her agitation, she replied, 'Yes, she was, Jiji! That is why she wrote in her suicide note, "I am so damaged that I should go away. You cannot accept me as I am, and I could not become what you wanted me to be. But I have one question. Why so many expectations? Is it not enough for a person to be a person? Why do we judge just by the body?

---

* Paramahamsa, literally 'supreme swan', is an enlightened Hindu teacher. Ironically used here.

† A way of addressing or referring to an older sister.

Why? In any case, may the leader of the opposition and the entire clan forgive me. There are two signed cheques in my drawer, and please send my jewellery to Suhani."'

The bearer came up with juice on a tray. I dismissed him with a wave of the hand and eagerly asked, 'What? What do you mean? Why did she refer to Phupha-ji not as Babu-sa* but as the leader of the opposition? What does this mean?' This information was new to me, so I was surprised. 'Why didn't Bua tell me about this?'

'Babu-sa probably stopped Amma from telling you, Jiji. He didn't want any further disgrace. Lado was angrier with him than with anyone else. I'll tell you one more thing, Jiji. Lado also flung another taunt at us. She wrote, "We were Rajputs before we became Jains, and Rajputs have a tradition of sacrificing daughters, in the name of either honour or protection. I pray to God that this be the last such sacrifice!"'

'What? She actually wrote that? Why did Bua hide so many things from me?' I was really astonished. I felt as if I, too, had been betrayed. Nevertheless, I doubted whether the twenty-four-year-old Lado could have been fully acquainted with the truth of which the changing times had made us aware. Was she really a *lesbian*, or was a deprived man seated in her heart, pining for union with a woman?

Bimla insisted, 'Jiji! She was aware. That's why she kept fighting with herself and with all of us. But she didn't trust us.' Her voice quavered as she spoke. 'We also drank poison, Jiji, and are still drinking it, but if only at that time we had drunk the poison of breaking social norms and traditions, maybe we, too, would have become Shiva.'†

*　*　*

---

* Father.

† In Hindu narrative, Shiva drank poison and held it in his throat in order to save the world from being destroyed by it; he thus overcame death. The word 'Shiva' also means 'auspicious.'

'Come, do come, dear son-in-law! / Your mother-in-law invites you to her house.'

The bride, Pinky, in her long, heavy, gold-embroidered skirt, was dancing with her girlfriends to the strains of a Rajasthani folk song. Watching Pinky, I could hear and see the past. The same house, and more or less the same scene. Yet how different Pinky and Lado were. Lado had sat with downcast face, as if all the butterflies within her had died. How far was spread the waiting in her wet eyes—waiting for Suhani.

Yet we had turned our faces away from her pain.

Some moments in life never pass away even when they are in the past. The flame of such moments follows one all one's life. Late into the night, we two sisters kept opening and closing the bundle of sorrow.* We kept flowing, straying and wondering why, even though we had her welfare at heart, our eyes had not been able to see the truth that she had lived. Perhaps truth is too big for any eye to see.

Suddenly, it occurred to me—what had happened to the heroine of the story that began in friendship and that ended the story of her life? I asked Bimla, 'What became of Suhani? She must have been shaken up by Lado's death?'

'Yes, Jiji, she was not just shaken but uprooted. She was in a state of shock for a whole year. She shut down her free school for children. Two or two and a half years after Lado's departure, they got rid of her too. I heard she had a daughter last year.'

'So was Suhani not a *les-* . . .?' What was the prohibition in my conditioning that prevented me from articulating the full word? It remained stuck in my throat.

'No, no, Jiji, Suhani was absolutely normal. She didn't need Lado. That's why she obeyed her father and humiliated Lado that day, even if unwillingly.'

A couple of heavy moments later, she whispered, 'Shall I tell you something, Jiji?'

---

* In north Indian languages, cousins are addressed and referred to as siblings.

'Yes, yes, tell me.'

'Sometimes I feel that if Babu-sa were not so highly placed, Lado wouldn't have died.'

'How can you say that?' Then I remembered that Lado had once told me that she could not carry the weight of her father's prestige: 'Bai-ji, my father being a political leader is my misfortune.'

'Yes, Jiji. What upset Lado the most was that without consulting her, Babu-sa got her transferred to Baroda. Had Babu-sa been an ordinary man, could he have got the transfer done within a week? The sorrow and humiliation of this were more than she could bear. Think about it, Jiji—all the mess was made by Babu-sa. Had Babu-sa not threatened Suhani's father, would Suhani have insulted her? Lado didn't care about the world. She cared only about Suhani. Lado lived only for Suhani, Bai-ji. By cutting her off from Suhani, Babu-sa closed the casket of her life. I think that when she came from Baroda and went straight to see Suhani, Suhani refused to meet her for fear of Babu-sa. This despair . . .'

'Perhaps Babu-sa would have accepted her, had he known that she was a *lesbian*. It was our ignorance that destroyed her. Perhaps Bua even today is not aware of Lado's reality.'

'Yes, Jiji, I dare not tell Amma. She may not be able to understand the truth about Lado.'

The anguished pages of the past kept fluttering, and the birds of thought kept pecking at me.

'Just think of it, Jiji, she had no dreams for herself. She kept linking herself with Suhani's dreams. She never asked for anything for herself. It was only in name that she was Lado.* We mistreated her, even though there was so much that was beautiful, tender and human about her. We never grasped the whole Lado, only the Lado who gave us trouble.'

Then she softly said, 'I also saw her only from afar. I never looked closely at her life, even though she wrote to me, "You think

---

* Lado is a short form of *ladli*, which is an endearment for a girl, meaning a cherished and pampered child.

the problem is inside me, but I know that I am made this way. The cause of the problem is outside me.'"

I had travelled a long way within when Bimla again spoke. 'Jiji! It's not a sin to be a *lesbian*.'

I muttered, 'It's not a sin to be anything. But we have made a measuring tape of morality, by which we measure everything. We start cutting and throwing away anything that does not fit our measurements. We don't realize that every bird has the right to sing its own song.'

She was looking to me for comfort. The sorrow that had diminished for a moment returned. I turned my eyes away. What could I say? My heart, so far wrapped in detachment, was filled with a strange annoyance, hurt, regret and guilt. Truth had not been spoken as truth, nor had it been heard as truth. Not even when the cat of death struck with its claws and all of us sat like pigeons with eyes closed.

Here was Bua, busy entertaining guests, playing the hostess and paying respects to everyone. She was doing everything, yet she was nowhere. Scattered in fragments, Bua's body displayed signs of untimely ageing. She had even respectfully invited Lado's former husband.

I asked Bua quietly, 'Why did you invite him? Lado did not accept him so . . .'

Bua sighed deeply, as if living had tired her out. Straightening the end of her sari on her head, she said in a deadened voice, 'Your Phupha-ji insisted on sending the invitation. I tried my best to stop him. But has he ever listened to me? He said, "After all, he did strike the arch over our gateway."'*

So saying, Bua wiped her eyes with the end of her sari and again got busy attending to the guests.

Lado's voice resounded in my ears, 'Bai-ji, my father isn't able to be a father. Life has made him a businessman.'

---

* A ritual whereby the bridegroom strikes with his sword the arched gateway at the bride's house before he enters for the wedding.

Mrs Raizada's Corona Diary[*]

Kinshuk Gupta

15 June 2020

Through the window I see a flame of the forest tree, the blazing red flowers on its bending boughs beginning to scorch at their edges. Are they not touched by sorrow at the swiftly passing final moments of their brief youth? I, still youthful, racked by corona, was admitted to hospital, all alone. [. . .] I didn't have breathing difficulties, at least no more than I have when I quickly climb a flight of stairs, but because I had seen Mrs Singh and heard her daughter shriek, 'Take my mother—hurry up, hurry up, take her quickly,' I insisted that I be admitted to hospital.

I keep thinking of Mrs Singh—if a healthy woman like her, who woke up early to exercise every morning and, for fear of pesticides, grew her own vegetables rather than buying them, could fall so ill, what chance do I have? [. . .]

Sonal's distraught face keeps flashing before my eyes. [. . .] For hours, I watched her embrace Mrs Singh, sobbing. I kept wanting to tell her to move away, not to invite the cursed corona. But how could I—I who have suffered the pain of losing a mother? I felt

---

[*] Excerpts from 'Mrs Raizada Ki Corona Diary', a long story published in *Vagarth*, May 2022.

like embracing her myself, but a screech of worldly expediency
warned me that blood is thicker than water. [. . .] I sent food over
in a basket and declared myself a sensitive person because I had
done my duty. [. . .]

I am nothing like Mrs Singh . . . I used to envy her when I saw
her setting out for school, in a pastel-hued cotton sari, carrying a
parasol, and sometimes wished I could be like her. But the cool
breeze of the AC, my troop of servants and all the comforts my
husband secured for me felt so good that I would dismiss those
thoughts and fall into deep slumber.

Until evening, no one came to collect Mrs Singh's corpse, and
gradually its odour began to penetrate my kitchen. I closed the
doors and windows, turned on the exhaust fan and sprayed in the
room half to three-quarters of the Italian perfume my husband
had bought me, but the distinctive smell of death filled my nostrils.
That was the moment when I decided I do not want to die in this
manner. I want a dignified death. I am not as afraid of death as I
am of decaying. [. . .]

19 June 2020

[. . .] It must have been around three at night when I felt a strange
restlessness. [. . .]

'Dr Shivesh, I don't want to die so soon. Please save me,' I
whimpered like a two-year-old.

'Mrs Raizada, your oxygen level is perfectly fine. [. . .] Please
go to sleep.' [. . .]

At around seven or eight in the morning, I felt the same
restlessness—the heart again beating like a galloping horse, the
breath growing fainter. I screamed again.

Dr Shivesh came, and when the oxygen level turned out fine
again, he said somewhat irritably, 'You don't realize that you are
not the only patient here. For one thing, rich people like you have
occupied beds so that those who are most in need are deprived,
and on top of that, this pointless drama.'

I shrank like a mouse in a lab. [...]

Ever since I arrived here, everyone in the city who knows me has been calling me up, the bell rings every minute, and if I have even a slightly lengthy conversation with someone, there are at least four missed calls. [...] But I grow bored after a few calls. All their voices are dry as hailstones, drenched in fear [...]

When Shivesh came on his evening round, he was embarrassed and apologized. 'Mrs Raizada, I'm sorry. There were complications in my wife's delivery.'

Then, like a child who has won a prize and wants to announce it to the whole city, he asked, 'Would you like to look at pictures?'

Before I could reply, he opened up his phone and began showing me pictures of his newborn son. Seeing the lines of joy on his face dimly through the face shield, I too felt a wave of joy. Then suddenly sorrow overshadowed his face.

'What's wrong, Dr Shivesh?'

'Who knows whether I will get to meet him?'

'Why do you say that?'

'My close friend died in the blink of an eye. I talked to him on the phone in the morning, he was perfectly well, laughing and chatting. Two hours later his wife called up. Who knows if I too ...'

22 June 2020

Today, for the first time, I enjoyed the patch of sunlight that fell on my face; I kept stroking its shining light on my cheeks. I felt an emptiness, an incompleteness in the heart's deep valley, I felt that swinging in the spiderweb of familial existence, I had never known the deep sensations of a woman contending with contradictions.

That is why my desire to live has grown strong today. I want to hold someone's hand, sob on someone's shoulder. [...]

There is no hand, no shoulder here, not even a drop of love. Since I was admitted, no one has come from home to see me.

My husband called a couple of times, but we hardly talk, we just say, 'Yes, hmm.' [. . .]

Except for my husband, I can't expect anyone else to come. [. . .] I send my husband messages, telling him not to come. He has diabetes and high blood pressure. If he falls ill, it will be hugely expensive.

When Shivesh comes, he tells me about his wife and son. She has named the child Vikrant, but he's not happy because he prefers Atul. Then he says, 'Delivering a child is as painful as breaking thirty bones, and she suffered it all in my absence, so she has the right to name him.' When he speaks of his wife, his voice grows dreamy and his face glows. I wish I could imprint his face forever on my eyes.

[. . .] Today, when Shivesh came, I had a strong desire to hold his hand tightly and feel the sharp sensation of touch, of which I have so far been deprived, hear him voice the hollow hope that I will recover completely.

But when I moved my hand towards him just a little, he backed away slightly, and I remembered that I am nothing but a middle-aged patient of his, the wrinkles on whose face have become deeper and whose body is daily being defeated in this battle against a terrible illness.

24 June 2020

[. . .] Today, the nurse informed me that Shivesh had tested positive and was in quarantine, so he would not come on his rounds for some days. [. . .] I kept praying to God all day: O supreme father, put all Shivesh's bad deeds from former births into my account. [. . .]

In the evening, a nurse told me that a boy asks about me, saying, 'My mother is in there. I must meet her, however long I have to wait. I won't leave until I've met her.'

I thought it must be Sarthak.

I ask the nurse, 'What did he say his name is?'

'Jacob.'

Jacob's coming here and calling me his mother overwhelms me. I want to embrace him because, as my condition worsens every day, I think I may not get another opportunity to do so. But this infirm heart cannot face up to those timid eyes which once yearned for a mother's love.

I read somewhere that being ill is like wearing someone else's spectacles. Today, lying here completely unwanted, when everyone is afraid of coming near me, I understand how those two suffered.

I want to tell Jacob that his love has given me a deep breath of air that I want to draw into my lungs, and that I will always be grateful to him for this. I try to look through the glass door, but I can't see him; I sternly instruct the nurse to tell him that I am exhausted and do not want to meet anyone.

27 June 2020

[. . .] I woke up, panting, my hands and feet trembling, and my body bathed in sweat. I felt it was another panic attack and tried to breathe deeply, but I had trouble breathing. [. . .] Had Shivesh been here, I would have called him right away. [. . .] After a while, I saw a nurse going down the corridor and beckoned to her. She got so upset when she saw the monitor reading that she ran to call a doctor.

I was terrified when I saw her run. I thought they would soon start a countdown, give me CPR and electric shocks, then draw a straight line on graph paper and declare the end of my life's journey. Ward boys came and started dragging my bed out of the room. I was about to ask where they were taking me, but seeing their eyes wide with fear, I lay curled up like a small child.

Outside the room was a sign: ICU. As we entered, my hair stood on end at the extreme cold, the complete darkness and the beeping machines with their red lights blinking on and off. [. . .]

I lay for a long time with eyes closed—I was bewildered by the fact that in those moments when I had thought I was dying, all I could think of was Shivesh. [. . .]

30 June 2020

Someone called out, 'Mrs Raizada.'

I was startled. The voice was Shivesh's. I was more delighted than taken aback. 'Doctor Shivesh . . . Shivesh, how come you are here? The nurse didn't tell me you're in the ICU. So suddenly, but how?'

Ignoring my questions, Shivesh said, 'Mrs Raizada, will you pray once, just once, for me to be able to embrace my wife and child to my heart's content?'

Defeat in his voice, tears in his eyes; I was struck by his passionate tone, and I mentally prayed for him.

My blood test showed sky-high levels of CRP and ferritin, and 25 percent of the lower lobe of my right lung was destroyed. Dr Mirchandani told me, 'You need plasma, but because of the rapidly rising cases, we don't have it.'

I called my husband, but he began to scold me for creating a new problem. I said tearfully, 'No, no, there's no need, absolutely no need to arrange for it. I've understood my value in your lives. The strangers here seem like my own. I'll depart, carried on their shoulders.'

He challenged me, 'Think whatever you like, but these strangers look after you only because I'm spending money like water. Do you know how much this is costing me every day?'

I cut off the call with a jerk. I feel as if someone has slapped me hard, my cheeks are burning and my ears ringing. [. . .]

Shivesh asks in a frightened voice, 'What's the matter, Mrs Raizada? Are you having trouble breathing?'

He holds my hand lightly. I want to remove my hand but am unable to do so. His touch is like hope sprouting in the heart's dead valley. A ripple in my heart says, Shivesh, you are my only companion in the withering garden of my life, my Adam!

Before I can gather my thoughts and find words, he removes his hand with the speed of lightning and apologizes gently. The warmth of his gentle touch and the pain of so soon being deprived of it churn the waves within me, and I burst out crying.

In the unmoving silence, the only sound is the sad cry of birds returning to their nests and the tumult of my thoughts. Although Mrs Singh was mocked for the way she lived—fearfully double-locking her doors at night, buying 250 grams of okra instead of half a kilo, drinking the local brand of coffee instead of Nescafé—she lived with self-respect and departed with the same self-respect. Where is the dignity in this death—lying in a posh room in a posh hospital, paid for with your husband's money, where a short-skirted nurse is always at your service while you listen to your husband's taunts and are finally burnt on a sandalwood pyre?

I felt that no one would cry when I went. [. . .] Yes, I would be cremated with speed. My husband will be happy when I die, and the problem will be over, so he won't have to spend more money. Sarthak hates me so much that he has not phoned even once.

A woman who has always lived like a sprout in her husband's banyan-like shadow, and has thought it her good fortune and destiny not to be able to grow—can such a woman have the right to a dignified death?

In the evening, he sends me a message, 'It seems difficult to find plasma anywhere. Jacob told me on the phone that Sarthak had corona two months ago. Talk to him. I'm busy.'

The heavy fog of sadness seemed to lift for a moment. I dialled Sarthak's number as if it was my right, but as soon as the phone began to ring I disconnected. No, I won't be able to talk to Sarthak. What right do I have? I lost a mother's right on that rainy night when I forbade him to enter the house, and he sat scrunched up all night on that part of the ramp where fewer drops fell, wracked with hunger and whimpering like a puppy. My husband kept telling me that a twenty-two-year-old who has never earned properly would find it hard to live—where would he go, what would he eat?—but I wouldn't listen. I stayed awake late into the night; I wanted to call him in, but my ego wouldn't let me yield to my husband. Sarthak left, taking with him all hope and leaving behind a home that was like rice eaten by weevils, ready to fall apart at a touch.

My heart is sorrowful; I keep remembering that girl whose laughter echoed through the house, who was highly aware of her rights and kept fighting for them—how did that girl become so cruel after getting entangled in marriage? [. . .]

1 July 2020

[. . .] I ask, 'Dr Mirchandani, why is plasma needed? I feel all right. The nurse says my saturation and pulse are normal.'

Mirchandani looks amused, as if he knows my son has refused to help. With great cunning, I look at my phone and say, 'Look, Dr Mirchandani, Sarthak is longing to come, but it's hard to travel forty kilometres in the lockdown.'

As if stripping me naked, Mirchandani says, 'Don't worry. Plasma will be found somewhere or other.' [. . .]

2 July 2020

I don't want to call Sarthak . . . perhaps I don't want to strangle the hope that Sarthak still loves me, which I hold in some corner of my heart. Without thinking, I dialled the number; my heart was hammering as the bell rang; it stopped only when the call was picked up.

'Hello, who's speaking?'

'Hello,' I said in a tearful voice.

'You . . . why have you called now? *Please don't call here again.*'

He was about to disconnect when I pleaded, 'It's not like that, Sarthak. You're a part of me. I've always been thinking of you. Only now did I pluck up the courage to call.'

'Whenever I fell ill, Jacob called you again and again. Do you know why? Because he was under the illusion that no mother can be so cruel as not to visit her son who is burning with fever, just because she wants to uphold her social reputation. When I was admitted to hospital the first time, I too expected you to come. Now I expect nothing of anyone.'

'Son, what happened was not easy for anyone. But what's the use of digging up the past?'

'Only one whose breast is wounded knows the pain that is suffered until the *scar* forms, the desire to wrench at the skin that throbs day and night. But now, the *scars* have formed and will remain forever.'

'Will you come and see me just once? I want to ask your forgiveness.'

'How can you be so selfish? Now that you need plasma you want to ask forgiveness. Jacob took a big risk when he went to visit you, but you flatly refused to see him. Jacob is everything to me. I won't go where he's insulted.' He was exploding like an active volcano whose lava consumed the hope that lay buried in the ruins of my heart.

Next morning, Mirchandani asked the same question, and I acted out the same drama.

My husband sends a message, 'Did Sarthak give plasma?'

I think for a long while about what to message back. I don't want to once again appear helpless before him. If I tell him the truth, he'll somehow persuade Sarthak into giving it. But I don't want to tell him. I know he'll find out from Mirchandani, yet I text, 'Yes.'

4 July 2020

A strange fear sits coiled and waiting—more for Shivesh than for myself. If Shivesh dies, whom else will I be able to love so steadfastly? [. . .]

I wonder if Shivesh, too, has begun to love. [. . .] I reassure myself—I love, that is the only truth.

Shivesh awoke and, feeling on half his face the sun's rays filtered through leaves, rubbed his eyes sleepily and looked unblinkingly at me. [. . .]

He perhaps sensed my self-consciousness and said, 'Mrs Raizada, did you sleep well? I dreamt of you last night.'

I'm very happy to hear this and feel excited, wondering what happened in the dream, but I keep my face expressionless and ask, 'How did you sleep?'

'Quite well.' [. . .]

I ask him, 'Do you get food from the canteen every day? Don't they bring food from home?'

With a faint smile, he says, 'We both are very busy, so it's not possible every day. I don't know how to cook; she often gets up early to cook, but then she gets irritable. Also, I don't much enjoy what she cooks. Why squabble every day over food?'

Then he chirped, 'I'm learning to cook. I've started making some things—Italian, etc. Sometimes I go and eat at Ma's house.'

'One cannot carry on like that all one's life. It's strange not to take an interest in the kitchen. We have servants to do all the housework, but I cook and serve him food myself,' I say with pride.

'Not everyone likes cooking. And how do you know your husband likes what you cook?'

For the first time it occurs to me that I've never looked at things from my husband's perspective. He may have made all kinds of adjustments to live with me. Thinking about it, I understood that I had never thought about him with intimacy, as I've been able to think about Shivesh for many days now. All I have felt is responsibility— bread and butter for breakfast, food with less salt and chilli, getting clothes ironed, arranging clothes in the wardrobe. Is this because I know Shivesh is with me for just a short time? Is it not possible for the husband–wife relationship to be an evergreen tree?

Perhaps love is just a seasonal creeper.

10 July 2020

Yesterday, Dr Mirchandani told me that Shivesh is stable; his Covid test was negative, and he will be discharged in the morning. [. . .] I've never been so happy for anyone; I feel as if life is once again inviting me to smile flirtatiously.

I expected his wife to come and wanted her to come, but at night, when he was on a video call with her and enthusiastically told her about getting discharged the next day, no expectation lit up his face. She didn't come, and Shivesh said she must be busy. When he was leaving, he said jokingly, 'Mrs Raizada, I'll call every day to find out how you are. You won't forget me, will you?' And quietly measuring the depths of my heart by looking into my eyes, he left.

After he left, I wondered why Shivesh did not get annoyed—no one visited him either; perhaps his wife, too, considers the relationship a responsibility, and no one loves him. [. . .] I blame my incomplete relationship for my deadened state. Why, then, is Shivesh so complete in himself, as if he has a treasury of love within him? [. . .] I know and understand so much, thanks to Shivesh—Shivesh, I cannot forget you even if I want to; you've brought me to the threshold of a new life. [. . .]

The nurse tells me plasma has been obtained through the hospital's blood bank. I say, 'Dr Mirchandani said the blood bank could not provide plasma due to the increasing demand for it. How did they find it?'

'I don't know, ma'am. Sir told me to inform you.'

The nurse leaves. Through the glass door, I see a boy who looks just like Sarthak walking with long strides towards the lobby. I think it must be Sarthak and am about to call his name, but then I think it cannot be Sarthak.

How intensely I wish for him to be Sarthak.*

---

* The name Sarthak means 'meaningful,' 'significant'.

Shadow[*]

Shubham Negi

He had become a hotel *corridor* rather than a person. In him was a straight path ending in a wall which he could neither leap over nor even leap from in order to end his life. Rooms opened to the left and right. In each one was a different world. No inkling of the world in one room reached the suffocating world in the adjoining room. He was part of and yet not part of the mysteries hidden in those rooms. Looking at him, one would never know that so many rooms were part of his personality.

There were long rows of rooms on both sides of the *corridor* in which he now stood. He checked the number on his key and walked ahead. The cameras on the doors pierced him with stares. He felt as if all the doors would open with a crash and a crowd would catch him red-handed. The answers to all the questions that he could be asked swam in his brain. For instance, why was he in a hotel at that hour? He moved faster. How long could a *corridor* be, after all!

When he reached the room, he put down his luggage and began his *routine* check. He put a finger on the cold mirror to check whether it concealed a camera. Then he climbed on the bed and closely examined the smoke alarm. Getting off the bed, he switched off all the lights and took his mobile out in the dark.

---

[*] 'Parchhai', published in *Hans*, May 2022.

With the mobile camera, he looked all around the room, searching for a red light. He had read somewhere that the UV rays of a night camera appeared red to the camera. After this *basic check*, he sat down on the bed. The room was wrapped in a dim yellow light. There was a large French window on one wall, from which the whole city was visible. The bed was close to the window, and above it hung a large painting. Across from the window a mirror took up half the wall. The window and the mirror layering the walls gave the room a pleasant openness.

He looked at his mobile. No *reply* yet from Manav. A terrible suspicion came upon him. His mind seemed to sit down and scrutinize the last couple of hours like an unresolved lawsuit. Such scrutiny was an unavoidable, depressing part of his daily existence. Every breath he drew was one-third life and two-thirds distress.

Emerging from the bathroom of his flat, he had looked into the other two rooms. Perhaps his friend had returned while he was bathing! He had locked the main door of the flat from inside and checked it several times. Even so, he felt reassured only after he found the two rooms empty. No closed door in the world could prevent fear from making its way into him.

With time, the fear had diminished, but he still sat in the car as if hiding from the driver. To begin with, he would repeatedly glance at the rear-view mirror. What if the driver knew why he was going to a hotel? What would he do if he found out? All kinds of scenes would appear in his head. His body would shudder but would not be able to shake those scenes out of itself.

He would feel that the whole world's eyes were always fixed on him. Whenever he set out to meet a new person, he would be troubled by a strange unrest. What if the person turned out to be fake? What if this was a conspiracy to catch him red-handed? It was as if there was a gang somewhere waiting for him to embrace a boy so that they could all come and shout—we have caught you! Was he a criminal? Loud laughter would echo around him. When he came back to himself with a start, he would find the driver looking at him. His body, soaked in sweat, would claw at him from within. He usually alighted at some distance from the hotel.

With time, this fear had gradually diminished. In childhood, he had played with a jigsaw puzzle that had the picture of a man on its box. But when the puzzle began to resemble the picture, he would scatter all the pieces. Now he was putting them together in a different order. For what picture was he searching?

* * *

When he had come to Delhi two years ago, he had stayed in a PG with Ankit.* In those days, he didn't dare tell anyone anything. He often thought how strange it was that one had to gather up one's courage to talk to the world about love but bullets could easily be fired at any crossroads. Perhaps his *straight* friends could never understand any of this. All around were fortresses of male–female love, into which a large part of the population was forbidden to enter. Male–female love was everywhere—in poems, stories, plays, films, songs. All the advertisements, propaganda, speeches dedicated to building society had forgotten parts of that society. So loud was the din of this propaganda that one was forced to shout on the streets in favour of same-sex love, and when one did, the world thought this shouting too noisy.

The Supreme Court had just delivered its historical judgment. Those were the days when people said that now everything would be all right for 'those people.' Those were the days when his friends in college kept making *homophobic* remarks. Those were the days when he would pretend to laugh at those remarks. Those were the days when, for fear of being caught, he would come up with acerbic slurs about *gay* people. Those were the days when everything was fine on paper. Those were the days when a swamp had appeared inside him, into which countless corpses kept being pushed. Those

---

* 'PG' is an abbreviation for 'paying guest accommodation'.

were the days when the past was an ugly mirror of present and future, in which centuries lay suppressed. Those were the days when, one despairing day, Ankit caught him.

In their first days at the PG, Ankit had an old mobile that could only make calls but had no Internet capability. He was waiting for his new mobile to arrive. In their fresh enthusiasm for the new city, he shared his phone with Ankit and they both used Tinder. Those were childish days.

One day, Ankit picked up the phone when he was out and tried to open his Tinder account. Messages from dozens of boys popped up. Ankit told him about it some days later.

They were going together to get their hair cut at a salon that was walking distance from their PG. On the way, Ankit asked for his phone. Although this was a regular affair, there was a mischievous smile on Ankit's face. He had veiled himself behind a heavy secretiveness all his life. He had felt that if he threw off the thick, scratchy blanket that covered him, he would be naked before the world and would die of cold, but if he did not remove it he would keep sinking beneath its crude weight all his life. So heavy was the pressure of that secret that if anyone behaved in a strange manner, the needle would immediately shoot to the question— does everyone know? A list of scores of questions would appear before him, and he would start searching for answers. Ankit's smile released a pungent odour of sorrow and suspicion within him. He refused to give him the mobile.

'What happened?'

'I have to show you something.'

The swamp in him began to boil like lava. In a roundabout way, Ankit told him. Black blotches swam around him. He himself had become a blotch and fallen somewhere between them. They took a few more steps together, silent. Then, suddenly, he turned around and arrived at the PG.

He lay on his stomach all day, with his face in the pillow. If only there were a deep well in the pillow, into which he could roar aloud. When we step out into the yard, the foraging birds fly away, making room for us. When we drive on the road, animals move away for us. When we go into the fields, we push the plants aside. We have forced the whole world to make way for us, yet we have not been able to make space for a defeated person to openly, unhesitatingly weep.

When Ankit returned, he was still lying down. He kept lying all day. Silent. At night, he suddenly got up. Ankit, sitting on the other bed, turned towards him. Ankit was looking straight at him when he began to speak.

'Look, there are many things no one knows about me. At home, you, people at college, people at school—no one. *So I would really like this to be a secret. I know*, you won't tell anyone.'

Ankit was still silent.

'It's new to me—anyone knowing about this. I'm still trembling. I can't deal with it.'

He clenched his fists. For a moment, all his sadness was enclosed in his fists.

'I'm *bisexual*. This is the first time I've said this. I've said it to myself in my heart, but I've never said it aloud.'

As he said this, tears ran down his face. Ankit came to his bed and took his hands.

'*Yaar*, I didn't know you would *feel* so *sad*. I would never have spoken of it had I known. I never thought about all this. I thought someone had played a *prank* on you by *swiping* boys. But it's *chill. Please* don't cry.'

He felt better. But he also felt dejected, realizing that even after seeing everything clearly on his phone, Ankit's first thought was that it was a *prank*. The stories all around us had had their tongues cut off. Such was the silence encompassing these things that even when the curtain was drawn away, spectators saw only the curtain. What a world we have created!

When Ankit took his hands, something in him melted into tears on his cheeks. Ankit stood up and hugged him tight.

He realized how many lives could be saved by a hug! After being
hugged for quite a while, he grew calm. Joking, he reproached
himself, '*A friend would have been better*. Why didn't I think of it?'

They laughed. He felt as if the walls of this ten-by-ten room
were speedily expanding. The roof had touched the sky. Never
before had he felt so open.

* * *

As soon as he got into the cab, he had messaged Manav—*on
my way*. He looked at the phone again. Manav had read the
message, but there was no *reply*. A strong gust of doubt rose from
the screen and spread through the car. Had this been his first
meeting with Manav, he would probably have turned back. He
was trying to explain things to himself in this fog of doubt when
the mobile vibrated.

Papa was calling. How did he get to know? That was the first
thought that came to him. Drawing a deep breath, he took the call.

'Hello, Papa. Namaste.'

'Hello. What are you doing, son?'

'Nothing—why?' He was disconcerted.

'No reason. I mean, everything's fine, right?'

'Oh! Yes, everything's fine. And you?'

'Here too. Your mummy wanted to talk to you.'

Papa gave the phone to Mummy. They exchanged pleasantries
and that was it. Mummy could not talk freely in front of Papa. And
Papa had nothing much to talk about.

If they actually got to know, what would happen? This question
often confronted him like a maze. Agitated, he would look for an
exit, run around, scream, but wherever he went he would finally
find himself back where he had started. The script had not yet
been invented to write the answers to certain questions.

Things at home were not great. Family relationships were like
thorns stuck in the feet. Walking even two steps without crying

was difficult. How could he add to everyone's burden? He had seen
an English film in which, after many problems, everyone supported
the boy in the end. He had wept heartily that night. After that, he
had stopped watching *queer* stories with *happy endings*. This was
not his reality. This was not his ending.

Sometimes, when he was feeling cheerful, he would consider
telling them. Wouldn't those who cared so much for him and
bragged about him understand? They had always considered him
an ideal child. Would this one thing put an end to that? If it did,
so be it! Why have a relationship with those for whom one thing
could change everything? But how many relationships could he
break off? Should he put everything at stake? At stake! Was this a
game? What was this? What was this darkness into which no ray
of light found its way? What mirage was it? What was it that kept
arising in his heart? He felt as if a long line of red ants was passing
through his windpipe to come and sting his eyes. He would break
into sobs.

Turning the pages of countless tears, he had decided that
he would never tell anyone at home, even though this meant
that he would always be alone. He could not unnecessarily push
anyone else into this furnace. That was why he did not want any
relationship to become *serious*. This had been going on for two
years. After a couple of meetings with someone, he would stop
himself. But Manav?

Manav! Trying to fathom the last few hours, he looked again
at the mobile. No message yet from Manav.

He took a picture of the room key and sent it to
Manav—'Where?'

This time, a reply came. '*On my way. Sorry* to be *late.*'

Doubt leapt out of the window, and a smile appeared on his
face. He had met Manav *online*, but it turned out that they worked
in neighbouring offices. They had first met at *lunch*. This was
different from his other *dates*. They had met outside a *restaurant* in
Nehru Place. Manav was one of those people whose smile is their

signature. When he smiled his eyes crinkled. His smiles seemed like
the doorway to another, more beautiful world. Manav was a few
years older than he was. This was evident in his entire being. His
personality was like two long arms that could save the world from
every danger. That afternoon was like a long, intimate embrace.

Today, for the first time ever, he had arranged to meet someone
in the day. Usually, he met people in a hotel room in the evening or
at night. The path to walking on the street together began in bed.
As they dressed, they would make a plan for dinner, and then he
would return to his flat. A new day, a new person, or if an old one
then with '*no strings attached.*'

This did not happen with Manav. That afternoon they had
not spoken of the body. They had shared their pasts, dreams had
spilled from their eyes on to the table, they had woven something
spun from their smiles. He had always wondered why humans who
had made everything had not made a place to cry. That day he
realized that this was that place. This was that place where one
could cry, could fall to pieces, could sob. But this was also the place
where one did not feel the need to do this.

They met many times after that but only in the afternoon.
When he asked to meet for dinner, Manav would make an excuse
to postpone it. Manav wanted to meet in the day, during office
hours. He couldn't understand this, but he went along with it.
Then one day, Manav on his own suggested that they go to a hotel.
Yet as he suggested it, Manav's eyes did not meet his; he looked
down, which was unusual.

Taking Manav's hand, he had said, 'If you have a *problem* with
it, it's fine. Let it be. Where's the need?'

Lifting up the burden of his smile, Manav replied, 'No, *I really
want you.* It's just that—*nothing.*'

He had found Manav's hesitation strange, but he knew that
he, too, had felt that way when he had met a boy for the first time.
He remembered the hesitation and fear of that first meeting and
tightened his hold on Manav's hand.

He had been waiting in the hotel for over an hour when Manav finally knocked at the door.

'*I am so-o-o sorry!*'

Closing the door carefully, Manav embraced him. He held him even tighter and forgave him. Manav looked all around the room, crinkled his eyes and smiled.

Now they were sitting on one side of the bed, legs dangling side by side. He wanted to ask Manav whether he was all right. Manav perhaps understood this, so he took his hand. A current ran repeatedly through both their bodies. He was about to speak when Manav's face came close to his. Very gently, Manav placed a shy kiss on his cheek. A tremor ran from his cheek and spread into a smile on his lips. He put his right hand around Manav's waist and drew him close. Manav's body gave up its resistance. Their faces came still closer and finally only one face remained. Which are whose lips? Which is whose face? His left hand slid down from Manav's face to his neck. His fingers moved to Manav's chest and opened his shirt buttons. His hand kept sliding down. Manav's body opened and closed like thousands of touch-me-not plants. When his hand reached Manav's belt, Manav's hand stopped it. Their lips were still finding their places. His eyes became question marks before Manav's eyes. Manav closed his eyes, moved his lips away and drew a deep breath, as if he were giving permission to someone within himself. Then Manav gave him a gentle push. He was half reclining on the bed. Manav sat by his legs and began to open the buttons of his pants. At this, he bent his arms and put them under his head. When Manav took him into his mouth, flowers rose and burst from many volcanoes in him. He felt as if someone was pouring hot light on him. He caught hold of Manav's hair. The upper part of his head sank back on the bed, and his chin lifted towards the ceiling. The movements of his breath kept pace with those of Manav's head. Every corner of the room began to release long, high-pitched moans.

As their wound-up bodies unwound, Manav gradually slowed
down and then stopped. Manav threw himself off the bed. His
body lying on the bed came back to consciousness. He got up.

'What is it?'

He gazed at Manav, who was sitting on the floor, trying to
read him. Had he done something wrong? He bent forward and
put a hand on Manav's shoulder.

'What is it? *Something wrong?*'

Manav glanced at him briefly, then turned away and shook off
his hand. Manav's body looked like the verbal meaning of guilt.
He pulled up his pants, buttoned them and stretched his hand out
towards Manav. Manav stood up and went to the window. His toe
was scratching the floor as he looked out of the window. As if he
was suffocating, he opened the window. Then he closed it, as if
afraid to reveal some secret. His shadow cast by the recessed light
above the window looked very small. The room had completely
forgotten the flowers that had burst from volcanoes a short
while ago.

After a long silence, both of them spoke at the same time.

'*You know* you can tell me anything, *right?*'

'*I have something to tell you.*'

* * *

Standing at the window, Manav was trying to bring the steam
bubbling inside him up to his tongue. Manav moved from one
foot to the other, as if trying to first tell every part of his body what
he was about to say. His shadow kept changing its position. After
much toil, words emerged.

'*I'm really sorry!*'

'What is it?'

'I knew this would happen. I shouldn't have come.'

'*Arey yaar*, why are you frightening me?'

'*I'm sorry.*'

'Tell me. It's OK!'

Manav gripped one hand with the other, let it go and then gripped it again.

'I . . . *I am married.*'

He felt as if an axe had struck the thick trunk of a tree within him. Then another blow, and another, many more. A whole forest was felled in him. The room that had been silent seemed now to officially announce its silence. Manav was still speaking in that silence.

'*I know* I should have made this *clear* from the start. *It's all my fault, but* what am I to do? *I care for her.* How is she to blame? But am I to blame either? We are tied to each other, that's all. *I don't know . . .*'

Manav kept speaking. He looked at him steadily. What kind of life is this? Who is being sacrificed and to whom? How many lives are scattered and wasted after being tied to one another? How many forests have been felled and in whom? On whose hands are the marks of axes? In whose eyes are there memories of sharp edges?

'The drama goes on. We are the actors. So many bodies acting. Bodies can act. But what about hearts? How long can the heart live a lie? But whatever it was, I should have told you. *Please* don't tell anyone . . .'

He went and held Manav to his heart. Embracing can save lives. He knows that. Manav burst into tears. Manav knew all his questions. He knew all Manav's answers. A meteor had descended and fallen between them. For a long time, they tried to quench it with each other's presence. Manav's shadow merged with his. He felt for a moment that he was playing both characters, as if Manav was not someone else but his own shadow formed by the sun of another time. This thought was terrifying. He kissed Manav's forehead and stood beside him.

One of the shadows on the floor, although with the other, turned in the opposite direction.

Acknowledgements

I am grateful to (in alphabetical order by surname) Pankaj Bisht, Kinshuk Gupta, Madhu Kankaria, Shubham Negi, Akanksha Pare, Sara Rai, Geetanjali Shree and Surendra Verma, for granting permission to translate and publish their works; to the following for permission to translate and publish the works over which they have copyright: Rajkamal Prakashan for 'Bhugol Ka Prarambhik Gyan'; Kailash Detha Kabir and Mahendra Detha for 'Dohri Joon'; Rachana Yadav for *Prateeksha*; and to Oxford University Press for permitting me to reprint my translation of Ugra's story.

Many thanks to the following for helping me to find stories and to contact authors: Nandita Basu, Kashish Dua, Kinshuk Gupta, Kuldeep Kumar, B.S.M. Murty, Tejpal Saini, Geetanjali Shree, Rachana Yadav and the inter-library loan staff of the Mansfield Library, University of Montana. Thanks to Harish Trivedi for various conversations and for reading the draft introduction, and to Mona Bachmann for discussing possible titles.

Some of the translations in this book were earlier published elsewhere, mostly in abridged form. I have acknowledged these sources in footnotes accompanying each story.

Ruth Vanita

About the Authors

Pandey Bechan Sharma (1900–67), pen-name 'Ugra' (meaning, extreme), was a Gandhian nationalist who was jailed twice for his journalistic writings. He wrote fourteen novels, thirteen short-story collections, ten plays and several prose works, including a pioneering autobiography, *Apni Khabar* (About Me). *Chocolate*, his 1927 collection of stories on male–male desire, ignited the first public debate on homosexuality in modern India. Fellow nationalist litterateur Banarasidas Chaturvedi dubbed Ugra the founder of an inflammatory school of literature, which he labelled *ghaslet* (kerosene oil). Ugra's work inclines to the didactic and the satirical.

Premchand was the pen name of Dhanpat Rai (1880–1936). He is regarded as one of the greatest twentieth-century Indian writers. He began writing in the Urdu script under the pen name Nawab Rai and later switched to writing in the Hindi script. Premchand wrote about 300 short stories, a dozen novels and two plays. He was a Gandhian nationalist and one of the few who responded to Gandhi's 1921 call by quitting his government job. In 1910, his collection of stories *Soz-e-Watan* was declared seditious and all copies were burnt. Premchand was also a prominent journalist; he founded and edited the literary journal *Hans*.

The little that is known about **Asha Sahay** comes from Acharya Shivpujan Sahay's foreword to her first novel, *Ekakini*. She was

from Bihar, and she authored short stories in the weekly magazine
Aaj, published from Banaras, and also wrote another novel entitled
Azad (Free).

Rajkamal Chaudhari (1929–67) was the author of seven novels,
two short-story collections and three books of poems in Hindi, and
three novels, two short-story collections and two books of poems
in Maithili. He translated two novels from Bangla to Hindi. Both
his bohemian lifestyle and the focus in his writings on the seamy
side of sex created controversy, despite his mostly didactic and
satirical intentions.

Rajendra Yadav (1929–2013) was a prominent writer and critic
of Hindi fiction. He wrote four novels, several short stories and
numerous essays on literature and society. Yadav was a pioneer
of the *Nayi Kahani* (New Story) movement. His first novel, *Sara
Akash* (translated as *Strangers on the Roof*), was a bestseller and has
never been out of print; it was adapted into a movie in 1969. He
co-authored an experimental novel, *Ek Inch Muskaan*, with his
wife, the novelist Manu Bhandari. In 1986, Yadav revived *Hans*,
the literary magazine founded by Premchand, and edited it until
his death.

Shobhna Bhutani Siddique (died 1974) studied at the National
School of Drama, New Delhi. She wrote several short stories, three
plays and a couple of short articles in Hindi before her untimely
death by drowning.

Vijaydan Detha (1926–2013), who belonged to a clan of
traditional storytellers (*charan*), wrote more than 800 short
stories. His *Bataan Ri Phulwari* is a fourteen-volume collection
of stories that draw on Rajasthan's folk literature. Many of his

works have been adapted for stage or screen, and translated into other languages. In 1960, he and Komal Kothari founded Rupayan Sansthan, an institute that collects and preserves Rajasthani folk tales, folk songs and art. Detha won the Sahitya Akademi Award and the Padma Shri, and was nominated for the Nobel Prize for literature.

Surendra Verma is the author of fifteen novels and plays, and several short stories. He won the Sangeet Natak Akademi Award in 1993 and the Sahitya Akademi Award in 1996, for his novel *Mujhe Chand Chahiye*. He had a long association with the National School of Drama. Varma's historical play, *Surya Ki Antim Kiran Se Surya Ki Pahli Kiran Tak* (1972) has been frequently enacted and was adapted as a film in 2018. His works have been translated into many languages.

Sara Rai is the author of four collections of short stories and a novel in Hindi. She has translated several works, including *Premchand's Kazaki and Other Marvellous Tales* (Hachette, 2013) and, with Arvind Krishna Mehrotra, Vinod Kumar Shukla's *Blue Is Like Blue* (HarperCollins, 2019), which won the Mathrubhumi Book of the Year Award in 2020. *Im Labyrinth* (Draupadi Verlag, 2019), the German translation of her stories by Johanna Hahn, won the Coburg Rückert Prize in 2019 and was nominated for the Weltempfänger Literaturpreis, Frankfurt, 2020. Her memoir, *Raw Umber*, appeared in 2023.

Geetanjali Shree won the International Booker Prize 2022 for the English translation (by Daisy Rockwell) of her novel *Ret Samadhi* (*Tomb of Sand*). The French translation of this novel was shortlisted for the Émile Guimet Prize. She is the author of five novels, *Mai*, *Khali Jagah*, *Hamara Shahar Us Baras*, *Tirohit* and *Khali Jagah*, and four short-story collections. Many of her works have been translated into Indian and foreign languages. She also writes playscripts and non-fiction in English and Hindi, and has had a long association with theatre.

Pankaj Bisht is the author of three novels, six short-story collections and a children's book. Several of his works have been translated into other languages. He worked for the Ministry of Information and Broadcasting, and edited the magazines *Akashvani* and *Aajkal*. He now edits and publishes the magazine *Samayantar*. He won the Rahi Masoom Raza literary award.

Akanksha Pare Kashiv is a Hindi poet, playwright and short story writer. She won the 2011 Ramakant Smriti Award, the 2015 Rajendra Yadav Award and the 2019 Krishna Pratap Award for her short stories. She works as an assistant editor with *Outlook*.

Madhu Kankaria is the author of seven novels, four short-story collections and two non-fiction works, and has won numerous awards, including the 2021 Bihari Puraskar for her novel *Ham Yahan Thhe* (We Were Here). This award, named after the major Hindi poet Biharilal, is awarded to a writer from Rajasthan. *Ham Yahan Thhe* is about Jharkhand tribals, and her 2022 novel, *Dhalti Sanjh Ka Suraj* (The Sun at Twilight) is about suicides among Maharashtra farmers.

Kinshuk Gupta is a medical student. His Hindi and English poems have been published in journals and anthologies. He won the Dr Anamika Poetry Prize (2021), and was shortlisted for the Bridport Prize (2022) and Srinivas Rayaprol Poetry Prize (2021). He writes non-fiction for *The Hindu*, *Caravan*, Live Mint, *Hindustan Times* and *Deccan Chronicle*. He edits poetry for *Mithila Review* and *Jaggery Lit*, and works as an associate editor for *Usawa Literary Review*. His short-story collection, *Yeh Dil Hai Ki Chor Darwaza*, appeared in 2023.

Shubham Negi is from Himachal Pradesh and works as a data scientist. His Hindi stories and poems have appeared in *Hans*, *Sadaneera*, *Bahumat*, *Chakmak* and other magazines. He has acted in, written and directed several street and stage plays. He was awarded a special jury award at the Hans Katha Samman competition in 2022.